THIRSTY GROUND

By Hazel Mattice The Books of *The Chosen Five*

The Green Door
Where there is no Whisper
Thirsty Ground

Thirsty Ground

Hazel Mattice

Cover by Anna Grotberg

ISBN (SC) 978-1-7351054-4-4
ISBN (e) 978-1-7351054-5-1

For God who chose, saved, and continually reprimands me.

And for the sons He's given me, Connor, Jeremiah, Xavier, and Jack Mattice who have all taken a stand against evil in this world.

Author's Note:

A writer's voice is a unique signature in fiction which includes a specific dialogue style and character development.

Ephesians 6 tells us of a battle *"not against flesh and blood, but against… rulers of the darkness of this age, against spiritual hosts of wickedness in the heavenly places."*

In Thirsty Ground, the author uses italics for the voices of Good and Evil as a random thought or a ghostly whisper in Simon Anderson's mind.

It is this author's belief it is in the mind where the war is ultimately won or lost.

Part I

A man is one whose body has been trained to be the ready servant of his mind; whose passions are trained to be the servants of his will; who enjoys the beautiful, loves truth, hates wrong, loves to do good, and respects others as himself.

John Ruskin

July 31, 1975

His wife wasn't right and hadn't been for a while.

Merle Anderson stepped out of his bedroom and halted, drinking in the scene before him:

Light spilled through the wispy lace curtains in the nursery. Christy had a pale pink paintbrush in hand and a splash of pink on her nose. The euphoric look on her face, disturbing.

"Do you like it?" she asked.

"It's very...pink."

Sneakers, freckles, straight hair parted down the middle, and bellbottom jeans made him think of the woman he first met. Vacancy in her eyes reminded him she wasn't.

The reason, in Merle's opinion, wasn't the cows as she would like him to believe. Rather, he was wrapped around her leg, and three years old. Riotous curls black as midnight splayed across their son's forehead.

Merle cleared his throat. "What does Doug think about giving up his room?"

Christy absentmindedly rubbed their toddler's head. "I know it's a girl this time. I'm not sick like I was with the other two."

The "other two," eight-year-old Kevin and Charles, shy of six, stood outside their bedroom door painted white. Their room was over the landing, and up the next four stairs across from them.

"...I don't crave pickles or ice cream," she was saying. "I'm carrying lower than with Doug or the other two."

He ran a hand over his dark blonde matted hair. "I think there's time to paint afterward, when we know for sure. Then we…"

"I talked to Selene."

"The hairdresser?" he asked, startled. An image of the dark-haired gypsy came to mind.

"The *midwife*. She's delivered hundreds of babies. She said she would bet a fortune in hair products it's a girl."

He opened his mouth, caught the toddler's eyes, and let it snap shut. Without a word, he turned and retreated down the staircase.

At the landing, Merle saluted his two older sons before descending the remaining stairs. He ticked off the list of disturbing details in his head.

Pink walls and curtains of lace.

His wife's folly, continual and growing daily.

His toddler's blank stare. The empty feeling Merle got in his son's presence.

The dark spirit resting on a boy so young.

1
Valley City, North Dakota
December 13, 1975

Beyond the glass in Mercy Hospital nursery, five infants were cradled in bassinets and wrapped in blankets: three pink and two blue.

While Chief of Angelic Hosts Michael gave charge over an infant wrapped in blue to a Guardian angel in another realm, a delivery nurse retrieved the warrior.

Pushing the bassinet into his mother's hospital room, she said, "I'm sure you can exchange the blanket."

"Whatever for?" Christy Anderson fingered the pink edges.

Ignoring the question, the nurse smiled down at the baby boy in her arms. "What are you going to call him?"

"Denise Rae."

Her head shot up. "What?"

Christy frowned. "Jennifer Jane?" A pause. "Sue Marie."

"A boy name Sue?" the nurse continued with a twinkle in her eye, "My name is Sue! How do you do! Now you're gonna…" she trailed off.

Christy's stare was blank.

Clearing her throat, she set the innocent in his mother's arms. "He looks like Simon Peter to me. A fine Christian name."

***

The babysitter was late.

In a long-sleeved yellow housedress with orange polka dots buttoned to her neck and a yellow star, Christy primped her pageboy-style brown hair in front of the full-length mirror hanging on the dining room wall.

It was the third outfit in a matter of an hour. This one seemed to flatten her stomach more than the blue jeans.

Merle was a fourth-generation farmer in Barnes County. He ran cattle northwest of Valley City. Black Angus weren't bad.

It was the Holsteins.

Twenty head.

Wind blew outside their two-story red farmhouse, whipping snowflakes in dust devils across the field. Inside, newborn Simon Peter lay in a metal crib painted white.

Merle might be married to the cows, but she wasn't going to be stuck raising his boys all day every day. It was her night out.

She deserved it.

***

Darla Tyre arrived and put pizzas in the oven. She got to work on the breakfast dishes piled high in the sink.

The front porch outer door opened, and voices could be heard along with the stomping of boots. Soon, Kevin and Charles opened the inside door. They stepped into the living room, made their way through the dining room and into the kitchen.

"What's for supper?" Charles asked.

"Pizza." Darla sniffed, wrinkling her pert nose. "Get washed up first."

Kevin's chin came up. "Daddy says the cows smell like money."

"Yeah. Like a thousand dollars," Charles supplied.

Darla pointed to the wooden door painted white, leading to the basement stairs. "Go to the tub. Go directly to the tub. Do not pass go, do not collect $200."

"Aw, man," Kevin protested, even as he swung toward the door. "We're hungry."

"Make sure to wipe up the floor when you're done," she called after them.

"We will," they called back in unison.

A half hour later, they emerged, clean, with dry clothes pulled on over wet bodies. Their hair dripped water on the floor.

Doug emerged behind them. The three-year-old made his way around the table. "I'm bored."

Darla ruffled his head. "Then you can set the table."

"No way." Doug ducked, running off to the living room.

Kevin grabbed a bag of bread. He and Charles rolled slices into golf-sized balls and popped them into their mouths.

"Guys," Darla said. "Ten minutes and the pizza will be ready."

Doug returned from the living room where Simon was sleeping, his face screwed in hot anger. "I don't want that baby anymore. Take that baby back. Bye bye, Baby."

Abandoning the dishes, Darla retreated to the living room. She crossed over to the record player and set the needle. "Angel of the Morning" began to play.

Simon was wrapped in a pink blanket.

Darla decided he couldn't possibly be in it when neighbors arrived in the future, and made a mental note for a newborn Christmas gift. She picked him up and sat down on the gold couch.

Charles huddled close, touching his baby brother's nose with the tip of his small finger.

6

"Can I hold him?" he asked.

Darla patted the yellow paisley cushion. "Sit here."

Charles obeyed. Darla set Simon on his lap.

The baby opened his eyes.

Darla glanced over at Kevin. "What about you? You want to hold him?"

Before Kevin could respond, Darla took the infant from Charles, and placed him in Kevin's arms.

Kevin immediately got good and angry. He didn't care for the baby. The nursery was still pink. Their father told Darla to paint it something else. Mom hadn't allowed anyone to go in. Not even Simon, and pink it remained. The baby slept in the crib in the living room.

Kevin was working himself up into a real scowl when he happened to glance at the baby.

The infant stared right back.

Enraptured with the newborn, no one noticed Doug silently fuming in the corner, red-faced and eyes boiling with rage. He dashed across the small space, and without warning, dipped down, sinking his teeth into Simon's eye.

Simon screamed.

Kevin jumped up, nearly dropping the newborn.

A bead of blood formed on Simon's eyelid.

Darla sprang to her feet. "Why would you do that?" she cried.

"…*I won't be blinded by the light*," Juice Newton's voice built momentum.

Charles rushed Doug.

"*Just call me angel of the morning, Angel. Just touch my cheek before you leave me, baby.*"

Doug laughed, ran behind Darla, wrapping himself around her leg.

Charles' brow was furrowed. "Baby's bleeding."

Darla's eyes widened at the blood on Simon's brow. She took the baby from Kevin. "It's a flesh wound. A scratch really," but she looked scared, "Charles, go get me some toilet paper from the upstairs bathroom."

Charles hurried off.

Kevin glared at Doug. "You're gonna get it when Dad gets home from cow chores."

"What's he gonna do?"

"He'll spank you good."

Fear shadowed Doug's eyes briefly before he stuck out his lower lip. "Mommy won't let him."

They heard an engine pulling into the yard as Charles returned with a bit of toilet paper.

"You guys get to bed," Darla said, holding the tissue to the baby's eye. "I'll explain what happened."

"What are you going to say?" Kevin asked.

"If it's your mom, we'll tell her the truth. If it's your dad, Thomas the Cat did it."

"Hey," Charles cut in. "He's my kitty. Besides, he's not allowed in the house."

"We'll tell him Doug let him in."

Instantly red-faced, Doug screamed at the top of his lungs.

Darla stepped back. "All right, all right. Charles left the door open."

The anger suddenly disappeared from the toddler's face, replaced by a rather snide grin. "Yeah."

Darla glanced out the window once more. "It's your mom."

The tomcat was never seen again.

2
December 13, 1981

"Happy Birthday, bud," Doug burst into my bedroom. "How old this year?"

"S-s-six." I took a quick step back, scanning for escape.

"S-s-six?" He grinned, and took a step toward me.

My gaze flicked to the space beneath the stairs between my bed and the wall. Instead, I made a dash for the door separating his room and mine. Clutching the back of my shirt, he pinned me to the cement floor.

"One," he spanked my backside, "Two." The stench from his armpit shoved in my face took the cake.

"Four, five…"

I twisted beneath him. "Let me up."

"Not quite." He reached over and pinched my forearm. "A pinch to grow an inch," His fist landing on my arm, "And a sock to grow a block."

I wiggled out from underneath, stood, and backed up against the wall. Feeling the painted wooden surface of his closet door, I jerked away.

"Whatsamater?" Doug eyed me carefully. "Scared of the witch?"

The darkest creature on earth resided in there. It wasn't always in his closet, but often. And when it was….My heart began to pound.

He made claws with both hands and held them up. "She's coming for you, Barbara."

I paled. Doug convinced me to watch *Night of the Living Dead*. Ever since then, the scene from the horror movie haunted me.

Claws in the air, Doug took a step toward me. I turned, ran out the door, and dashed up the stairs. He was right behind me as I burst into the kitchen.

Kevin and Charles were sitting at the breakfast table.

"…I'll take the grapple fork. You can cut the twine on the bales," Kevin was saying.

Doug strolled to the fridge like he hadn't been chasing me. "Can I help you guys?"

"Nope." Charles looked up from his cereal. "Happy Birthday, Simon."

"It's not my birthday," I said.

"Today's the thirteenth."

"Yeah, but I don't get to celebrate until December 26."

"What's December 26?" Kevin asked, reaching for the Cheerios.

"My birthday." Doug took the carton of orange juice from the fridge, drinking straight from the container.

"Still his birthday today." Kevin poured the milk to the top of the cereal bowl, Cheerios spilling over the sides.

"Dad said he would take us ice fishing after chores." Charles held the bowl to his lips, slurping milk.

"I wanna go," Doug said.

"Simon should get to go since it's his birthday." Kevin wiped his mouth with the back of his forearm.

"Can I?" I jumped up, spilling the milk.

Charles shot to his feet, the white liquid running down the table and onto his lap.

"Dude." Doug smacked the back of my head.

10

"Sorry." I got up and went to the sink for a dishrag. "Can I go fishing?"

Kevin and Charles exchanged covert looks.

"You'll have to ask Mom," Kevin said through a mouthful of Cheerios.

***

"I'm ready," I announced when Kevin and Charles emerged from the basement midmorning, showered and dressed from chores.

"Where are you going?" Mom's voice stopped me short.

"Fishing." I held up my fishing pole. "Kevin gave me this for my birthday."

"How thoughtful, Kevin." Mom smiled. "Don't the Morris' live nearby the slough you've been going to?"

Disappointment was quick and heavy as the morning snow fog. Ever since Jeffy Morris had called me cyclops, I avoided him at all cost.

"No one goes out there, Mom," Charles said. "Pretty secluded."

"Kids can be so mean." She sighed. "Jeffy Morris takes after his father."

I hesitated. "Maybe I shouldn't go."

Mom's brow arched. "You sure? I was going to ask Doug to watch the twins so you could go. I'm going over to the Frank's place to see Pearl's new kitchen floor. "

Doug watching my baby brothers? "I'll stay home. I can watch the twins."

Her eyes took on a shine. "You're so thoughtful."

I glowed beneath her praise.

"Nice, Bro." Kevin ruffled my head. "I'll catch extra for you."

Doug strolled in and asked, "Can I go?"

Kevin and Charles exchanged another glance.

"Not this time," said Kevin.

"Can I, Mom?" Doug rushed over where she was fixing her hair in the dining room mirror.

Charles said, "You need a pole."

"I'll use Simon's." Doug flashed me a grin.

"I wonder if Simon would let you use his," Mom mused.

"But he'll wreck it!" I cried. I'd gotten it for my birthday and hadn't even used it. Something about him using it first got under my skin. I snatched a glance at Mom. "I guess you can."

She gave me a brilliant smile. "Good boy."

"I'll take excellent care of it," Doug said, a gleam in his eye.

Kevin and Charles exchanged another cagey look.

After everyone left, I headed to the living room, a warm bottle of milk in each hand.

Under a shadow of loneliness, I scooped Harry out of the crib, sat down, and popped a bottle in his mouth. Half the reason I was stuck in the house instead of fishing.

My mind wandered to the fishing trip and outing I was missing. I should have gone. Resentment crept inside.

Suddenly, I felt a tiny grasp on my finger where my hand held the bottle to his mouth. Startled, I glanced down. Harry gazed up at me with trusting eyes. Hans lay, cooing.

My chest swelled with something powerful.

Pride.

***

I finished tucking Hans and Harry in the old metal living room crib as they returned from the fishing trip with a slew of fish.

Doug made a beeline for the basement. "See ya, wouldn't want to be ya."

Charles spread tin foil across the breakfast table. "Want to learn how to clean fish, Simon?"

"Sure," I said eagerly.

Kevin pulled out a sharp knife. "When you're older, I'll get you a knife for your birthday, and you can clean fish all by yourself."

"When I'm seven?"

"Maybe." Kevin chuckled. "First, set the fish on the cutting board." He inserted the knife tip into the fish's belly, moving the blade up along the lower end. "Cut to the head. Don't dig too deep or you'll cut intestines."

"What's intestines?" I asked, feeling sorry for the gutted fish.

"The digestive tract."

"Poor worm."

"Night crawlers are bait, Simon."

"What's bait?"

"Like a trap. Now pay attention." Kevin spread the body open and removed all of the entrails and innards. "Some fish have a kidney by the backbone." He scraped it out with his thumb.

Charles pulled out a frying pan from the cupboard above the kitchen stove. "I'll let you cook the fish if you clear the table."

"Okay." I grabbed the garbage pail from the kitchen, pulling it up to the edge of the dining room table.

After the table was cleared, Charles kicked a stool over to the stove. "Stand here."

I stepped up on it.

"Now, pay attention." Charles flipped on the burner and greased the frying pan.

And I stood a little taller.

3

December 26, 1981

Doug got a bike for his birthday and a Beach Boys record. I got a record too, *Music Machine*.

"This is for you too, Simon," Mom said with a serene expression, walking over to a large box with a picture of a yellow Easy Bake Oven on the front.

I ran my hand over the top. "Can we bake something?"

"Not today," she said, primping in the dining room mirror. "Daddy and I are going to the Martin's."

My heart sank.

"Hold on. I think there's a special on tonight." She crossed over to the TV.

Tears brimmed my eye, spilling over and down my cheek.

A burst of laughter escaped her lips. "What are you crying for?"

I wiped my cheek with my palm.

Charles walked into the room. "What's with Simon?"

"I told him there's a movie on." Mom giggled.

"What?" Charles chuckled. "Oh boy."

***

The living room TV blared the Tuesday night special *Pinocchio*.

"*...Hi diddly dee an actor's life for me.*" The show was back on.

"Whatcha got?" Doug snatched Monchhichi from me.

I reached for the stuffed toy. "It's mine."

He held it out of reach. "And now it's mine."

I started to reach for it and stopped. Between Christmas presents, and my birthday presents, there was enough stuff to play with.

Besides, it was just a toy. Not like a book or anything.

I returned my attention to Honest John convincing Pinocchio to skip school and become an actor.

Shut your ears, Pinocchio. Don't listen.

Head in the clouds, Pinocchio listened, following Honest John down the road.

Doug marched over and changed the channel.

Quick tears burned my eye. "Excuse me, I was watching."

Blocking the TV, he snorted. "There's no excuse for a guy like you." He glanced back. "Hey look, it's an Andy Kaufman special."

My gaze shifted to the TV and the guy in a suit with a high robotic voice said, "*I would like to imitate for you the Elvis Presley,*" and turned his back to the audience.

"Watch." Doug's eyes were fixed on the TV. "See? He's going to rip the sides of his pants off."

Soon, he turned around, looking like Elvis, and danced to an Elvis ballad before taking a drink of water. "Thank you, thank you very much," his voice was low.

My gaze was now glued to the screen.

Hans began to cry.

Doug flicked an annoyed glance at the crib. "He's fine. Just watch."

I hurried over to check on my twin brothers.

Doug threw Monchhichi at Hans. It bopped him in the head and Hans screamed.

"I'm telling," I cried.

"What did I do?"

"You threw a toy at him."

"Did not."

"Did too."

"Prove it." A sinister look crept over his eyes. "Anyway, not like it hurt him." He pushed me hard and I landed on my butt on the floor. "Later, loser."

After he left, I spread a blanket on the floor and set my baby brothers on it. I got them fed and changed their diapers.

A spirit of heaviness covered me. Doug tormented us with no remorse. He was heartless, throwing objects at the babies for the fun of it.

Because you paid your attention to Hans instead of Doug.

At least he hadn't hurt them.

Yet.

***

"*...So if your hand or foot causes you to sin, cut it off and throw it away,*" Pastor Johnson was saying as he gripped the pulpit in front of him. "*And if your eye causes you to sin, gouge it out and throw it away.*"

In the front pew at the Methodist church in Wimbledon, I sat between Mom and Doug, kicking his feet back and forth.

Church: The one place Mom was delighted to take me. I knew she was embarrassed by my eye.

"*Beware that you don't look down upon a single one of these little children. For I tell you that in heaven their angels have constant access to my Father. And I, the Messiah, came to save the lost.*"

The offering plate was passed around.

Two ushers walked down the aisle with full plates. The congregation stood as one, singing, "Praise God from whom all blessings flow."

After the service, we made our way to the foyer.

In a form-fitting black dress with aqua stripes, Audre Fredrick made her way toward us. "Hi Christy. How are you doing?" She snatched a glance at me. "Everything going okay?"

"Good," Mom said.

"This is Darwin and Brenda Mattson and their family," Audre introduced the couple next to her. The woman had long platinum hair. The man wore a red sweater with a white butterfly collar beneath and gray slacks. They were surrounded by kids.

A girl with brown curls around my age stared at me.

"I bought the fifty acres next to my folks near Welcome," Mr. Mattson shook my dad's hand.

"What brings you here?" Dad asked.

"No luck buying land around Oakes. Kids go to school there in the winter and we farm up here in the summer."

Staring at me, the brown-haired girl tugged on her dad's sleeve. "Did he pluck his eye out because Jesus said to?"

"Rosemarie, don't be rude," her dad said.

"It's okay," Mom was always eager to regale the tale to whoever would listen. "When Simon was a baby a cat scratched it and it got infected."

The result of the tomcat scratch changed a little every time Mom told the tale. Last time, it was where my eye filled with blood and detached from the retina. Larry Lichte began asking a lot of questions. The next time, the story was my eye got infected and eventually withered.

As Mom regaled the story of the tomcat, the brown-haired girl's words drifted through my thoughts. *Did he pluck his eye out because Jesus said to?*

I often wondered why God took my eye. Could it be I was to be an example of Jesus?

It was then I decided what I would be when I grew up.

A preacher.

4
November 2, 1983

President Ronald Reagan signed a bill that established the Dr. Martin Luther King Jr. holiday.

The sun shone through the trees on the unseasonably warm fall day.

There wasn't a puff of wind.

I nodded, showing my dad I understood his instructions on how to operate the rifle. My hands trembled. The animal stopped suddenly, ears perked. Another larger animal emerged from the bushes, clomping toward the first.

It wasn't a deer at all, but a moose.

"There it is. Like we talked about," Dad whispered. "Ain't it a beaut?"

Thick neck and awkward tromp, the cow was magnificent. I'd never killed before and wasn't entirely certain I had the stomach for it.

My palms grew sweaty.

As though reading my mind, Dad said, "You can do it. Easy peasy, Japanesey."

I concentrated on the target. The gun shook. A bead of sweat rolled down my forehead and hung on my eyelash. Opening my eye, I drew my head back, and muttered, "I can't."

A rifle blast echoed across the distance.

Dad dropped next to me, pulling the bolt back. The empty shell popped out. "Figured you'd chicken out."

Defeated, I rubbed the sweat off my forehead with an impatient hand.

Dad stood, smiling big. "This is it, Simon," he clamped his hand on my shoulder. "A moose! Clean shot, too. Went down like a sack of rocks."

A war waged inside me between the thrill in my dad's voice and the majestic animal on its side as the last breath of air escaped.

A leg twitched.

I struggled to stand, watching lifeblood flow from the cow's neck.

"It's the nerves," Dad explained. "We don't want them to suffer, we do it real quick-like. We kill to eat."

I paled. I was unable to conceal the devastation I felt at the animal's death.

Dad handed me a knife. "We need to gut it here, otherwise the meat spoils. Now watch me." Pulling the hair and extra skin away from the animal's chest, he made a slit and began to cut down the stomach and toward the backside. "Have to be careful around the butthole. Don't cut it or you'll have a mess to high heaven."

I watched for a few fascinated minutes before grabbing Dad's arm.

Dad glared at me with eyes of rage.

I stumbled back. "You said not to cut into the butthole."

He glanced down where the knife had nicked the yellowish sack between the legs. "For a kid with one eye, you don't miss a thing. Maybe you want to try."

The knife shook in my hand. I knelt alongside the moose, ignoring blood pooling.

You can do this.

I picked up a fold of hair and skin, digging the blade in as Dad had instructed.

Dad sucked his teeth. "Don't cut yourself."

I rubbed an itch on the tip of my nose with a clean spot on my forearm.

The salty smell from the carcass wafted toward me. Watching Dad cut skin away from muscle had been horrifying. Performing the task was humbling. I worked the knife, moving aside entrails and organs.

Dad wiped his knife on the leg of his jeans and stood. "I do believe you got this, Simon. You're a natural."

Elated, I sucked in a breath and puffed out my chest as I finished up the flank.

Dad rested his hands on his hips. "Imagine. A moose."

5

January 22, 1984

"On January 24, Apple Computer will introduce Macintosh, and you will see why 1984 won't be like 1984." The advertisement for the original Macintosh computer ran in its full 60-second length on national television during the third quarter of Super Bowl XVIII.

"Look, Mom got me a Swatch." Doug followed me into the kitchen.

"A watch?"

"No, dummy, a Swatch. Check it out." He held out his wrist, showing off a white watch.

I peered closer.

He snatched his hand away. "Want to play hide-and- seek?"

"No thanks." I'd gotten George Orwell's *1984* for Christmas. Not to mention Mom was going to coffee with Beverly Richards. I had a dream about cookies, and I might take a reading break to sneak into the pantry to bake some.

"Ah, come on. You chicken?"

There was a yellow ring around both sinks, dirty silverware, and leftover food lining the bottoms. "Did you do the dishes?"

"Yep," he said proudly.

"You didn't clean the sink. Also, you gotta wash the silverware."

"I'll be it." He closed his eyes. "One, two, three…"

He didn't listen at all.

"Nine...ten..."

No amount of refusing would deter Doug. Besides, I was good at hiding. I hurried down the basement steps and slipped between the cement wall and the stairs, crawling beneath my bed. He would find me for sure.

Doug's room.

I shimmied out from beneath my bed and crossed to the door separating our rooms. Reaching for the handle, my gut ached as I stepped into his room.

Chicken?

The closet door was open.

Unopened toys lined the shelves: Dungeons and Dragons figurines, a Lego clipper ship, model airplane, and a Tonka truck. I wondered if Mom knew he didn't open anything.

There was two boxes of broken ones on the floor. He didn't let me play with his toys, even the damaged ones, but refused to put them away. Every once in a while, he would go through them like he was taking inventory.

I took a step forward and stopped.

The closet beckoned. *Simon.*

"Ninety-nine...one hundred. Ready or not, here I come." Doug's voice was loud.

My mind was wiped clean of thought, palms aching with anticipation.

His footsteps descended the stairs. Before I could chicken out, I stepped inside the closet and shut the door. Slipping behind the hanging clothes, my heart galloped like a racehorse. He entered the room.

I held my breath.

He was outside the closet door and turned the handle. *Click.*

I gripped the knob. He locked it! "Hey! I'm in here."

"I wonder where he could be," his voice growing softer as he retreated. "Simon? Where are you?"

I pounded on the door. "I'm in here, Doug! In the closet."

I heard him snicker then his feet clomping up the basement steps.

"Help me." I banged on the door.

He knew! He knew I was in here and locked the door anyway.

The dishes. I'd told him to clean out the sink and wash the silverware. A niggle worked its way up my spine. Why had he done the dishes at all? He always got out of chores, especially anything to do with housework. He'd locked me in here because I'd corrected him. He'd been planning on getting me.

The whole time.

***

The next day, I met Doug at the blacktop after the bus dropped him off.

We walked the driveway in silence.

Mom said Doug was sorry about the closet incident, and told me he cried. I couldn't imagine him crying. All the same, anger radiated from him, and I wanted things back to normal.

"You told Mom I locked you in the closet," he said at last.

I didn't answer.

At the house, he reached for the porch door handle. "You can't take a joke."

Heat prickled the back of my neck. How would he like being locked in there all afternoon? I kicked my boots off in the enclosed porch.

He tossed his coat on the floor. "Admit you did it and I'll forgive you."

"What?" I blinked, confused.

"Look, Simon it's not your fault. It was an accident. I'm over it already." Suddenly, he turned and pinned me with a long look, one which made me take a step back. A cold sensation delved in the pit of my stomach.

Then he turned and walked away, leaving me with my thoughts in a whirl. Of course it wasn't my fault.

He's fine.

Maybe, but he sure wasn't sorry.

6

January 27, 1984

While filming the sixth take of a pyrotechnical shot for a
Pepsi commercial, sparks landed on Michael Jackson's greased
hair and set it on fire.

Doug's hair was cut in a shiny black mullet. Digging
through the kitchen cupboards, he pulled out a box of Gremlins
cereal and shook it. "Save some next time, Pillsbury
Doughboy."

Ignoring him, I sat at the table, eating my cereal.

Dad entered the kitchen. Over six-feet tall, he wore horn-
rimmed glasses, and a checkered shirt with a butterfly collar
and white pearl buttons. His brown bell bottoms were topped
off with a large brass belt buckle.

"You need a haircut, Simon." Dad set the tea kettle on the
stove.

Doug snickered. "You should get a couple hairs cut."

Doug wasn't scared of Dad. He told me once the fear had
been beaten out of him, but I figured the real reason was
because he wasn't smart enough to be afraid.

Dad's mother died in childbirth. Then his dad, the grandpa
I had never known, sent him to live with his brother Bernard.

"I'll head to the bathroom," I said.

"Better not." Dad opened the cupboard, retrieving items for
tea. "Last time I buzzed your hair, your mother had a fit. I'll
sign you up for a real haircut."

"What about Harry and Hans?" I asked. The twins were rambunctious. They paid no attention to the Mr. Yuck stickers I'd put on all the cleaning supplies. What if they left the house?

"He can watch them." Dad waved a carton of orange juice in Doug's direction.

"You can't leave them alone outside," I told Doug, horrified at my father's words, but knew better than to question him.

Doug winked at me. "Don't worry. I'll put them on a leash."

Fear wiped my mind clean of all caution. "I'm telling Mom."

Just then, Charles walked in.

Dad shut the fridge. "Charles, watch your brothers. I'm taking Simon to get a haircut."

I exhaled.

In Wimbledon, Dad dropped me off at the beauty shop. "When you're done, I'll be parked at the bar. Wait for me in the van."

Selene Tomson, Mom's hairdresser, had big blonde hair, a bright pink shirt, and a smile as I walked into the shop.

Something in her smile didn't sit right with me.

Selene tied a black cape around my neck.

I kicked, draping it over my knees.

A pair of scissors in one hand, and a comb in the other, she got to work.

"You have pretty hair." Her voice, a near whisper.

She worked away at my hair with the scissors. Stepping around, she stood in front of me, reaching the back of my hair. Was that her fingers on my neck?

I flicked a quick look at her.

She smiled again, an unsettling grin. "Nice and wavy." She smoothed a lock.

I didn't say a word.

27

"Nice long eyelashes too," she said, her face close to mine. *Snip. Snip.*

A thunderbolt of fear shot up my spine. I endured the haircut in silence, a loud sigh escaping my lips at the end.

***

Smelling of cheap whisky and alfalfa, Dad was in his quiet mood. I kept silent.

There was a flash in front of the car.

Gripping the wheel with both hands, Dad slammed on the brakes.

I braced my hands against the dash.

The van weaved from one side of the road to the other before finally coming to a screeching halt.

"What was that?" Dad shifted into park, peering out the windshield.

I reached for the door handle and got out.

Dad met me at the front of the truck. The front headlight was smeared with blood. Scattered shards of broken fiberglass littered the pavement and nearby snow-covered ditch. We made our way around to where the animal lay crumpled at the edge of the blacktop.

I dropped to my knees on the frozen asphalt.

It was a dog.

A wire terrier, thin and long, curly brown hair, and eyes wide with shock. Blood ran from a deep gash on its head, down the side, matting his hair, and into a puddle on the blacktop.

"Can I keep him?" I asked, shedding my parka and slipped it beneath the puppy, gently gathering him in my arms.

Dad approached me from behind. "Your mother would have a fit."

The terrier whimpered.

Dad held a rifle in both hands.

I jumped back. "Wh-what are you doing?"

"Ending its suffering."

My lower lip trembled. "But I…"

Dad scowled. "Tuck your lip back in, or the birds will perch on it."

"Yes sir."

"Men don't cry," he said gruffly. There was hesitation in his eyes. "We don't even know whose dog it is."

"I could keep him until someone comes looking for him. You won't even know he's around." I gave him my saddest look. "I could keep it in the tool shed."

Dad's eyes were focused on the road to the north. "Car's coming."

The vehicle closed the distance.

I rose on my haunches.

"We'll keep the drinking and bar to ourselves," he said more to himself than to me. "No need to get your mother involved."

Mom met us at the door when we reached the house. "Did Selene say anything about his eye?"

"No," he muttered.

"She told Deanna Morris we hide him." Mom moved in, quick and angry toward him. "Plus, she's got the biggest mouth in town. If she hasn't heard something, it didn't happen."

Dad threw his hands up in exasperation. "Why let her cut his hair then?"

Mom's eyes narrowed to slits. "Don't be so stupid. We have to put out fires. She…" she trailed off, glancing over at me. "Take your dog into the shed and clean him up. And if I see him in the house, I'm going to lose my cool."

Guilt slid into me as I slipped into the tool shed. Then the terrier licked my hand, and regret disappeared.

"Daddy said you got a puppy…" Harry and Hans erupted into the tool shed, stopping short when they saw me cleaning him up. "What are you gonna name him?"

"Eddie Van Halen."

7
Saturday

"The Youngs are coming over," Mom announced, entering the dining room. "I want this house spotless in an hour."

Ben Young was a farmer five miles south, two miles west. He had three kids. Daniel, Kevin's age, Stephen, Charles age, Sean, my age, played basketball, and hung out with Doug. They kept to themselves, in Mom's words, and were over to our house often.

"Simy got a haircut at Simy-girl's place," Doug strolled in, chanting for the hundredth time.

Mom caught my eye in the dining room mirror. "Your hair was so pretty before. Selene usually does a better job."

A memory of the barber chair came flooding back, along with it, an image of the hairdresser's smile. I immediately hung my head and got to work on clearing the dining room table.

***

The Youngs arrived, their footsteps thundered above my ceiling below the living room floor.

Stepping on a folding chair, I cranked open the small basement window. The blonde wire terrier tumbled into my arms. Eddie Van Halen slept underneath the enclosed porch outside the bedroom I shared with Harry and Hans.

Harry and Hans squealed.

"Shhh," I handed Eddie Van Halen to Hans. "We don't want Mom to know we let him in the house."

The puppy licked his chin.

31

Hans stroked the fur on the terrier's head. "How come? Doesn't she like him?"

"She said he can hardly be called a dog," Harry said, holding him against his chest.

I set them in front of the TV. "Captain Kangaroo just started." I adjusted the bunny ears until the picture cleared.

"We're hungry," Hans said.

My mind went to the kitchen and the usual cold cereal and dough balls.

"Are we having Lucky Charms?" Harry asked.

Looking in two pairs of trusting eyes, compassion swept over me like wind across the prairie. "I'll see what there is. You two stay here and keep Eddie Van Halen out of trouble."

"We will," they chimed in unison.

I made my way to the kitchen. Mom was making coffee.

I took a step back, glancing down. "I was going to feed Harry and Hans."

"Shall we make pancakes?" Mom said in her happy voice.

My head came up. "Really?"

"Yes really." She smiled then, and she was the most beautiful woman in the world. Her brown hair was feathered, dark eyes gave her a look of mystery. "Grab a silver mixing bowl from the bottom cupboard and the milk from the fridge."

"But it's sour."

"Exactly."

She demonstrated how to make a light and fluffy batter, pouring a pancake and waited until the surface was full of bubbles before flipping it.

My turn. I watched the bubbles, and turned it over.

"You got a fold in it," she said. "Let me show you again."

Two more were golden brown on the outside, gooey batter on the inside.

Moving between me and the grill, Mom sighed. "I'll finish."

"I-I'll do better." This time, the fold was on the edge.

She took the spatula from my grasp and made five more light fluffy ones with ease. "Why don't you set the table and tell your brothers it's time for breakfast?"

I reached for a stack of plates.

"Don't drop them," she warned.

Time for the silverware.

"Don't forget the fork goes on the left, knife on the right. You'll need a stick of butter on a plate and the syrup."

After setting the milk pitcher out, I yelled from the top step, "Harry, Hans. Breakfast!"

Mom shot me an irritated glance. "I could have done that."

The twins thundered up the stairs.

Two large stacks of pancakes were in the center of the table. We said grace and dug in.

Harry and Hans ate them up like it was their last meal.

"Guys. Elbows off the table," I said.

Their elbows came off.

I poured syrup over the top of the fluffy one in front of me, and took a bite. I immediately reached for another, and yet another.

Doug strolled into the kitchen. "Save some for the rest of the world, Tubby." He pushed the back of my head.

Mom eyed my plate. "You don't have any butter on your pancakes. Here," she placed three pats on the top.

I took a bite, and another.

"Slow down," Mom said, setting her fork down.

"Yeah, Simon," Doug chimed in. "Don't eat like a pig."

I flushed. I ate quickly, anxious to get away. From the looks Mom was giving me, she wasn't happy. I was pretty sure it had something to do with Doug. He put her on edge.

Something I understood.

8
Sunday

Wearing an apron over her lime green dress, Mom was spreading flour on a rolling pin in the kitchen. Sunflowers decorated her ears.

In a Western shirt with the top three buttons undone, a tuft of chest hair poking out of his white undershirt, Dad leaned against the kitchen counter.

My gaze caught the driftwood above the kitchen table. *Welcome to Mom's kitchen. There are three rules: Take it, leave it, or make it yourself.*

Soaring on the memory of pancake making, I asked, "Can I help bake cookies?"

Mom absentmindedly handed me the rolling pin.

"Ben Young's wife ran off with Dale Roberts," Dad told her, peeling an orange.

Dale Roberts was one of the pit-pumpers who cleaned out Ben's farm lagoon.

"Serves him right for having all those hogs," Mom said.

"Ben shacked up with a new gal. Cute little thing, not more 'n twenty-five," he said, popping a slice of orange in his mouth. "Ben being close to fifty if he's a day."

Mom's eyes shone like the morning sun. "You're kidding. Who is she?" she asked, crossing to the coffee maker.

"Name's Rachel Toogoody. Ben said she's from Oakes."

Coffee pot bubbling furiously, the rich aroma of coffee drifted through the air.

"I wonder how they met," Mom mused.

Dad shrugged. "You can ask when they get here."

Mom's eyes narrowed. "I wish you would have told me yesterday. Now I'm going to have to vacuum and wash the walls."

"Just found out."

"You can't do anything right." She sighed.

"I hope your next husband is perfect." A dark look flickered in his eyes.

There was a gleam in hers. "So do I."

He opened his mouth to speak and let it snap shut.

Mom turned to me. "Simon, I need you to wash the walls on the way upstairs. Afterward, the living room needs vacuuming."

"Aw. But it's Sunday."

Dad turned and shot me a murderous look. "Don't argue with your mother."

Fear raised the hair on my forearms. "Yes sir."

After I was finished vacuuming, I scrubbed the walls with soapy water in an ice cream pail. Halfway up the olive green wall was white. Everyone dragged their hands on the white half when they climbed the stairs. Scrubbing grimy fingerprints off the glossy white surface, I thought about baking.

Afterward, I tucked the soap bucket beneath the sink, and headed to my room. Reluctant to be assigned more chores, I emerged only at lunch time before slipping to the basement once more.

It was late afternoon when I heard voices above me.

The Youngs had arrived.

Mom greeted them. Dad boomed about the weather. I tiptoed up the stairs to hear Kevin and Charles asking if they could go with Daniel and Stephen Young to Jamestown.

Doug announced he and Sean were going tobogganing, and I crept back down the stairs.

Harry and Hans were driving toy trucks across the cement floor, making engine noises.

"You guys want to go sledding?" I asked them.

"Yay!" they said in unison, abandoning the trucks.

We bundled up in snowsuits and headed outside. Harry sat in the front of the red plastic sled, Hans behind him. I pulled them through the field. Packed snow would make for good sledding.

The snow-covered hill glistened in the moonlight at the section's end. Dead prairie grass poked through snow caps.

I headed toward the highest peak, slowing when we saw Doug and Sean Young with a wooden toboggan at the top. There was another boy in a red hat and matching scarf with them. I lined our sled up alongside his.

"I want to ride on the toboggan," Hans said.

"Sleds are better." I set him in the front and Harry behind. "They go faster."

I squished behind them, snatching a glance over at the new kid. He was watching us. I glanced away, shielding my bad eye from him.

Squeezed together, we pushed to the ledge.

Harry and Hans squealed with glee as we sailed down the hill, through the ditch and over the road. We got out of the sled, laughing.

I reached for the string and started walking back.

"The farthest we've ever gone," Harry said.

The other sled flew over the road and down the ditch toward us. The new kid's hat flew off, exposing blond pigtails.

"He's a girl!" Hans cried.

I slowed to a halt.

37

Hans ran up to her and asked, "What's your name?"

"Nora."

"How old are you?" Harry chimed in.

Snuffing up a stream of snot, she said, "Nine."

"We're twins," Harry motioned between him and Hans. "We're four."

"My birthday was yesterday." She plucked her hat from the snow.

Harry glanced at me. "When's our birthday, Simon?"

"October 19."

They turned back to her. "October 19." Harry draped his arm around Hans. "Right, buddy?"

"Right." Hans returned the gesture.

Harry and Hans chatting behind, I made my way back up the hill. I knew nothing about girls. The ones at church avoided me, giggling whenever I walked past. The older ones Kevin and Charles brought over giggled constantly.

I guess I knew one thing about girls.

They were giggly.

***

Back at the house, there were items on the counter to make Russian tea.

Mom was talking to Rachel Toogoody over coffee at the dining room table. Dad was watching the game with Ben Young. Harry and Hans returned to the basement and their trucks.

Doug snatched the basketball from the wooden bin in the enclosed porch. "Let's go to the garage and shoot hoops, Sean," he said, pronouncing his name *Seen*. He knew the right way to say *Sean*, but didn't care, and Sean never mentioned it.

Suddenly, I realized I was alone with her.

Without a word, I turned around and made my way toward the living room and the puzzle I'd been working on.

She followed and sat down next to me. Her eyes were the color of a Sunday dress Mom called periwinkle. "Your eye looks funny."

Words lodged in my throat.

"What's wrong with it?" she asked, twirling a short pigtail with small fingers.

I touched the spot. "An old tomcat scratched me when I was a baby."

She sat back. "I got double pneumonia once, and was in the hospital for a month. Another time while sledding, the sled hit a hard patch of ice, and I flew in the air. I was heading straight for the ground, head first, when my body did a summersault."

I nudged puzzle pieces with an index finger.

"Do you like comics? I do. *Calvin and Hobbes* is my favorite."

My head came up. She read comics? I wondered if she liked reading.

"I like books too," she continued. "I finished *The Hobbit*."

It was my favorite book. Better than *Lord of the Rings*.

"It was better than *The Lord of the Rings*," she said as though reading my mind. "I couldn't get into the first one." She fit a piece together. "Hand me the box. I need to see the picture. I don't know where this piece goes."

"Pick a different piece." I never looked at the picture. It was too easy.

"Okay." She reached for another.

A warm feeling, one I'd never felt before, started in the bottom of my stomach, filling my entire being.

Acceptance.

For the first time, the sun peeked through gray gloomy clouds in the world in which I'd lived.

9

"What smells like pancakes?" Mom asked, entering the kitchen.

"Pancakes," I said. I woke at six and couldn't go back to sleep. I imagined everyone's mood when they woke to pancakes. I couldn't wait for Harry and Hans to try them.

She crossed to the coffee maker. "Did I say you could make breakfast this morning?" she asked, her voice heavy with suspicion.

"N-no. I didn't mind. No folds in them. They're perfect."

Mom frowned, "Pride cometh before the fall."

"I…"

Doug walked in and sat down. "Simon made pancakes? What a good little housewife."

Mom giggled. "Doug."

She often reacted to his obnoxiousness with a giggle.

To appease him.

There was no appeasing Doug I knew of.

He forked three onto his plate, slathering the stack with syrup. "Bon appetite," he said, taking a bite.

My mother glanced at my plate. "How many pancakes are you going to eat?"

Eyeing the tall stack, I suddenly wished for an escape hatch like on Bugs Bunny.

"Oh you love to eat!" My mother clapped her hands with glee. "Here," She cut a pat of butter, dropping it on the stack before me, and cut another.

Three pats of butter later, my throat tightened, threatening to choke me. "I don't want more butter."

"There are starving people in Africa, you know," Doug piped in with his authoritative voice.

"I thought you loved butter," Mom said, her eyes pleading.

The hope in her voice had me taking a bite. The flavor of maple syrup, welcoming. The butter not so much. I chewed and stopped. It was thick, cold, and waxy. How was I supposed to swallow?

My gaze lifted to hers. "Mm," I mumbled.

"You don't have to be shy." She cut another wedge and dropped it on top.

I glanced over at Doug's plate. He didn't have tons of butter on his cakes. It didn't even look like he had any.

Doug grinned at me. "You are what you eat, you know."

"Shut up."

"No shouting at the breakfast table," Mom said, shocked.

"See you around." Doug pushed away from the table, stood, and grabbed the basketball from the seat next to him. He bounced it off my head and left the kitchen.

Bile reached my throat, and I swallowed back vomit.

Harry and Hans hadn't even eaten breakfast yet. Would Mom pile butter on their plates?

What if she did? She didn't mean any harm. She just liked butter.

Really? Did you see any butter on her plate? So what? It was fine. She was my mom. Probably didn't know I didn't like all the butter.

I made a mental note to tell her next time.

10

"The Youngs are coming over this afternoon." Mom hung up the wall phone. "Doug, make sure there are enough ice skates for everyone. Kevin, you and Charles see about starting a bonfire."

Kevin's eyes lit. "Yes ma'am."

She turned to me. "Simon, clean the bathrooms and empty the garbage."

Hoping Nora would be with them, I was never as happy to clean toilets. Drawing a deep breath, I tried to calm my pounding heart. But there was no stopping its hopeful beat.

When I heard a commotion in the back entryway, I knew the Youngs had arrived. The boys were loud enough to know all three had come.

Dad wasn't in from chores.

Mom was talking to Rachel Toogoody.

I paused, dying to see if Nora was here, and having no clue what to do if she was. I hurried over to the baking cupboard and pulled out a mixing bowl to appear busy.

Behind me came her soft voice, "Hi Simon."

"Hi." I didn't turn around.

"What are you doing?"

"Baking."

"Can I help?" Nora asked.

"Y-yeah." I placed a mixing bowl on the counter and pulled out a bag of sugar and a carton of eggs. Tapping the egg gently against the side of the mixing bowl, I used my thumbs to break the shell in half.

"Can you show me how?" she asked.

I handed her an egg and cracked another.

Nora followed suit. "I got a shell in there."

I dragged it out, grabbing a bowl from the cupboard. "Crack them in here first. Then scrape out the shells."

"What are we making?" she asked, cracking another.

"Mini-cakes." I scooped a cup of sugar, shaking it to level the top.

"I moved here from Oakes with my mom," Nora said. "We live with Ben Young. His house is nice. It has a fake fireplace."

I opened the door of my Easy-Bake Oven.

"I'm a little scared of the rug," she said.

A polar bear rug covered the entire floor of Ben Young's den.

"Can we frost the tops?" she asked.

I nodded and stood on a chair, reaching up in the top cupboard for the frosting tips I saw my mother use. I thought about asking her, and remembered there was company. You didn't interrupt her when company was over. Besides, I was more likely to get away with using them.

"You don't talk very much," she said.

"You're not giggly." I stepped back down. "I thought all girls giggled."

"Time to go, Nora." Rachel Toogoody entered the kitchen as the cakes were cool enough to decorate.

"A little longer?" Nora asked. "We were about to frost the cupcakes."

"Another time," her mother said, slipping into the coat Ben held up.

Nora appeared crestfallen.

I would send some with her. I reached into the lower cupboard for the orange Tupperware container for cupcakes, and grabbed a little green one for the frosting. After shuffling through the lid drawer for a painful minute, I found the lids. I turned to fill them with cupcakes.

Doug stood, grinning at me through frosting-stained teeth.

***

"Doug ate them all," I lamented, lining my fork up across from my knife, and glanced at Doug. "Elbows off the table, this is not a horse's stable."

"Prove it," Doug said, sitting across from me.

"You can't be serious," Mom's eyes widened eyes. "All of them?"

Kevin poured himself a glass of milk. "The ones he didn't eat he licked his finger and shoved in them."

Charles snickered.

Harry glared at Doug. "You're mean."

"He never even asked," I mumbled.

Dad cut the last piece of his steak in two. "Ask next time."

"Nora helped Simon bake them." Hans took a long swallow of his milk.

Mom looked like she was about to say something and changed her mind at the last minute.

Dad shifted in his chair, and stood. "I'm stuffed. I think I'll go watch the game."

Supper was finished in silence.

***

Afterward, I cleared the table while Mom finished her coffee.

"I'm sorry about the cupcakes," she said.

Mini-cakes. "It's okay."

"About Nora Toogoody." She took a sip of coffee. "She's alright and all, but maybe a little dizzy."

44

I remained silent, waiting for her to continue.

"You're special and she's not an original." She put her cup down. "Girls like her are a dime a dozen. Mean, keep secrets, and talk behind your back."

"I'll tell her not to."

"An aspiring preacher needs to be careful." Mom gave me a look that could peel the skin off a tomato. "You don't want to wind up with Jezebel."

Jezebel? I realized we'd reached the point in the conversation where I agreed or she would make it an issue.

"You know I thought you were going to be a girl." She giggled. "Have I ever told you that before?"

Only like a hundred times. Not something I was going to say, and laughed instead.

To appease her.

45

11
March 21, 1984

The Republican-controlled Senate rejected President Reagan's proposed constitutional amendment to permit organized spoken prayer in the public schools.

Regardless, I found myself wishing I could go to school with Nora.

I did a little research on Jezebel. Turns out she was an evil woman who killed God's prophets while she fed and cared for prophets of false gods, Baal and Asherah. *You don't want to end up with Jezebel,* Mom's words floated through my mind. I didn't know what she had to do with Nora. It didn't mean she thought Nora was Jezebel.

Oh yeah? Then why did she say it?

Glancing at the radio clock on the dresser, a cold fist of fear gripped my chest. The glowing orange digits were blurred.

I dashed up the stairs and burst into the kitchen. "I'm going blind!"

Pouring herself a cup of coffee, Mom giggled. "Oh Simon. You probably need glasses."

***

Two weeks later, my glasses were ready.

The ride home revealed a whole new world. There were leaves on the trees. Details were sharp, clear as a polished mirror. By the time Mom pulled into our yard, I was flying high above the clouds. I exited the car in a hurry, throwing my arms around her.

Mom held herself back. "You need a shower."

"Sorry." I stepped back, my face flushed.

She waved a hand at me. "Go put on some deodorant."

***

The cool spring day melting the nearby snow-crusted field turned into a gentle thaw on Mom's mood.

Larry Lichte from church stopped by. "There's Youth Group tonight in Dazey," he said. "We're having a guest speaker."

"We're calving," Mom told him with a smile. "Kevin and Charles help Merle, and we don't leave the farm during calving."

"I understand," Mr. Lichte said. "Doug and Simon could go. There's nursery tonight for the little ones and a van picking up kids. I could have them pick up your boys."

"I don't know…"

"Dave Roever is supposed to be pretty funny."

No good. Mom didn't have a sense of humor.

"Eight months into his tour of duty in Vietnam, Dave Roever was burned beyond recognition when a grenade exploded in his hand. His survival was miraculous."

"And he tells jokes about it?" Mom asked, aghast.

"He's from Texas."

Better. She'd find it interesting and want to meet him. Probably even tell the neighbor ladies about it.

Mom gave him her brightest smile. "I don't see why not."

***

The March sun was low, melting snowdrifts into hard black mounds.

Doug sat in the back seat, ignoring me. Mom stopped at the Youngs. My heart pounded so hard I was nauseous. By the time Sean got into the van, I was nearly ill with a wave of disappointment.

"Just you?" Doug asked.

"Yep," Sean said, sitting down next to him. "Stephen and Daniel are helping Dad get stuff ready for planting."

A mile down the road, Doug snickered behind me. "You got on the wrong bus, Tubby. This isn't the short bus."

I never understood the short bus insult, other than it had something to do with being slow.

Sean began singing, "The wheels on the bus go round and round..."

Doug pushed the back of my head. "Ride the short bus next time, Tubby."

"That's Reverend Tubby to you," Sean snickered.

The van stopped and a girl from our church, Lisa Dawson, got in. Dangly earrings hung from Lisa's ears and her red hair was punk-rock style.

At the last stop in Dazey, another girl from our church got in, Gretchen Roth. She sat next to Lisa. Gretchen's short brown hair was feathered and she wore large dot earrings that looked like pills. Both girls had on matching lined jean jackets with collars flipped up.

Snatching glances in my direction, they leaned toward one another, whispering and, of course, giggling.

At the church, Doug sauntered over to them, Sean in tow. Sean said something to Doug who laughed loud and fake.

The girls giggled some more.

I went to the sanctuary, sat down, and opened my Bible.

Then Nora walked in. I felt her presence before I turned around and saw her. She wore her blonde hair in two pigtails and cowboy boots. In old-fashioned clothes, her cheeks were as rosy as her coat.

Then she saw me.

I turned back around, knowing it was one thing to work on puzzles and bake with me in privacy, but to sit by me in church where everyone could see was sure to be sudden death.

Pushing my nose in my Bible, I pretended not to care.

She slowed next to me, the scent of cigarette smoke radiated from her. I stared at the page in front of me, sweat forming at the base of my white butterfly collar beneath my red sweater.

I thought she wasn't coming.

"My mom brought me," she answered my unasked question. "I like your glasses. Do they help your bad eye?"

I shook my head. The right lens was a normal glass lens, the left one prescription for my good eye.

"Did you know Jesus healed a blind man with mud? We could go look for mud."

"I don't think so."

"Why not?"

"Because you're not Him."

Nora continued, "Ben smokes like a chimney. My real dad didn't. My Dad died at four o'clock. He was the oldest in his family."

I pushed my glasses up my nose.

"Daniel, Stephen, and Sean have a trunk full of Lincoln Logs. Sean and I built a house for my Barbies," she pressed her hands between her legs, "My favorite Barbie is Barbie on Vacation. Have you ever played with dolls? I suppose not. Hans and Harry like trucks. I play trucks too sometimes. But I like Bugs Bunny too."

I glanced over at her.

Nora continued, "I like to read too. Especially history and books about dogs. Have you ever read about *Titanic*? It was sad. Did you know lots of daddies died?"

"Yes."

"Women and children only." She leaned closer. "Some people think there's one, two, three, even five or six gods."

Why would she say that? Did she believe in Baal or Asherah? "There's only one God."

"The one-eye preacher." Doug sat in the pew behind me. His finger was in his mouth and then my ear.

I jerked away. "Please don't."

"You are way polite." He laughed, glancing at the girls in the pew across the aisle. "What sermon are you going to preach today, Reverend?"

Gretchen Roth giggled.

He laughed loud. "I know, an eye for an eye."

Like I hadn't heard that one before.

After the service, there were chips and cookies. For what seemed an eternity, I scanned the tables.

Nora was sitting at a table with Lisa and Gretchen. I took the far end with three spaces between me and Roger Martin. Roger didn't talk to me in front of other people.

Lisa stood and came over to me. "Gretchen wanted me to give you this." She laid a folded piece of paper on the table in front of me.

I stared at the note. What did it say? I saw her looking at me during the service. Earlier, I'd taken care picking out the red sweater in case Nora showed up. Gretchen must have noticed it.

Lisa returned to her place, giggling.

I opened the note with shaky fingers.

"You have so many double chins you look like you are staring at us over a pile of cookies."

Swift disappointment churned in my gut. Soon, anger pounded through my veins. I crumpled the note.

Gretchen's laughter rose over Lisa's, but not over the rage roaring in my ears.

I looked down at my belly, hanging over my pants, my gaze lifting to the pile of chips and three cookies on my plate.

Nora stood up and walked past them, stopping in front of me.

I shoved a cookie in my mouth so I wouldn't have to answer any questions.

Nora said, "I'm going outside. Want to come? We could look for mud."

I looked up, swallowed hard, and said, "But you're not Jesus."

She smiled, a warm, happy one that made me feel real good.

12

It was a late afternoon in May when Mom loaded us kids into the van, minus Charles and Kevin, and drove to Wimbledon. We picked up Sean and Nora on the way. Mom dropped us off at the park and went to Red Owl grocery store.

Doug and Sean headed over to the basketball court.

Hans and Harry played teeter-totter.

Pigtails glistening like winter wheat, Nora sat on the merry-go-round. I sat next to her, the metal surface beneath me, both warm and cool.

"Did your mother cut your hair?" she asked, leaning closer.

Leaning away, I shook my head.

"What happened to it?"

I didn't know how to answer.

She sighed. "You gonna play basketball?"

"I don't know the rules."

"The ball may be thrown in any direction with one or both hands. The ball may be batted in any direction. You can't use your fist. You can't run with the ball. You have to throw it from the spot on which another..."

For a girl, she sure knew a lot about basketball.

"...No shouldering, holding, pushing, tripping, or striking in any way shall be allowed..."

I cut in, "I know the rules for basketball. I just don't know Doug's rules." Which changed daily. He hogged the ball, bounced it in the house, and was never guilty of a foul.

A light came on in her eyes. "Like Calvinball."

"Yeah." *Calvin and Hobbes* described it perfectly. "Wanna go for a walk?"

"Sure."

"Come on." We wandered over to a row of trees. A yellow baby warbler hopped past, flapping his wings.

"Oh. Look! His wing is hurt." Nora dropped to her knees. "Will it die?"

I shrugged. "Not sure, but it'll have a better chance if we leave it alone."

We watched it for a few moments in silence.

"I'll call him Hamlet," she said, and quickly added, "Even though I can't keep him."

"Hey Preacher," Sean called as they made their way over. "You read anything besides the Bible?"

Doug snorted. "I like to read Berenstain Bears."

I stiffened. I should have known they wouldn't leave us alone.

Sean laughed loud and long. Doug pushed his shoulder. Sean pushed him back. I tried to push them both from my mind. Sean strolled over and smacked the back of my head.

My eye smarted. "Stop it."

"Oh, is the widdow Preacher sad?" Doug rubbed both eyes with his fists.

Sean laughed.

Doug dropped down. "What's going on, guys?"

"Nothing."

"This doesn't look like nothing to me." He reached out to pick up the injured bird.

Without thinking, I knocked Doug to the ground with one swipe. *What are you doing you fool? You'll be creamed. He'll make lunch meat out of you. You'll...*

"Of all the stupid…" Doug stood, brushing dirt from his pants. "I can take you down with one hand tied behind my back."

I clenched both fists at my sides. "You can try."

"Tough guy, huh?" Sean drew his fist back and slammed it into my right temple. I saw stars.

Suddenly, Mom appeared from nowhere. "What on earth…? Are you okay? What happened?"

I glanced away, my head throbbing in pain. "Yeah, I'm okay." Any other response would have Doug on my case when Mom wasn't looking. Besides, I didn't want Nora to think I was a sissy.

"You sure?" she reached out to touch my cheek.

I managed a wobbly smile. "I'm sure. I've got a hard head."

"Look Mom," Doug said, picking up the nest. "Can I keep it?"

My smile faded.

Mom's eyes softened. "Oh, sweet."

Nest in hand, Doug poked Sean. "Come on." They turned and headed for the van.

"Let's go, guys," Mom said, trailing behind.

Defeated, I climbed into the van.

"Simon, over here." Nora patted the window seat next to her. "You dropped these." She handed me my glasses.

I sat down and put them on.

"Your good eye's bleeding," she said. "Is your dad gonna be mad?"

He was probably out with the cows. When he came in, he would be tired, and head for the shower. If Mom was in the mood, they'd drive to Jamestown for supper and drinks. I doubted he would notice.

Not something I was going to let her know.

I shrugged. "Probably." Then without warning, a hot tear leaked from my eye. And another. I took off my glasses, and turned away, swiping my cheek with an angry wrist. A roll of self-loathing hit me full force.

"We're a lot alike," she said.

Struck, I looked over at her. Nora talked nonstop and liked basketball…and was a girl. Did she mean I acted like a girl? Cried like one?

"You stood your ground even though you had no chance of winning," she answered my unasked questions. "You're the bravest boy I know."

Smiling through my tears, I turned to stare out the window once more.

It was a small victory, but still a victory.

13

May 16, 1984

In the news, Andy Kaufman died.

If I were to die, I wouldn't mind it being on such a warm, sunny day. In our freshly tilled garden, I dug my fingers through rich upturned soil alongside night crawlers. A beetle. Joyful songbirds in chorus fluttered about nearby bushes.

"Whatcha doing, Simon?" Dad's voice came from behind me.

"Looking at worms."

His mouth twisted in a thin line, and I knew it was the wrong thing to say. He watched me for a long, silent moment.

"Grandma will be here any minute," he finally said in a tight voice. "Why don't you go and help your mother."

I quickly stood, brushing my hands on the sides of my jeans, and headed toward the house.

My mother's dad died before I was born, and her mother, Grandma, moved out to California. I'd been to visit Grandma once last year. I didn't remember much about her house except for the dolls. Various kinds lay upon her bed and a shelf above her headboard. Instead of novels, dolls lined bookshelves in the living room. Raggedy Ann sat upon a highchair in her sitting room.

The path homeward was scattered with dandelions. I picked a careful bouquet for my mother. Entering through the porch by the living room, I made my way to the kitchen.

Mom was cracking eggs into the mixer bowl.

At the breakfast table, Doug ate a peanut butter sandwich noisily. How anyone could make noise while eating a soft sandwich was beyond me.

"Doug, you add flour before the yeast when baking bread, otherwise you'll kill the yeast with hot water."

"Hmph," he said through a mouthful, looking about as interested as a student in a classroom full of elementary classmates on the last day of school before summer vacation.

"I picked flowers for you, Mom." I put the dandelions in a cup of water and set it in the center of the breakfast table.

"That's nice," she said.

The cup looked off-center. I adjusted it. Too far. I moved it back a little.

"Leave it," Mom ordered.

I backed away quickly. "Can I help bake bread?"

"Maybe later."

"Hello, anyone home?" Grandma called from the front door. She wore a frilly white shirt and pale blue slacks. Sunglasses made her look twenty years younger.

Mom abandoned the bread. "Hello Mother. Simon, help Grandma carry in her suitcases."

Doug leapt from the table. "I'll help Grandma."

Mom turned, her eyes shining. "Thank you, Doug. You're a fine young man."

"Hi Grandma," Doug said, giving her a hug. "How was the trip?"

She hugged him back. "Good. Your mom tells me you're captain of the basketball team."

"Yeah."

"I'm proud of you, darling."

"Better get those suitcases."

After he left, Grandma turned to Mom. "He's darling."

"Thank you." Mom gave her a shy smile, the kind reserved for Grandma only.

"How are your other children?" Grandma slid me a probing glance. "What sports does he play?"

It wasn't uncommon for Grandma to talk about me indirectly. I think my eye bothered her.

Mom shook her head. "Simon doesn't play sports. His eye you know."

Grandma's chin came up. "What about an instrument?"

"He goes to school at home."

"I'm going to be a preacher when I grow up," I said.

"Simon, don't interrupt."

Grandma eyed me beneath lofty lids. "He could play the piano."

Mom frowned. "I used to beg you to let me take piano lessons."

"It wasn't your thing, darling," Grandma patted her arm. "What about the other two?"

"Kevin will be a senior in the fall. He plans on taking elementary education at North Dakota State University next year. Charles will be a sophomore. He's the quarterback for the high school football team."

"How wonderful." Grandma painted on an easy smile.

"Would you like to go shopping?" Mom asked. "Jamestown has a mall. We could go out to eat afterward."

"Sounds lovely, darling," Grandma said. "Let's hope it's better than the place you took me last time. They really need to hire a chef who knows how to cook a steak properly."

"Paradiso has Mexican food."

My mouth watered. I'd never been to Paradiso but always wanted to try it.

"Shall I put these in the nursery, Mom?" Doug toted two large suitcases.

"Yes. Thank you, Doug."

"Doug should come with us," Grandma said.

"Simon, do you mind cleaning up the kitchen for me?" Mom asked.

"Sure."

After they left, I eyed the mixing bowl. I'd watched Mom make bread a couple of times.

How hard could it be?

***

Turns out baking bread was tricky, dependent on the weather, the flour and the applesauce.

By the third day of Grandma's visit, I had it down to a science. I didn't measure the flour according to the recipe. I watched the sides of the mixer bowl until it looked right.

Mom looked at the array of breadstuffs on the table. "Oh my. What are we going to do with all this?"

Suddenly, the front door burst open.

"Hold it," Dad grunted in an impatient voice.

Dad never came through the front door except to and from church on Sunday. Kevin was behind him. Together they hauled in an upright piano, pushing it against the living room wall where the old metal crib used to sit.

Dad took a step back. "Takes up half the living room."

"It's perfect." I sat down on the bench.

Doug pushed me off. "Move it, loser. It's mine. Grandma got it for me." He sat down, pounding random keys.

"What?" I looked up, startled.

"I couldn't help myself," Grandma said. "Doug is so darling." Her cool, unapproachable expression sent a chill up my spine.

"Larry Lichte gives lessons," Mom told Grandma. "He's from Dazey."

Lessons too.

"I'll expect you to be able to play Mozart by the time I come back, darling." Grandma watched with a triumphant smile.

It clicked in my head finally. Grandma was playing a game. The piano was the equipment needed to score points. I'd bet she didn't really expect Doug to play, nor would she care if he did. Next year when Grandma visited and Doug couldn't play, it would be a victory.

With a natural athletic ability and grace in social situations, life came easy for Doug. But I'd never seen him practice anything.

There must be some way for me to learn how to play the piano. Then I could surprise Mom. Maybe, just maybe, she'd see the piano really should be mine.

14

July 1984

Since the United States had boycotted the Moscow Olympics in 1980, the Soviet Union and its allies boycotted the Summer Olympics, also called the "Games of the XXIII Olympiad" in Los Angeles, Calif.

Doug was in his room with Hamlet. Mom let him keep the yellow warbler in one of our rabbit cages.

"He looks good today. Wing's nearly healed," I said the same thing I did every day as I fed him table scraps. "Don't you think you should set him free?"

"What do you care?" Doug said, not looking up from the *Sports Illustrated* magazine.

The cage was small. Doug fed him when he remembered, but otherwise ignored the bird. I felt sorry for Hamlet and guilty at the same time.

***

Larry Lichte was a thin man with a crooked nose. His hair, white as a sheet, and eyes gray like a summer storm. Mom let me sit and watch piano lessons. Then Mr. Lichte struck up a bargain for lessons for two.

Turns out, learning to play the piano was a task proving to be quite challenging. Doug didn't practice, but he also didn't want me on his piano.

***

The house was quiet.

I sat at the piano and began practicing piano scales.

Playing "Happy Seal" in F Major position, I concentrated on Mr. Lichte's instructions: steps and skips, playing teeter tottery and not bouncy — staccato — until my fingers were tired, and my back, sore.

Finally, I stood and stretched.

Mom was in the yard having a conversation with Ben Young. I pulled my cowboy boots on and ran outside. Neither paused when I reached them.

I looked around and found Nora in the backyard by the horse pasture where our new Welsh ponies grazed.

Nora had a carrot in her hand, and bridles over her shoulders. "Ben gave my ponies to you guys," she said, her voice filled with sorrow.

I didn't know what to say.

She fed the closest horse a carrot. "This is Clyde." She pointed to the other. "She's Petunia. Clyde is the fat one, Petunia has the sloped back."

I shoved my hands into my pockets.

She glanced over at me. "You want to ride?"

"I don't know how."

"I'll show you," she said, leading Clyde out of the pen.

Holding out my hand, I waited as the gelding's soft lips traveled across my palm and fingers, leaving a feeling of tickling warmth behind.

Nora held out a bridle. "This is his. See? It doesn't have a bit." Pulling the other off her shoulder, she held the bit to Petunia's velvety lips. "Hold her halter to keep her head in place." Then she grabbed a five-gallon bucket and flipped it over. "Stand on this to get on. You'll ride Clyde."

I stepped on the bucket and swung my foot over his back. Looking down Clyde's mane, I trembled. "But...how will I hold on?"

"With your legs."

I squeezed my legs together, and Clyde began to walk.

"Whoa." I clutched his mane.

"Not so tight," she said, and in a single leap, she was on Petunia.

"Okay." My voice shook.

"Don't fall," she said, and then broke into song, *"If you fall I will catch you, I will be waiting…"*

"I've heard a couple of Madonna's songs." I focused my gaze straight ahead.

"Cyndi Lauper sings 'Time After Time.'"

"Never heard of her."

"You've never heard of Cyndi Lauper?" Her tone, incredulous.

"I usually listen to country. Or Christian."

"That explains a lot."

***

"I rented movies, bud." Doug set rental tapes next to the VCR. "Want to pop popcorn and watch with me?"

"What movies?" I asked, making my way through the living room.

"Nightmare on Elm Street."

"No thanks." After learning to ride horseback, I was feeling pretty good, and wasn't in the mood to sit in front of the TV for two hours.

"Come on. What about *Karate Kid*?" Doug reached for the tape, and casually added, "By the way, I saw you riding with Toogoody."

"So?"

"I didn't know you could ride."

"Nora showed me how."

"You were owned by a girl."

"There's nothing wrong with learning from someone who knows how." I faked a yawn. "Kinda tired. I think I'll head down to my room."

Doug's eyes darkened, and with a wave of his hand, he said, "Forget it. I know you don't want to hang out with me."

"I don't like horror movies."

"I'll watch by myself."

"You don't mind?"

"I'm used to it." He sighed.

A surge of compassion slammed into me like a strong south wind. "I'll watch *Karate Kid*."

All evidence of sorrow on his face fled in an instant. "You mean it?" he asked.

Minutes later, I arrived with a large bowl of popcorn.

We watched *Nightmare on Elm Street*.

15
July 23, 1984

The first African-American winner in the history of the pageant, Vanessa Williams was stripped of her crown when nude photos she'd posed for previously were published in *Penthouse*.

Monday morning, about the time the sun colored the eastern sky golden, I heard my folks arguing in the kitchen.

"You can't baby him," Dad was saying.

"He's not like other kids," Mom sounded furious.

"Cows don't care what you look like, Christy."

"It's not just his eye." A pause. "He's…delicate. Everything has to be just so. Did you know he folds his underwear?"

"You turned him into a sissy by coddling him." Dad's voice was impatient. "He's got to grow up sometime. You can't keep hiding him away like he's some sort of freak."

"If the noise doesn't drive him crazy, the manure will."

"Nothing's wrong with him other than he has one eye."

Her eyes flashed fire. "He might not have lost it if you'd taken him to the doctor when I asked."

"When you what?" Dad roared. "You said nothing about it. The day I noticed it, I took him to Dr. Jones." He sighed loudly, his voice dipping slightly, "Some responsibility would be good for him."

"Fine. Don't come crying to me when he freaks out."

"I won't." Dad stomped over to the basement door.

I quickly stepped back down.

"Simon," he called down the stairs.

"Yeah?" I said, climbing them once more.

"Come with me."

"Yes sir."

Outside, the July sun shone brightly.

Our farmstead lay ten miles north of Wimbledon, ND. A two-story red farmhouse with shingles on the second story was surrounded by a deep cluster of trees.

Beyond, farmland. A large white and red silo stood across the yard, and beyond, the old red barn with the white milkhouse against its anterior.

Without a word, Dad got into his pickup. I climbed into the passenger seat. My curiosity overrode good sense, and I asked, "Where are you taking me?"

"You'll see."

He pulled up in front of Grandpa's old barn and got out of the pickup. I followed him into the small room at the front of the barn.

Inside, he stood in front of a stainless steel tub. "This is the bulk tank. This is the agitator. The paddle inside and the tank will need to be cleaned after the milk is drained. The milkman comes every other day."

He walked over to a see-through five-gallon jar mounted to the wall.

"The milk fills in here and drains into the tank when it's full. The pipe," he pulled a stainless steel pipe over from a washtub to the tank. "Make sure when you start milking this is in the tank."

His eyes were serious. "When you start the wash cycle for the milkers, it needs to be in the wash basin, or the detergent and bleach will drain into the milk."

He walked through a spring door to the barn. Heat blasted the aroma of manure. Dad waved his hand over one side of cows lined up. "Ten on this side and ten across. That's about enough cows."

I'd never heard my dad talk so much.

He turned and caught my eye. "It's going to be your job now, Simon."

"Me?" I'd never had anything to do with the cows or the farm. Housecleaning was what was expected of me.

"Yes you. Holsteins prefer girls, they have milder tempers."

I waited for him to say something like *since I don't have girls, you'll do it.*

I'm still waiting.

***

Milking cows was dirty work. Between manure-stained tails in the face and getting splattered with pies, bright green from the heifers grazing, I quickly realized jeans and long sleeve shirts were the way to go.

Doug's job was hauling hay from the lean-to and filling hoppers.

"Watch how strong I am." Doug grabbed the pitchfork in the corner. He raised it over his knee, and with two good whacks, broke it in half.

"What'd ya do that for?"

"Because I can." He flashed a look of rage, and then it was gone. "Dad's making me haul hay and corn and clean out the lean-to. Plus, I have to feed calves."

"So?"

"So, I was thinking we could trade jobs. You feed calves, I'll fill hoppers."

"I don't know…" It took three five-gallon pails full to fill one hopper and there were seven, three on each side of the barn in front of the cows.

There were only four calves, and feeding them would be way cooler. But Dad gave us specific jobs, and Dad always had his reasons why.

"Deal." Doug shook my hand.

"Wait! I didn't agree to anything," I called, but he was already out the door.

I couldn't shake the uneasy feeling creeping in my gut.

16

"Where's the beef?" Charles asked. Thanks to Wendy's restaurant, everyone was asking that same question.

"Funny," I answered, rooting around in the fridge, pulling out a Styrofoam container with holes poked in the lid. "You should keep night crawlers in the dairy barn fridge."

Harry and Hans thundered up the stairs, bursting into the kitchen. "We want to go fishing."

"Sure," Kevin said. "You in, Simon?"

"No thanks." Starving, I shoved whatever food available in my mouth. I finally understood why Kevin and Charles ate bread balls.

"Dude, slow down," Kevin admonished.

My face reddened. I remembered the stuff for sandwiches in the fridge and pulled out buns from the freezer.

There was a knock on the front door. My mother sailed down the stairs and answered it. "Ben. Good to see you."

Nora's gaze caught mine from behind him, and she crossed over to me. She was wearing cowboy boots.

"Mom doesn't like us to wear boots in the house." I swallowed the bread in a gulp and stood.

Nora draped her arm around me like Harry and Hans often did. "Then let's go outside. Want to ride horse?"

"Sure. How about a picnic?" I opened a bottom cupboard door. "We'll need a Thermos for ice water."

"Comics too."

"Right." I grabbed the bag of chocolate chip cookies I'd made the day before. "Kevin, can I use your backpack?"

He ruffled my head. "Sure little man."

***

The mid-morning sun was already high in the sky.

Clyde and Petunia waited at the gate for us.

Nora frowned, "Petunia seems to be limping. We'll have to ride double on Clyde."

Palms sweaty, I led Clyde out of the pasture.

Nora took a leap, swinging her leg over his back. Leaning forward, she pressed her nose against the side of his neck. "He smells good."

I set a five-gallon pail upside down.

Nora moved back and I slid in front. She wrapped her arms around me like I wasn't thirty pounds overweight. We headed for the hill, comics and specialty sandwiches in our backpacks.

"We have to ride in the stubble field." I pointed to the black rows scattered with cornstalks and clicked my teeth.

Clyde broke into a canter.

Eddie Van Halen followed us to the hill, tail wagging happily.

I pulled on the reins as we reached the bottom. "We'll walk from here. Too many gopher holes."

We dismounted and sat in the tall grass. Clyde grazed. I unzipped the backpack and pulled out picnic food.

"What kind of sandwiches are these?" Nora asked, taking a bite.

"Pastrami. I did the grocery shopping myself."

"They're good," she said through a mouthful.

"For a good sandwich, you need fresh ingredients."

"And bread."

An idea came to me. "You want to head back to the house after this and bake a batch? I used the last of what I baked yesterday on these sandwiches."

Her eyes lit. "Yeah."

We read comics and finished eating. Afterward, we packed up the remains and comics into Kevin's backpack.

"It's tricky. You'll have to pay attention and do what I say." I cupped my hands next to Clyde.

She stepped on them and mounted.

Sweat beading the back of my neck and under my arms, I searched for a way to get on.

"Here, I'll lead him to the slant," Nora said. "Go to the higher part of the slope. Then I'll help you."

My cheeks flushed. "I'm too heavy."

"I'm strong."

Walking around his haunches, I was relieved to discover I was much higher on the other side. Clyde's back was level with my midsection. Nora scooted back, and I jumped up, managing to get across his back without her help. Strong or not, I didn't want her help. Then she would know I really was heavy.

Clyde stepped forward. I took the reins.

Halfway home, she said, "You're good at riding horse."

I sat a little straighter. "We got Monopoly. We'll play while the bread rises."

We reached the pasture and put Clyde away. He trotted through the gate, kicking up as he ran off. Petunia limped behind.

Back at the house, Nora followed me downstairs. "I get to be the shoe."

"No fair. My favorite."

"I called it."

"Fine. I'll be the thimble."

Harry and Hans were in the room driving their trucks across the cement floor.

"Hi Nora," Harry said.

"We're playing," Hans added.

"We're going to play Monopoly," I said, grabbing the game off the shelf.

"Can we play too?" They asked in unison.

"Sure. But the thimble and the shoe are taken."

The game ended in less than ten minutes when Harry's foot caught the board, sending it flying.

"Sorry, Simon," Harry said, helping me clean up houses and hotels.

"It's okay." I glanced over at Nora.

The aroma of fresh bread wafted down the stairs. "We better check the bread."

They followed me to the kitchen, gathering around as I opened the oven. The tops were golden brown. After removing all eight loaves, I carefully sliced the two best-looking ones. They sat at the table and I set the sliced loaf in front of them along with jelly and butter. I retreated to the living room and set a record on.

"Everyday" by the Oak Ridge Boys drifted through the air. *"You know a smile never goes out of style..."*

Nora glanced at me. "You eat yours plain?"

"Fresh out of the oven, it doesn't need all the stuff on top." I noticed Nora never propped her elbows on the table.

"Delicious," she gushed through a mouthful.

I sat a little straighter. "Soon you'll be able to bake bread all by yourself."

Harry and Hans ate three pieces each, and ran off.

"...Let it shine and you just might find you'll lighten up the load that you bear."

Nora smiled at me then; a smile as genuine as she.

The front door opened and Mom walked in. I jumped to my feet, watching her eyes drink in the scene before her. Surprise flickered across her beautiful features, chased by annoyance.

"Simon, what do you think you're doing?" Displeasure, evident in her voice.

I shoved my hands in my pockets and swallowed hard. "We were baking bread. Harry and Hans just left," I added without knowing why.

Another long, uncomfortable moment ensued before she said, "Nora, it's time to go home. Ben is waiting for you in the front yard with the truck running."

Nora scurried away, and it was me left to face Mom.

"Clean this mess up," she motioned to the table, turned, and said, "And shut that music off. You know I don't like country," before heading upstairs.

Thoughts in a whirl, I cleared the table, making a list of the things I'd done wrong: baking bread, listening to music.

Having fun.

Guilt swept over me like a prairie gust. I should have asked. Mom always wanted to know what I was doing.

An image of Nora's smile, her cheeks full of fresh bread, worked its way through my shame.

I'd do it all over again just to see her smile.

17

Ben Young and Rachel Toogoody arrived at our house the next day. Nora was with them.

"Simon, why don't you take your little friend and work on a puzzle in the living room," Mom said.

To keep an eye on you.

Nora didn't seem to notice. She sat at the card table next to me, and picked up a piece.

The wall clock caught my eye. "I have to get ready for milking chores."

"Can I come?" she asked.

Horror flooded me at the image of her getting a tail full of manure or being pestered by a hundred flies. "It's a dirty, smelly place."

"I don't care."

"Ask your mom." I couldn't imagine her mother agreeing.

Mom was sitting at the dining room table across from Ben Young. Rachel Toogoody sat next to him.

"Can I help Simon milk cows?" Nora asked.

Mom's eyes locked with Ben's across the table.

Ben took a sip of his coffee. "I don't know, your mom will probably kill me if you get your clothes dirty." He turned and winked at Rachel.

Mom gave Rachel a winning smile. "We might have something she can wear."

"Okay then, if you really want to," Rachel said.

Nora clapped her hands. "I really want to."

***

We chased cows into the barn, heat from cow hide mixed with the muggy air zapped my energy. I locked the stanchions.

Nora followed.

Maybe I'd been wrong about Mom keeping an eye on me and Nora. After all, it was her idea to get Nora chore clothes.

Doug was topping off the last of the grain hoppers.

"Don't overfill them or the corn spills everywhere," I called.

Doug flashed me a dark look. "I'll do what I want."

After I started the compressor, Nora followed me into the milking barn. I set the washing pails down in the middle of the alleyway.

Kittens were piled on the ledge between the gutter cleaner and the door to the milkhouse.

"Look Simon, an audience." Nora petted the striped one closest to her.

"They wait until the end of milking when the jar drains leftover milk." I sat on a stool alongside the newest heifer, washed the cow's udder, and hooked up milker cups.

"That's it?" Nora asked.

"Yeah." I stood, and stepped out from between the cows. I tossed the dirty rag into the empty pail, waiting for her to complain about the work.

"Should I wash the next one?"

I stilled. Wouldn't she rather do something else? Like whatever other girls did. Go to movies, shopping, hit Dairy Queen...

"Simon?"

I felt the tips of my ears grow warm. "Uh, sure. You need to be gentle."

After she washed three, I no longer had to rewash the udders.

"I like the music," she said.

"Heifers do too. The reason I play classical music during milking. To sooth them into letting their milk down."

Following behind her, I put on milkers. All five on, we stood, watching milk swish into the milkers.

"You're a hard worker," I said, grabbing a narrow scraper to clean manure from behind the cows.

Then I noticed Doug standing at the end of the alley, watching us. Then, without a word, he disappeared into the lean-to.

Whatever that was about. I turned back to Nora, handing her the scraper. "You try."

Nora scraped behind the next one in line.

Just then, the heifer lifted her tail, eliminating a load of fresh green manure, splattering Nora from her neck to her feet.

I froze, waiting for her to flip out and go home.

A surprised laugh erupted from her lips. "Good thing I borrowed clothes."

I blew out the breath I'd been holding.

Holsteins prefer girls. I didn't know if Dad was right about cows and girls, but he was right about female temperaments.

Nora was peaceful as an early morning sunrise, and calm as a clear summer night.

18

The back door led to the basement. The dairy barn smell wafted toward me. Barn boots were lined up on the shelf next to the stairs. My new least favorite place in the house to clean.

I descended the stairs, tiptoeing past Doug's room, and stopped. Outside his bedroom door, I heard Hamlet chirping. I rapped three times. "Doug? You in there?"

No answer.

I turned the handle. The room was dark save one small basement window. The bright morning sunshine, a glimmer of light across his bed. "Doug?" I said, stepping inside.

In his tiny cage, Hamlet hopped toward the sliding latch when he saw me.

Now was my chance to set him free. Doug would lose his mind, of course. There was no way to measure on any Richter scale the repercussions of what I was about to do. But I had to do something.

"Hey Hamlet." I spoke softly, releasing the latch on the cage. He scrambled away from me. I gently scooped him up, stroking soft feathers, and stood. Making my way out the door, I headed up the basement steps.

Once outside, I gave him a gentle toss. "Here you go, little fella. Be free." He flapped his wings, and flew off.

Then from nowhere, Doug showed up. "What are you doing?"

Hamlet circled back around, landing on Doug's outstretched finger. "Good boy. I nearly lost you." He glared at me. Then suddenly, his expression changed and he began to laugh.

"How did you get him to come back?"

"Trained it," he said arrogantly. "Every day, I'd bring the cage out here and tie a string to the bird's foot. Just when it thought it was free, I'd yank it back."

I sucked in an audible breath.

Doug returned Hamlet to the cage. "Should have named the bird Dodo."

Pent-up anger and rage spilled over, and I flew at him. His eyes widened briefly before he laughed, easily pinning me to the cold floor in one, swift move.

"Let me up." I panted, forcing back angry tears.

"Promise to settle down?"

"Yes," I said, cheek pressed against the floor.

"Fine. You sink anyway." He stood.

I got up and brushed myself off.

Shoulders slumped, I retreated back down the stairs and to the bathroom straight ahead. We had a shower stall and a clawfoot tub. Unwilling to sit in my own filth, I chose the shower. I scrubbed my hair and beneath my fingernails.

After, I slipped through the adjoining door and into the bedroom. "In My Room" by the Beach Boys played on Doug's stereo while I got dressed. No matter how long I showered, I couldn't get away from the dairy barn smell.

Doug burst into my room. "I have camp pictures," he said in a sing-song voice.

He'd talked nonstop about his week at conservation camp and the dance the last day. The entire time, I thought about Hamlet. Did he actually enjoy the cage?

The time dragged on as Doug replayed the entire camp experience, flipping through pictures to back up his story.

He was looking at me expectantly, and I realized my mind had wandered. "What?"

"I said we should go to *Manhattan Baby*."

"Mom's not going to let us see a horror flick."

He grinned. "I told her I was going to *The Neverending Story*."

"What if she checks showings?"

"This is Mom we're talking about."

Man he was persistent. "I'm not allowed to go to movies."

"Really." He pinned me with a hard look, then his eyes shifted around. "Come to my room. I've got something to show you."

"I've got to make supper." It was Friday night, already close to seven, and I was starving.

"You can do it later. It's important." He gripped my arm. "Come on. It'll take two seconds."

"One, two," I counted, following him to his room.

He reached beneath his bed and pulled out a stack of magazines.

My gaze landed on the one on top. I gazed upon a woman with smooth straight strawberry blond hair, and my heart slammed in my chest.

Doug went through the stack like there wasn't a half-naked woman on the front of each one.

My collar grew sweaty. "They're not wearing much."

"I forget you're just a baby."

"Am not."

He looked up and grinned. "Which one do you want?"

I didn't know what to say, so I said nothing.

"You know you want to," he taunted.

"Dad would kill you if he saw these."

He gave me a long stare. "Who do you think I got them from?"

I shook my head. "We'll get into trouble if we get caught."

He shrugged. "So don't get caught."

"I better go make supper." I backed out the door before I could change my mind.

***

After supper was over and the dishes were done, I was on my back on my bed listening to the radio.

Staring at the back of the staircase, I began counting the steps to keep my mind off the magazines.

Fifteen stairs.

I counted from top to bottom, back up again, and multiplied. Thirty.

Then the staircase four times.

One hundred twenty.

I heard the van leave the driveway. My mind wandered to the magazine. The image drifting through my mind, my blood ran hot.

No one will know.

I swung off the bed, hurrying over to Doug's bedroom door.

Just a peek. One little look.

I crossed over to his bed, feeling beneath it for the stack of magazines. How many did he have? Where did he get them anyway? I couldn't imagine my mom actually letting Dad have them. Pulling the one from the top, fear laid a swift kick in my gut.

I shot a glance toward the door.

He wouldn't miss one from the middle.

Carefully restacking them, I saw another that looked good. What if he had inventory on them? He wouldn't. I scanned the room once more.

The closet door was open a crack.

My heart leapt to my throat. Two in hand, I hurried back to my room. Scrambling in bed, I shoved the magazines beneath the covers. After four deep breaths, I pulled one out. I flipped to the middle picture while Steve Earle sang, *"…he never came back from Copperhead Road."*

19

"Gremlins Gremlins bite after bite, what a tasty way to satisfy a gremlin appetite." Another morning, and the Anderson brothers sat around the table eating sugared cereal.

I sat down and reached for the box. It was empty. I shook it. "Guys, you didn't leave me any."

Doug stuck his finger in my protruding belly. "You'll survive, Pillsbury Doughboy." He laughed.

I turned away and started rummaging through cupboards.

Doug stood, a minute ticked by. Two. Then, "Later loser."

I found a container of rolled oats.

Hans came rushing in, crying. "Doug's mean."

Anger surged through my gut. I draped my arm around him. "What happened? What did he do?"

"He took my truck away."

"Are you okay? He didn't…" I forced an air of nonchalance, "…spank you, did he?"

"No."

Of course he didn't spank him. You're the bad one, Simon. You deserve the spankings. Anyway, he never really spanked you, did he?

Of course he had.

Birthday spankings. Not real ones.

Hans' brown eyes were on me.

I blinked. "What did you say?"

"Are you going to tell Mom?"

I rubbed his head. "I'll take care of it. How about some cereal?"

He pushed away the bowl on the breakfast table, Cheerios floating in the milk. "Can I have a peanut butter and jelly sandwich?"

"Sure. If we…"

The kitchen door burst open, and Nora stood, eyes wild. Her cheeks were grimy and streaked with tears. "My dog killed your dog!"

The room around me buzzed. I thought of the Young's Blue Heeler, then of my little terrier, and my heart slammed in my throat. "Eddie Van Halen?"

"My dog killed your dog," she repeated, sobbing.

A flurry of questions ran through my mind. Slightly dizzy with fear, I opened my mouth and no sound came out.

Finally I managed, "He's *really* dead?"

"Is there any other kind?"

***

With sweat, grit, and determination, I put my foot to the flat part of the spade.

"Fred ran after Eddie Van Halen," Nora said alongside me. "I thought he was going to chase him. Then he picked up Eddie Van Halen in his mouth, and with a flick of his head, killed him."

Chik (pause) *chik* (pause) *chik,* the sound of steel against dirt.

A tremor shook me. I was relieved not to have been there to witness it and sorry Nora had.

The display of raw emotion on her face propelled me forward. Giving her a hug in front of Harry and Hans didn't seem appropriate, but gawking like an idiot didn't either.

"My mom put Fred down," she said.

Anger burned through every fiber of my being. Still, seemed a harsh punishment for an animal who acted out of instinct.

I scooped a shovelful.

Chik (pause) *chik* (pause) *chik.*

Following the last shovelful of dirt with a firm pat of the spade, I swiped my cheek with the back of my hand. "I suppose this is deep enough."

Harry and Hans watched in silence.

I was sorry to say goodbye to Eddie Van Halen, but not so much my pink baby blanket he was wrapped in. After placing them into the hole. Side by side, we four stood at the edge of the grave.

"Do you think he's in heaven?" Nora asked.

"Yes." I placed a flat hand on the shovel.

"Can we bake with your oven again?"

"Not today."

"Why not?"

I didn't answer.

Tears spilled over and ran down her cheeks. "I'm real sorry."

"It's not your fault. He was living on borrowed time anyway."

Shovelful by shovelful, we covered a brother and friend in the midmorning sunshine.

At last, we stood alongside the fresh mound of dirt. Eddie Van Halen's eternal resting place.

I swiped off my hat. "Dear God, please accept Eddie Van Halen as your dog now, Amen." I started to put my hat back on and stopped. "Oh yeah, and Fred too."

Nora shook her head. "It's too late for Fred. I mean, we can't make him not dead." Pain flickered in her eyes, and she looked as if searching for something to say to make things better.

There was nothing she could say.

The reality crashed into me at once, and I realized this was forever. I would never have Eddie Van Halen back. The ground was an awful place, cold and lonely. I hated it. I hated he was there. Forever was too long.

I would never again see him in this life.

20

September 14, 1984

MTV held its first Video Music Awards at Radio City Music Hall. "Like a Virgin" by Madonna was a feature performance and she emerged from a 17-foot wedding cake.

In the dairy barn, Mozart "Turkish March" played on the tape player I'd brought from my room. It was the perfect place to practice memorizing Bible verses. "*For I am not ashamed...*"

"And the award for Video of the Year goes to..." Doug's loud voice boomed from the east lean-to. "Like a...'" he trailed off. "What are you listening to?"

"Classical." I moved a milker from Minerva to Bess. "*...for it is the power of God...*"

"Preaching to cows." He made his way into the west lean-to. "You are one weird little freak."

I clenched my fists in anger.

He chuckled. "I suppose cows won't call you Reverend Cyclops."

I imagined standing in front of a large audience, everyone laughing at my eye. Humiliation flooded through me at the names they would call me. Fury welled inside, and my mind disengaged. "I-I-"

"I-I-I," Doug parroted, laughing.

***

In church on Sunday as the offering plate was passed around, I imagined standing behind the pulpit.

Hair, shiny and black, feathered neatly, Doug's eyes were on the pew in front of him. The collar of his white and blue striped shirt flipped up in Elvis style.

An impulse to tell Doug he needed to be saved from his sins was quick and unexpected.

Do not reprove a scoffer, or he will hate you.

The desire remained.

An idea was born. I glanced around the sanctuary, doing the math. Twenty-five kids attended Sunday School regularly. Even if only half showed up, I'd still have twelve or thirteen.

"Praise God from whom all blessings flow" began and the congregation stood.

After I cleared the lunch table and the dishes were done, I approached Mom. "I want to start a Bible Study."

"With whom?"

I shrugged. "Whoever. Tuesday night seems to be a time when people aren't busy."

She gave me a skeptical look. "What would you talk about?"

"The Gospel."

"Everyone knows that, Simon. Why don't you talk about something they can relate to?"

"Like what?" I didn't know anyone other than Nora Toogoody and the Youngs, and I didn't relate to the brothers.

"Like sports, for instance."

"I really don't…"

"Or movies. Concerts, maybe."

"Mom, I want to start a Bible Study, not a club."

She leaned toward me, sniffed once, twice. "You stink."

"Can I?"

"Fine." She huffed.

I couldn't help but add, "Oh, by the way, Doug doesn't take care of Hamlet, the bird you let him keep. Did you know he doesn't always feed him? He even said…"

"Then you feed it."

"But how will I…?"

"If the bird chirps, feed it."

The tone of her voice told me she was done discussing it.

***

Brownies cooling on the counter, it was fifteen minutes before seven o'clock. Fear gave me a stomachache and sweaty palms. A 1975 blue Oldsmobile drove into the yard. My heart picked up, then quickly returned to normal.

It was Nora.

I answered the front door. "You're right on time."

"For what?"

"Bible study. You can sit here." I led her to the kitchen table.

"I didn't bring a Bible."

"You can use one of ours."

Ten minutes after seven, a gold Cadillac drove into the yard and stopped at the door. Five minutes later, an angry-faced Gretchen got out and she stomped up to the door.

I answered it.

She answered me with an angry glare.

I cleared my throat. "Mom said we can use the kitchen table." I turned toward the dining room, and the door opened once more.

Harry and Hans raced into the kitchen, and reached for a brownie. "Can we have one?"

I put my hand out. "They're for the Bible Study guests."

"We want to go to Bible Study," they chimed in unison.

"Alright, but you have to pay attention."

Gretchen stared at the tabletop.

"Brownie?" I held out the pan to her.

"No thanks."

I glanced at the wall clock.

Seven twenty-five.

I'd better get started. I opened the passages I'd prepared ahead of time. I read John 3:16 and said, "If anyone here is sorry for their sin and ready to believe in Jesus, raise your hands and I'll pray for you."

Harry and Hans hands shot up in unison.

Gretchen's mouth twisted in a sneer.

I waited another minute, and prayed for the two of them.

Harry and Hans ate a brownie.

The clock said it was seven-forty.

Seven-forty?

What was I supposed to do until eight-fifteen?

"Are we done?" Gretchen asked.

"Yes. Unless you…"

"Great. Can I use your phone to call for a ride?"

After Gretchen left, I turned to Nora. "At least Harry and Hans came."

"Your message was good," Nora said.

"The only one who showed up from church was Gretchen Roth."

Nora smiled. "Not the *only* one."

"She's horrible."

"Simon, no one needs Jesus more than Gretchen."

***

Throughout the rest of the evening and into breakfast, I soared on Nora's words. *Your message was good.*

Mom was in the kitchen making coffee. "I'm sorry about Bible Study. I tried to warn you."

My enthusiasm faded.

"Just because her husband Frank has money, Joan Roth thinks she's better than everyone," she said, her back to me. "She brought Gretchen to look good. Appearances are important."

"To some people maybe."

"To everyone." She turned, her beautiful eyes, full of pity, met my gaze. "You tried hard."

"But..." I trailed off, unwilling to hear further criticism of the event.

After all, no one needed Jesus more than Gretchen.

When I was a child, I talked like a child, I thought like a child, I reasoned like a child. When I became a man, I put the ways of childhood behind me.

1 Corinthians 13

21
November 6, 1984

Ronald Reagan won 49 out of 50 states against Walter Mondale for presidency of the United States.

"You want to drive?" Doug asked as we got into the pickup. Grocery shopping was my job, and he was the only one around to drive me into Wimbledon.

"I don't know how."

"Dude. You're nine years old. I learned when I was like six."

"Mom thinks I don't have good depth perception."

"It's easy." He slid the key into the ignition. "I'll show you." I stared at him in horror.

He sat back in his seat. "Relax. You're such a girl," he said, cranking the key.

When we returned, Dad was in the kitchen pouring a glass of whisky. "Hey Simon. Did you buy Coke?"

"Yes." I handed him a bottle. Maybe Dad could teach me to drive. "Doug did doughnuts through the yard. I was sure we were going to die."

"I remember doing doughnuts," Dad said wistfully. One glance at him told me he was dead serious.

I'd ask Kevin to teach me to drive.

***

King of the Hill was a horrible game where you pushed and shoved each other to remain on top.

The hill: a pile of snow Kevin had pushed to the side of the feedlot.

The King: Doug. Always Doug. Which was fine. I just wanted to get it over with and go home.

Doug insisted. Harry and Hans joined us after bringing us cookies for a snack.

I climbed to the top and before I could utter a word, Doug came up behind me and pushed with all his might.

One minute I was at the top, the next, on my back on the bottom. I tried to draw a breath and couldn't. Clouds drifted slowly by. I was dying.

"You killed him," Hans and Harry cried in unison.

"He'll be fine." Doug was leaning over me. He actually looked scared. "Breathe, Simon."

His fear only made my situation grimmer. Fear based, of course, on Mom and Dad killing him if I died.

I was able to draw a tiny breath, then a little more.

"There you go," Doug coaxed. "Take another breath."

I did.

Then he clutched the front of my parka and pulled. "Get up."

I struggled to sit.

He laughed. "What a girl."

It was laughter of relief. At least, that's what I told myself. Anything else was …too horrible to think about.

"Got the wind knocked out of you, Preacher Cyclops. You would have been preaching to the angels in another minute."

I sucked in tiny breaths. "You take things too far," I gasped. "You always do."

"What are you worried about? You of all people should be welcome at the pearly gates."

I drew hiccupping gasps, Harry and Hans watching me.

"It's not that bad." Doug draped his arm around my neck. "Then again, maybe you wouldn't be ready to meet your Maker. Might be awkward to explain to The Almighty about the magazines you stole from my room. He might not give you your eye back."

My belly flipped. "I'm…" *Oh boy.* I leaned away from him. "I'm sorry. I was going to bring them back anyway. I…"

"Don't bother." He laughed. "I'm sure you got jizz on them."

Jizz? "What's that?"

He pushed the back of my head. "You're such a girl."

Right. I should have known. I couldn't wait to get home and throw the evidence in the trash. Doug may not want them back, but there was no way I was keeping them now. How did he know? Had he cataloged them all?

Likely.

Which led me to a bigger question, one I didn't have an answer for: what if I had died with that stain of sin on me?

I shuddered.

22

December 19, 1984

The United Kingdom and China decided that Hong Kong would be given to China. Hong Kong had been under British control after the First Opium War.

Dad said Crabs Golden Kingpin Cat was a Christmas present to himself. The six-foot, two-thousand pound bull was led by a nose ring into the lean-to. Crabs, as we called him, was mostly black with a single white strip by his tail.

Dad tossed me a braided whip. "He's not like Lancelot."

Lancelot was our shorthorn bull. Also huge, but very gentle-natured.

"Now watch." He held a whip in his hand, and flicked his wrist.

Crabs shook his massive head, backing up.

"You don't want to mess with the bull. When you go out to get the cows, you'll need the whip." He handed me the bullwhip. "Here, you give it a try."

I took the handle and snapped the whip like he showed me. No sound came out. I tried again, the end landing in the dust without significance.

"No, like this," he seized the whip from my grasp, flicking his wrist. *Crack.* He tossed the whip to me.

I tried again, and again. Nothing happened.

Dad rubbed the back of his neck. "Something to work on, I guess."

***

Three o'clock rolled around and Nora arrived for chores. From the fence, we watched Crabs at the feeder.

"I don't want you chasing the cows in," I told Nora.

"Why?"

"Because he's in there," I pointed toward our new bull.

Two-thousand pounds of pure swagger, Crabs sauntered over to the feeder.

"But how will we bring the cows in?"

"I'll bring them in." I cracked the short whip a couple times, watching Crabs back up. "I got this."

With an occasional crack of the whip, I chased the cows from the feeder into the lean-to.

The last of the cows pushing through the doorway, the back of the hairs on my neck rose.

I turned around slowly.

Crabs was directly behind me, his head close to the ground. Visible puffs of air emerged from his nostrils.

Sweat beaded my forehead, dampened my underarms beneath my jacket. After more furious attempts at cracking the whip, it shook in my hand.

Crabs charged.

I whirled around and ran for the gate, hurling myself over, but he caught the back of my knees, grinding them into the gate with his enormous head.

I heard someone screaming, and as Nora was trying to get past a cow in the barn door, I realized it was me.

The cows jammed up the passage.

"I'll get your dad," she hollered.

My life flashing before my eye, I was happy I hadn't stolen any magazines since I last made things right with God. I prepared for pain, and with it, my demise.

Suddenly, Crabs dipped his head, tossing me over the fence.

Then Doug was there, helping me up.

I staggered to my feet. "Where is he?"

"Dad went to Aberdeen and won't be back until later."

"I mean Crabs."

"He left, and I slid the barn door shut behind him."

Legs wobbling, I limped over to the door. Nora was inside the barn, flipping a five-gallon pail upside down. "Sit here."

I plopped down on the bucket, dragging in breaths.

"You gonna cry?" Doug rubbed his eyes with both fists.

Nora turned on him, her eyes dark with anger. "Back off," she roared.

Doug backed away. "Get to work, or Dad will be ticked I let you go in there," he said, disappearing into the lean-to.

"Are you okay?" Nora's eyes were filled with concern.

"I'm fine," I said on a shaky breath. Inside I was terrified, but couldn't show Nora, and swallowed back tears.

I was done showing weakness to Doug or even Nora.

To anyone.

23
December 21, 1987

"The piano recital is in Fargo at the Methodist church," Mr. Lichte told Mom after lessons. "On Christmas Eve."

"What time?" Mom asked. She had on a new dress that was black and made her look like a teenager according to Dad.

"It starts at three and will go for about an hour. Mrs. Benson's students will be playing a few pieces also."

"I told Doug 'Moonlight Sonata' was my favorite," Mom gushed. "I've been encouraging him to practice."

Mr. Lichte looked like he swallowed a lemon. "We can have all the potential in the world, but it does no good without action," he said, glancing down at me. "The piece Simon has been working on is scheduled for three-twenty."

Mom appeared shocked. "But…" She sputtered. "Simon doesn't play the piano."

"On the contrary, Simon plays very well."

After he left, I braced myself for Mom's wrath.

Instead, a slow smile worked its way across her face. "Good for you to learn how to play the piano. I'm proud of you."

I grinned back. "I knew you would be."

***

After lunch, I slipped to my room and opened *Thinner* by Stephen King. I was at the part where the gypsy cursed him.

Thump. Thump. Entering my room, Doug bounced his basketball. "Hey loser. What's up?"

I didn't answer, my gaze fixed on the pages in front of me.

"When are you going to have your own birthday?"

"Ask Mom, not me."

Thump. Thump. Now he started bouncing it off the wall.

I looked up. "Do you mind? It's hard to read with you whistling and bouncing that ball in the house."

He drew back and whipped the ball straight at me. It smacked the bridge of my nose, and my glasses flew apart.

Out of nowhere, Mom was there, standing in the doorway. "What did you do?" she cried, snatching my glasses from me.

"Doug threw the ball at me," I cried.

Doug hummed "It's a Jolly Holiday with Mary."

Mom sighed. "I won't be able to get them fixed until next week after Christmas when I go to Jamestown."

Doug laughed. "Maybe you can get the next pair made special with only one lens, Cyclops."

"Why don't you go play someplace else?" I said. "Like I don't know, on the highway?"

"Did you hear what he said, Mother?" Doug's eyes widened with feigned shock. "He's talking about bodily harm to your favorite son."

"Simon, don't provoke him." Mom sighed.

"He started it."

She turned and caught my eye. "Well you finish it."

Doug glanced at me and winked.

I took a step toward him and stopped. Mom would cancel the concert. That's all I would need. Without a word, I turned and walked out instead.

24
Christmas Eve 1987

After chores the morning of the concert, Mom was nowhere to be found.

Kevin was home from college and was sitting eating breakfast cereal at the table. Maybe he could take me to the concert.

"Simon. Make me one of those whatchamajiggers like you did yesterday," he said.

"Scones?"

His eyes lit. "Yeah."

I made my way to the kitchen and grabbed the silver mixing bowl, glancing at the clock.

It was almost nine.

Where was Mom? Had she forgotten the concert? I reached for the wall phone and dialed Mr. Lichte's number.

He answered after two rings. "Hello?"

"I think Mom forgot the concert was today. You see, my glasses broke. I mean, Doug broke them…"

"Simon? Slow down."

"Sorry. What will I do if she doesn't come home until it's too late?"

"Is there anyone else who could give you a ride? Maybe one of your brothers?"

"I could ask Kevin. He's home from college, but he wouldn't like it if Mom didn't know about it," the words came out in a rush, "And anyway, I don't even have a tuxedo."

"You just be there. I'll take care of the rest."

I hung up the phone. Now how to get Kevin to agree to drive me.

Harry and Hans thundered into the kitchen. "Can we help make breakfast, Simon?"

Suddenly, the story about Esau selling his birthright to his twin brother Jacob for a bowl of soup came to mind.

"You two can set the table. I need you to let Mom know Kevin drove me to the concert. Okay?"

"We will."

"Don't forget."

The scones were perfection. Light and tender, soft, with white chocolate chips in each bite. I set them in front of Kevin.

He reached for one.

"Not so fast." I pulled the plate back. "I need a ride to my Christmas concert."

He shrugged. "Sure."

"Mom isn't around to ask."

"It'll be fine."

I set the plate of scones in front of him. "Thanks."

***

"Simon," Mr. Lichte made his way over, "Right on time."

"Yes sir. Kevin agreed to drive me."

The church was decked with balls of holly. Conversations hummed throughout the holiday atmosphere.

"I've got your tux." Mr. Lichte handed it to me in a plastic bag with a coat hanger. "It was mine when I was your age. Go try it on."

Reluctantly, I headed for the bathroom. Mr. Lichte was skinny. There was no way I'd fit into his old clothes.

Turns out, the pants fit perfectly. There was even a little room as I buttoned up the white shirt.

There was a knock on the door. "Simon? Did it work?"

I opened the door.

"Not bad," he said. Reaching into his pocket, he pulled out a bit of black cloth, and held it up. "May I?"

"What is it?" I asked as he pulled it on over my head.

"Take a look."

We stood in front of the mirror, studying my reflection. I felt like I was staring at a stranger. Copper hair combed, the waves tweaking up around the black eyepatch.

"I look like a pirate."

"The Phantom of the Opera."

I flushed. "I hope not. I hate opera music."

He patted my shoulder. "I know."

We made our way out of the bathroom. I spotted Nora. She wore a green dress with a white embroidered collar. Her blonde hair, brushed into waves around her face. Her eyes lit when she saw me, and she hurried over, her mom trailing behind.

"Hi Simon."

"Hi Nora."

"Is your mother here too?" Rachel asked, glancing around the room.

"She's on her way." *Please let her be on her way.*

"When do you play?" Rachel strolled over, reaching for my tie.

I cleared my throat. "Three-twenty."

Nora held her violin in one hand, bow in the other. "I'm on in ten minutes."

I sat a chair away from her mom in one of the Sunday School rooms. Nora played "Away in a Manger" on her violin.

The performance was painful. She started too soon, a screech across the instrument. Then screech after painful screech, she played out the ballad.

Afterward, she was flushed. "It was terrible."

"You'll be better next time," I told her.

The time flew by while standing still at the same time.

Five minutes before two, Mom was nowhere in sight.

My heart hammered, palms growing sweaty. Where was she?

Mr. Lichte fixed my collar. "Are you ready Simon?"

I scanned the room. "My mom isn't here."

He gripped my shoulders. "This is your night, Simon. Tune out the world around you, your eye, the room, and yourself. Become one with the music."

"Yes sir."

He ushered me into the sanctuary, parents and their child musicians in the front pews.

Per Mr. Lichte's instructions, I stood before the audience. I didn't see Mom, but Rachel and Nora Toogoody were in the second row. I took a bow, turned, flipped the coattail up and sat down on the bench.

A hush fell over the room.

My fingers shook as I set them to the keys. I drew a breath, let it out, and began to play Beethoven's "Turkish March."

Music flowing beneath my fingertips, I shut out the audience and my mom's absence. By the last song "Chariots of Fire" by Vangelis, I forgot all about the fact I was in a heap of trouble.

***

Afterward, Mom hurried over to where I stood beside Mr. Lichte. Doug was at her heels, looking shamefaced.

"Sorry we're late," Mom said, glaring me into silence. Her dress was violet and brought out the dark hues in her eyes. Her brown hair, feathered, and in spite of the fury furrowing her brow, she was a most welcome sight.

Mr. Lichte clamped his hand on Doug's shoulder. "There's always next year."

"You must be proud of Simon," Rachel told Mom.

Nora came up beside me. "You were magnificent."

Heat crept up my neck.

All rage disappeared from Mom's face in an instant, and she smiled. "His grandmother has quite the flair for the piano. Did you know she played with Dolly Parton at the Grand Ole Opry? She was quite the accomplished pianist," she said with a practiced smile.

Rachel's eyes lit. "Really?"

"You'll ride home with me, Simon," Mom said.

***

We rode in silence. Doug slept in the back. I sat in the passenger seat.

Passing Tower City, Mom spoke at last, "How did Nora's violin piece go?"

"Good. She's getting better," I lied, blushing. What was worse, lying to my mother or betraying Nora?

Mom let out a laugh. "You don't have to sugarcoat it. I've heard her in church. She should give it up."

"She's not so bad." I shifted uncomfortably in my seat.

A dark look shadowed her eyes, and then she smiled, a warm, tremulous one. "You have such a kind heart, Simon."

My insides glowed beneath her praise. "I know what you mean about Nora." I chuckled. "'Away in a Manger' brought tears to my eye for the first time."

She laughed. "Oh Simon! You're funny."

I smiled, flushing beneath her approval.

You were magnificent, Simon. An image of Nora floated through my thoughts, sucking out all the satisfaction of the moment in a millisecond.

Inside, guilt wielded itself in my gut.

As soon as we arrived home, I excused myself to my room. Underneath the weight of betrayal, I mentally justified my actions. Nora wasn't so great. She had even made a comment about my mother's absence at the recital. Hadn't she? Round and round, it went through my head. Until I slipped my hand beneath the mattress for the latest magazine Doug passed down.

I flipped through the magazine, images drowning out guilt and shame.

25
March 1, 1988

In the bathroom after chores, I stood in front of the vanity mirror, working on a smile to quell even Mom's melancholy.

Since I started milking cows, I felt my pants get looser.

I kicked off my boots at the stair ledge and hurried to the bathroom. Snatching a glance around, I stepped on the scale.

I'd lost another pound.

That made me one ninety-five.

For supper, I made asparagus, fresh bread, and chicken breast. After a sample, I deemed it perfection.

Seasoning was the trick.

I sat down to my own plate, setting my napkin on my lap.

My mother picked up a slice of warm bread and slathered it with butter. "Why don't you have a piece, Simon?"

"No thanks."

"You know a cook always has to taste what he serves to diners."

I glanced over at Harry. "How's the bread?"

"Delicious."

I took a bite of the chicken. It was tender and juicy, melting with flavor. I sat a little straighter.

My mom thrust the bread toward me. "I put plenty of butter on this slice. I know how you love butter."

"I said no." Everyone stopped eating, their eyes fixed on me. Had I actually yelled? "I mean, no thank you," I said in a near whisper.

Mom sat back, stunned. She set the slice of bread on her plate.

"Simon," Dad said, the awe in his voice told me I was in for it.

"She's always shoving butter at me. Do you know how much fat is in butter?"

Dad's eyes widened. "What's gotten into you?"

Then I made the mistake of catching Mom's wounded gaze. Her lower lip quivered.

My heart ached. "I'm sorry."

"Never mind." She held up her hand. "I won't do it again. I didn't mean to upset you. I try so hard, and you don't appreciate all I do."

"Yes I do. Pass me the bread."

She reached for the slice caked with butter, and handed it to me. I took a bite. It was one third bread and two thirds butter. I concentrated on the bread part and took another bite. When it was finished, I ate another. And yet one more.

Mom sat across from me, watching. I felt her satisfaction, deep and primal.

Suddenly nauseated, I asked, "May I be excused?"

Dad nodded with a flick of his head.

"Mom?" I glanced at her.

Her eyes remained fixed on her plate.

Dad looked at me. "Go to your room."

In my room, I flopped on my bed and began to count stairs. Ninety.

"Hey Simon. Want to play trucks with us?" Harry and Hans rushed in.

"In a bit. Kinda tired."

"Okay." They made truck noises, loading the back of their Tonkas with various toys.

For one crazy, hopeful minute, I imagined Mom hadn't really forced me to eat a ton of butter. Dad didn't really sit there like it was normal. And I wasn't a weak, fat, one-eyed kid.

Emotion choked my throat.

Be a man. A man doesn't cry.

Maybe I wasn't a man yet, because I could no longer stop the tears any more than I could speed up time.

26
March 16, 1988

A chemical attack on the Kurdish town of Halabja by Iraqi forces killed 5,000 civilians.

Early that morning, light flooded my bedroom with a flick of the switch. Doug burst through the door, and I glanced at the alarm clock. Four-thirty came way too early.

"Dodo bit the dust," he said.

Wide awake, I bolted up in bed. "What?"

Harry and Hans didn't stir. They could sleep through a tornado.

Doug turned around, retreating into his room.

In a sleepy haze, I trailed behind, gnawing his words. By the time we reached the cage, reality sunk in.

Hamlet lay on his side.

I didn't have to open the cage and pick him up to confirm he was dead, but I did.

Doug took the bird's cold form from me. "Did you feed it yesterday?"

My heart thudded in my ears. "No."

"How about the day before?"

"It's your bird," I said, even as guilt slowly eased into my midsection.

He shrugged. "I figured you were feeding it."

"How is this my fault?" I asked, but it was. I knew Doug wouldn't take care of it. I should have remembered.

"Just a bird." He walked over and tossed Hamlet in the garbage pail.

Horrified, I dashed to the trash can. "Why did you throw him away?"

"Who cares?" He raised his arms over his head, stretching.

Staring at Hamlet amidst candy wrappers and pop cans, I made a silent plea for forgiveness.

Doug yawned loudly. "We better head over for chores."

I stiffened with swift anger. He had all the shame of an alley cat.

I headed to the clothes washer for the cow towels. A pail of manure-packed rags greeted me. Great. I must have forgotten to put them in the washer last night.

Doug tugged on his boots by the back door.

My boots weren't on the ledge. "Where are my boots?"

"Probably where you left them." He reached for the door handle. "You're losing it. First, you forget to feed the bird. Then it's the cow towels. Now you can't find your boots."

"I left them here," I waved an impatient hand over the spot, "But they're not there."

"Better wear a different pair. It's almost five."

I searched through the far dusty ones, choosing a pair of old barn boots. My cramped toes cried for help, but I ignored the pain. I stepped outside, one arm in the sleeve of an oversized camouflaged coat.

Wind gusts had died down, and the early morning hung in soft silence. Puffs of air emerged from my lips as we made our way to the barn. Stars shone in the sky above. I spotted the Big Dipper. I could never find the little one. A crescent moon lit the way. Trudging through the dusty yard, we reached the milkhouse right before five.

Wincing at pain in every step, I couldn't help but notice how things went missing whenever Doug was around. I crossed over and plopped the bucket of cow towels next to the milkhouse sink.

Doug disappeared into the barn.

I unhooked milkers from the wash basin.

The door burst open.

Doug stood, arms wide. "I think you'd better come with me to the lean-to." His tone was grave.

"What?" A stab of fear pierced my chest.

"I'll show you."

I straightened, following him into the barn and over the gutter to the south lean-to.

"You got a dead calf on your hands." He pointed to the far hutch.

The month-old calf lay on its side, mouth hanging open.

Horror filled me. "Poor fella. How do you think it died?"

"Did you feed it?" He pinned me with a hard stare.

I took a step back. "Of course." *Didn't I?*

He shook his head. "Dude, killing calves. Not cool."

"Me?" I blinked, moving further away. "I didn't kill it."

The next day, I went straight to the south lean-to first thing.

My mouth went dry.

The calf in hutch two was laying on its side.

"Simon," Doug admonished, stepping in behind me. "What did you do?"

"Nothing. I didn't do anything!"

He clamped his hand on my shoulder. "Okay, okay. Don't go loco. I'll take back the job."

"I fed them," I insisted.

"Was Nora here yesterday?"

"Yeah, why?"

"That explains it." He tapped his chin. "I wonder what Mom will say."

"Go ahead and tell her," I said, and then with less fortitude, "I fed them after milking. Nora wasn't even here."

He arched a brow. "Lying too? Maybe we should tell Dad."

Fear gripped the back of my neck, and I shouted, "No! I mean, sometimes calves die."

"Bend over."

"What?"

"Unless you want me to tell Dad."

I retreated further, feeling the barn wall against my back. "Dad will understand."

"Or Mom. She isn't as quick with the spoon as she used to be. Wait until she finds out what you two have been doing when you're alone out here."

"We work." Fear was a cold fist in my gut.

He grinned. "Is that what you call it?"

Mom would believe him. If she was mad enough, Nora would be banned from cow chores.

"Fine." I turned around, my back facing him.

I heard a shuffle behind me, then a burst of white, hot pain across my backside. "Ah," I howled in agony.

He laughed, holding the top half of the broken pitchfork handle. "Spare the rod, spoil the child."

Tears rolling from my eye, I held my hands against my backside, gulping air.

"We'll put these calves with the stillborn beef cow from yesterday," he said. "But I'll be feeding the calves from now on. You'll go back to filling hoppers."

"I never asked to switch," I gasped.

Dad and Mom didn't seem alarmed about the dead calves. I pushed the matter off as natural causes, all the while wondering what Doug had done.

There wasn't another dead calf that spring.

27
July 7, 1988

The Soviet Union launched Phobos 1 in an attempt to probe the Martian moon, which turned out to be unsuccessful.

The summer of 1988 was dry as a bone.

For weeks on end, there wasn't a drop of moisture. Then dark clouds rolled in, thunder rumbled in the close distance. Spirits lifted at the fragrance of promised rain.

Skinny drops began to fall, teasing the dried, cracked earth.

The storm clouds scattered, the relentless sun peeking beneath them. Clouds quickly evaporated, along with hope for rain.

It was two o'clock.

An hour before chores, and a nap was in order.

My bedroom door opened and Doug strolled in. He tapped the lid on a can of Copenhagen and twisted it off. Tucking a pinch between his lower lip and gums, he mumbled, "Got something to show you."

"Mom know you chew tobacco?" I followed him to his room.

"She doesn't care as long as it's not in the house."

"You're in the house."

"Never admit to anything." He shut the door behind us, and sat at the edge of his bed, motioning to the chair next to him. "Sit down."

"Why?"

"Because I said so." He dug around under the bed, and pulled out a stack of magazines, handing me the one on the top.

My blood went hot.

A blonde woman, hair the color of wheat, was laying on white sheets, her back arched. Bunched beneath her breasts, a gray tank top. The naked half-globes intoxicated me. If only her shirt were a quarter inch higher... She wore a matching gray pair of panties.

I laid it on his bed.

"Take it." He tossed it back.

It shook in my hand. "Really?"

"Have fun," he said, his eyes on the one in his hand. "Don't let the door hit you on the way out."

Slowly backing out of his room, I started to toss it in the garbage, and glanced at the cover once more.

Her bedroom eyes beckoned me. The slopes of her breasts teased my senses.

Once won't hurt.

I could throw it out afterward. No one would know.

Yes. Just this once.

With trembling hands, I opened the magazine to the centerfold and a world from which I didn't want to return.

There was three knocks on the door before Mom burst in.

"Get out." My voice, high-pitched and desperate.

Mom's eyes widened in shock. Was there a hint of a smile on her lips? Abruptly she turned and walked out.

Afternoon waned to evening. After chores, I returned to my bedroom. No way was I going to supper. I was too mortified. What had Mom seen? Maybe she wouldn't mention it. Maybe she'd forget by breakfast.

And maybe I would die before then.

28

"I made you an appointment for a haircut," Mom announced the next morning when I arrived in the kitchen. "At nine."

My gaze flicked to the wall clock.

Eight thirty-five.

Unease made its way up my belly and through my fingertips. "I got done with chores and haven't eaten breakfast yet."

"I can't cancel or she'll charge me twenty-five percent."

"I'll drive," Doug sauntered into the kitchen, wearing a farmer's cap with the inscription *If I said you had a beautiful body would you hold it against me?* "I want to get snacks at Red Owl."

Snacks? We weren't allowed to buy junk food. And anyway, Doug was the last person I wanted to take me to the hairdresser.

"Thank you, Doug." Mom's eyes sparkled. She made no mention of his cap.

Doug gave me a triumphant look. "You bet."

***

Doug pulled up in front of the beauty shop, turned to me, and said, "If you're done before I am, meet me in the truck."

"Where are you going?"

"I told you, Red Owl to get snacks."

He was lying. However, the impending haircut was foremost on my mind, and I exited the pickup. When I reached the beauty shop, I drew a deep breath and opened the door.

George Michael was singing "Faith."

Selene wore a hot pink tank top and Daisy Duke shorts. She caught me looking at her, and I averted my gaze.

I told myself there was nothing provocative about the way she wrapped the cape around my neck. Or the slow way she went about cutting my hair.

Every nerve ending in my body came to life. I couldn't speak a word.

Snip. Snip. "You sure turned out gorgeous."

My heart thumped wildly in my chest. No one had ever called me good looking, let alone gorgeous. Most couldn't get past the eye.

Slowly, she straightened, her breast next to my cheek.

Imagining her topless, my blood pounded through my veins. I looked away, praying she wouldn't notice my arousal.

"Already ninety-five and barely nine o'clock," she purred, blowing on my neck. "It's hot out there isn't it?"

Not as hot as it was in here.

"I'm burning up," she said, sliding her hands up my thighs. "Are you?"

My skin felt like it was on fire.

Spots flashed before my eye, and my palms ached. When her hands moved higher, I stopped breathing.

Her eyes lowered to my groin. "You're sweet," she breathed in my ear.

Then I felt her hand brush my crotch, the lightest of touches, and I couldn't think at all.

***

"What's with you?" Doug asked as I got into the pickup.

My cheeks flamed hot. "Nothing."

"Oh." He glanced through the window. "Dang, did you see the shirt Selene's wearing?" He whistled. "Makes you wish you were a baby."

"I don't know what you're talking about."

"I don't suppose you do." He chuckled. "Last time I got a haircut, she was wearing a pink sweater the color of cotton candy. The neckline...let's just say how low can you go."

I shifted in my seat.

"Best hand job I ever had." He slid the key into the ignition.

Did hand jobs mean you were no longer a virgin? I wasn't going to ask. I wanted to forget the whole thing.

You're supposed to make it last longer, Selene's soft voice, echoing in my heated thoughts.

It wouldn't happen again. I would get my haircut by someone else next time. It would be like it never happened. For now, I prayed to forget the whole thing.

How many hand jobs had she given Doug? He was a pig.

And now I was too.

29
Christmas Eve 1988

The air was Christmas festive. Lights twinkled. Presents were wrapped and stacked beneath the tree.

Mom walked in and grabbed her purse off the table. "I need to run to Wimbledon and grab cereal for Christmas morning."

Although common at the Anderson household, cold cereal was a rare holiday treat for Mom growing up. Her eyes always took on a shine when she brought home various kinds for Christmas morning.

"I was going to make spritz cookies," I said. Reading was on the schedule, but that was considered entertainment.

"You can do that later." She glanced over at me. "I made you an appointment for a haircut at two."

Desire, hot and unexpected, slammed into me. Followed by dread, making me weak-kneed and slightly light-headed.

***

Christmas was coming, and someone's goose was definitely getting fat. Consumers scurried about to get their first-and last-minute shopping done. Vehicles kept my focus on the holiday and not on the task before me.

Selene wore a red Christmas sweater with a tree on the front, ornaments hanging from the branches. It clung to her, the neckline dipping low.

"I hope you don't mind my not playing Christmas carols," she said. "Anyway you want It" by Journey began to play.

"You go to school at home?" She moved in toward me.

I mumbled an intelligible response.

117

"What's that like?" Her breath tickled my ear.

Every nerve ending in my body came to life.

I couldn't speak a word.

***

Afterward, I threw a ten dollar bill on the counter and dashed out the door.

Her laughter followed me.

30
Christmas Day 1988

Staring at the back of the staircase early morning, I blinked blurry edges of sleep away. I was at one hundred-twenty stair count, and struggling to stay awake.

It had been three months, two weeks, and four days since I'd looked at a magazine.

I reached for my glasses.

Yesterday came flooding back. Shame swamped me. I tiptoed up the back stairs.

Each minute and every hour of hesitation produced guilt. What if Selene told Mom? She wouldn't. Unless she lied.

Milking cows was a blur of activities. I couldn't stop thinking about Mom finding out. How she would look at me. What she would think.

After chores, I slipped into the basement and reached beneath my bed for the new magazine Doug had given me.

Then Mom's voice floated down the stairs. "Simon?"

"Y-yes." I bolted up in bed, shoving the magazine beneath.

Then she stood in the doorway, her silhouette outlined by the light in the bathroom. "Have you showered?"

"Just getting ready to," I lied. Truthfully, I was exhausted from chores, and all I wanted to do was sleep.

"We need to talk," Mom said.

I sank back down on the bed. My mind, slammed with fear. Had she talked to Selene? What was said? Would she listen to my side?

119

"When a boy gets older, his body begins to change," her voice rang like a clanging cymbal.

Realizing the topic of discussion, my gaze dropped to my feet. "Shouldn't Dad talk to me about it?"

"If you wait for your dad, you'll be thirty years old with a wife and kids before he gets around to it."

Sounded good to me.

"When a woman gets to a certain age, her body changes," she began. "She grows…tatas," She held her hands to her chest in cups, "And down there she has a jubie…when she…"

Jubie?

Focusing on the toes of my socks, I tuned out her rather shoddy, mechanical description of intercourse. Words she used to describe body parts, awkward and downright funny.

One thing was for certain, she knew nothing about what happened at the hairdresser's. Relief, swift and overwhelming, made me weak.

Her expectant look told me she was done talking. "Do you have any questions?"

"I'm good," I mumbled.

After she left, I headed for the shower. By the time the spray hit my body, I had myself convinced I'd made too big of a deal about it.

Mom would never have to find out. And I would never have to hear words like tatas and jubie. If I heard any nicknames for body parts again in this lifetime, it would be too soon.

The more I thought about it, the more certain I was I had overreacted about Selene.

Good.

It was good, really, Mom didn't know.

You can pretend it never happened.

That crisp winter morning, I dressed for the holiday in a cloud of shame. My companions, guilt and disgust, I prepared to celebrate Christ's birth.

31
New Year's Eve 1988

Fifteen-year-old Sam Dodson had a hole in his heart, and the Methodist church scheduled a potluck and bake sale benefit for him that evening.

Early afternoon, Mom was dressed in a new blazer pushed to her elbows, feather earrings, and matching pleated slacks.

The urge to see her smile, one saying she was happy with me, was all-consuming.

"You look nice," I said.

"Thank you." She applied red lipstick in the mirror.

"Where are you going?"

"Wimbledon for groceries." She smacked her lips. "You want to come?"

"Sure." My spirits lifted.

"When we get back, you can make the dish for potluck. I'll even let you use my new pasta maker."

Mom had wanted a pasta maker since she saw Deanna Morris, Jeffy's mom, had one. Christmas morning, she opened her gift from Dad with *"far more options than Deanna Morris'."*

"Cool. I wanted to try homemade mac 'n' cheese."

She frowned, "I got a brand-new pasta maker for Christmas, and you want to use it to make mac 'n' cheese?"

I smiled. "Trust me."

***

Doug invited himself along. Mom let him drive.

He put the right blinker on when taking a curve going right. On again taking a curve going left.

"Oh Doug," Mom giggled, like it was endearing. She always giggled when he turned the signal light while taking the curves.

Doug sped down the blacktop, Wimbledon emerging in the distance.

"Doug, maybe you should slow down," Mom said through gritted teeth. "There's not too much traffic on this road, but still…"

Doug ignored her. A mixture of dread and fear hit me with a rolling force. My heart began to pound with dizzying speed. By the time we reached Red Owl, I felt like a sailor who had been lost at sea, and resisted the urge to kiss the grocery store floor.

Mom began filling the shopping cart with jars of minced garlic.

Alarmed, I said, "A garlic clove would be better."

"These are on sale." Five cans later, she started wandering down the aisle once more.

I mentally came up with recipes requiring minced garlic. "We won't have to worry about vampires."

She gave me an incredulous look. "There's no such thing as vampires."

"I know, it's…" I trailed off. Nothing ruined a quip faster than explaining it.

We reached the freezer section.

I scanned the list. "A lobster tail."

She sucked her teeth. "It's too expensive. Twenty dollars for one small tail," she lamented, grabbing a bag of imitation crab instead. "This is half the price and you get a lot more of it."

I couldn't make proper lobster mac 'n' cheese with imitation crab. Mom would rather save a buck.

"I bet Deanna Morris isn't going to use imitation anything in her dish," I said, a niggle of unease creeping inside me as the suggestion left my mouth.

Sighing loudly, Mom returned the crab, and set a lobster tail in the shopping cart.

Rarely did she go with my choice, and satisfaction eased all remorse for the underhanded tactic used to secure it.

***

Sam's benefit was well attended, the dining area at the church was packed with attendees.

"Can you believe the Schmidts?" Mom was telling Clara Sharp.

Clara Sharp, in her late fifties, was a member of the Methodist church. Her husband Daryl Sharp was a local farmer.

Clara giggled. "Horas and Nelda Schmidt live in the nicest house in town, and don't pay for a single meal if they can get it for free."

"I heard they showed up at the Carlson-Steven wedding," Mom said. "Uninvited."

"I was there. The bride and groom did not look too happy about it, let me tell you," Clara returned eagerly.

Dave Bartlett, a Barnes County commissioner and owner of Red Owl, along with his wife Rita, approached the serving counter. They were members of the Methodist church.

Rita said, "The lobster mac 'n' cheese was the star dish, Christy."

"And the doughnuts for the bake sale were a clever addition," Dave added.

Even Audre Fredrick was impressed. "It really was fabulous. You always do such a good job." In her thirties, Audre was the fussiest lady at our church.

"The pasta maker was a Christmas present from Merle," Mom said in the voice of a schoolgirl.

Deanna Morris blinked. "You made the pasta from scratch?"

Harry rushed over. "I want some more mac 'n' cheese."

Hans held up his plate. "Simon said we could have seconds if there was still some left."

"He made this?" Audre turned to Mom with wide eyes.

"Yeah," I cut in.

Audre took a step back, avoiding looking directly at my eye. "You should be a chef when you grow up."

"Simon's going to be a preacher," Pastor Johnson clamped his hand on my shoulder.

My face heated beneath their gazes.

"Yes, and now he will be on kitchen duty," Mom said in a loud voice.

Everyone chuckled.

After cleanup, four untouched Christmas bags remained.

"Can I have them?" I asked Mom. I loved the peanuts, peppermints, chocolate marshmallow Santas, and most of all, peanut butter cups.

There was a twinkle in her eyes and warmth in her smile. "I don't see why not."

I carefully placed each smaller bag in a large grocery bag. The Youngs were coming tomorrow. Meaning enough for me, Nora, Hans, and Harry.

It was sure to be a happy New Year.

32

New Year's Day, 1989

"It was the maid in the billiard room with the candlestick," Harry said, shoving a peanut butter cup into his mouth.

Nora scanned the Clue board. "How can you tell already?"

"Because I'm good at this game." Harry grinned.

I took a bite of a chocolate Santa.

It was after lunch. We were in the basement on the floor in our room playing board games and eating the leftover Christmas candy. I hardly ever ate chocolate anymore, but it was a special occasion.

I reached into the bag for the last one. A peanut butter cup. Savoring each bite, it was gone all too quickly.

"I'm going to take these out to the trash," I said, cleaning up the wrappers around us, "I'll be right back."

When I returned, Harry said, "It's your turn."

I returned to my lotus position on the floor.

Mom called from the top of the stairs, "Simon."

"Coming." I jumped up, and headed for the space between the wall and the stairs.

Mom burst into the room from the bathroom door. "Simon, I need those Christmas bags from yesterday."

"They're gone." I stopped short, shoving a candy wrapper into my pocket.

"What do you mean gone?" She set her hands on her hips.

The bottom dropped out of my stomach at the look in her eyes.

Harry and Hans got up, slowly backing out of the room.

Nora stood next to the game of Clue, shifting awkwardly from foot to foot.

"We ate them." I fixed my gaze on my mismatched stockings. I'd been in a hurry after my shower, and couldn't find the match. Now they shouted at me.

"Ate them?" Mom threw her hands in the air.

"You said we could," I added in a small voice.

She sighed. "I'll need the wrappers."

"Here," I pulled the Reese's one from my pocket.

"We'll have to replace all of them." She gave me an even stare. "I'll need to know what to buy."

"All?" I echoed. "But… I emptied the trash into the burn barrel."

Her expression murderous, she whirled around without a word.

I hurried up the basement steps behind her, grabbing my boots on the way outside.

She strode over to the burn barrel and peered inside. "You're in luck. The trash hasn't been burned."

I glanced into the barrel. It looked like someone had dumped the slop pail on top. "But…"

She pierced me with a sharp look. "You didn't throw any of your magazines in the trash, did you?"

My heart slammed in my chest. "What?"

"If there's nothing to hide, I don't see why you can't find a few wrappers to make things right."

Right? As in punishment for the magazines or because of the praise last night over my cooking skills?

You made her look bad.

***

After Mom went back inside the house, I slipped into the basement where Nora stood waiting.

"I want to help," she said.

Panic swept my stomach. I hadn't thrown any magazines in the trash, but I didn't know if Doug had. What if Nora saw them?

"I can do it. You don't want to go through the trash."

"I ate candy too."

"You didn't know."

She stood, hands on her hips. "Neither did you."

"Someone dumped slop into the burn barrel," I said, betting a million dollars it was Doug.

"Then we'll need gloves."

There was no way to explain without looking terribly guilty.

"Uh s-sure," I stammered, rooting through the glove basket at the top ledge. I found a matching pair, thank goodness, and handed it to her.

We made our way up the stairs, outside, and over to the burn barrel. We dug for candy wrappers. With each piece of garbage moved aside, I grew more anxious until I thought I was going to throw up.

There were no magazines in the burn barrel.

Together we made our way to the house, a brown paper bag full of slop-soaked wrappers in hand.

Mom was having coffee at the table with Ben and Rachel.

"Did you need something, Simon?" she asked.

I handed her the bag.

"What's this?" She peered inside. "Looks like garbage to me." She stood and tossed the bag into the trash.

My mouth dropped open but no sound came out. What was that all about? The image of the two of us digging through slop made my cheeks burn. I didn't dare look at Nora.

Mom returned to the table. "Simon, why don't you go get a game of darts going?"

"Darts?" I echoed. Kevin put a target up in the shed, and Mom never approved.

"Sure." She giggled. "Then you two can burn the garbage. The matches are above the stove."

Burning garbage and playing darts. Two activities from which I was banned. Matches, because Mom caught me playing with them when I was six. Darts, because she said, *"You don't want to lose your other eye."*

On our way out to the shed, I walked a little lighter, and felt a lot better. If Nora thought the switch in Mom's attitude was odd she didn't mention it.

The humiliation and shame disappeared with a game of darts. After five rounds, we built a fire in the metal trash container.

"You sure are good at darts," Nora said.

"Thanks." I removed my work gloves.

"The fire is dying out." She grabbed kindling from the pile next to the shed.

I stoked the fire. "Sure was nice of you to dig through the," I swallowed hard, bile rising in my throat at the memory, "garbage."

"You're welcome." Her gaze, reflected in the flames, met mine. There was a gentle look there I'd never seen before. One that kicked my heart into high gear, making my palms sweat.

In a winter moment, everything changed.

All senses were captivated: her cheeks, ruddy with cold. Blonde waves tousled about her head. Eyes that danced, saw, and accepted. A smile warm as the firelight, melting every reservation.

There was nothing I wouldn't do for her.

129

33
March 25, 1989

Les Miserables opened at Auditorium Theatre in Chicago, and Selene's beauty shop loomed ahead.

I told myself it was relief, not disappointment, seeing another vehicle parked out front.

Inside Hank Jr. sang "Mind Your Own Business" and chemical for hair permanent wafted through the air.

There was a new hairdresser with long brown hair and blue eyes. "You must be Simon," she said. "I'm Beth."

Smoothing a hand over my hair, I glanced at Selene.

A man around thirty was getting a perm in her chair. She pretended not to notice me.

Beth motioned to the barber chair. "Have a seat."

Beth wasn't a small talker and I kept silent.

Every haircut I'd gotten here was by Selene.

She's cutting someone else's hair.

Not like she would kick him out of the chair. But why hadn't she even acknowledged me since I'd walked in the door? It was a relief of course.

Except.

Was it because of what happened last time?

And the time before that, and the one before that.

After I'd paid Beth, I turned to leave.

Selene glanced over, her eyes filled with contempt. *You're supposed to make it last longer.* "Tell your mother I said hi won't you, Simon?" she called in a mocking tone.

I slipped out the door without a word.

***

The Red Owl building cast a shadow over the side street. I entered through the back entrance and grabbed a bag of flour.

On my way to the front, I passed a magazine rack by the far shelf. A publication covered in blue caught my eye. My heart kicked up, followed by a surge of disappointment.

Mom gave me twenty dollars for a haircut and flour. I didn't have enough left. Plus, she'd expect to keep the change.

Walk away.

Flicking a glance toward the front of the store, I reached for the magazine. There was a pimply-faced teenager I didn't recognize working the till. Before I could think better of it, I slipped the magazine in my pants, pulling my shirt over it. Heart thundering, I held the bag of flour close to my chest, actually my salvation.

Your salvation?

Lost in thought, I nearly collided with a lady in the aisle ahead of me.

"Watch where you're going," she ordered.

"Sorry," I mumbled, reaching the counter.

Mr. Bartlett strode up, nudging the teen. "Why don't you take your break?"

He knows.

They switched places. I set the flour on the counter.

Scanning the item, Mr. Bartlett's gaze was fixed on me. I was used to stares because of my eye. This time, I felt his x-ray vision.

"Three seventy-five," he said.

My hands trembling, I handed him the remaining ten.

He popped open the cash register, eyes never leaving me.

It was the longest five minutes of my life.

Making my way out the door, I shot a wild glance behind me.

No one followed.

Scrambling inside the pickup, I stared at the grocery store front, catching a glimpse of my reflection in the rearview mirror. I barely noticed my stylish copper hair, feathered and parted down the middle.

Instead, my eye stared back.

I was ugly on the outside, and now, ugly on the inside. Hatred, damning and fierce, swept through my entire being. With hands of fury, I tore through my hair until it looked like I was attacked by wolves.

And changed nothing.

34
July 1989

It was a hot, dry Sunday morning when Sam Dodson killed himself. His parents found his body on their way to church. Apparently, Sam stuffed the crack beneath the garage door, got into his folks' gold Ford Taurus, and started the engine.

Mom and Dad were talking about it over coffee.

"He went to sleep and never woke up." Mom took a sip from her mug.

"His folks are about to lose their farm," Dad said, reaching for the paper. "A lot of farmers are going belly up."

"I guess they raised ten thousand dollars at his benefit. Deanna Morris said the family shouldn't accept the funds raised."

Dad pushed the paper away. "Now who's gonna tell them? You? What are you going to say? 'Oh, sorry your boy killed himself. By the way, we want our money back?'"

Mom's eyes flashed with fury. "I didn't say it, she did."

I cleared my throat.

Mom glanced over. "Church is cancelled today."

"Cancelled?"

"We aren't going."

I tiptoed back downstairs and flopped on my bed.

Doug burst into the room. "I'm going to the lake. You want to come?"

"No thanks." The holiest time of the week was Sunday between morning and afternoon chores. My only day to take a nap. Getting up at four in the morning was taking a toll.

A bed on wheels had become a morning fantasy. It was seventy-two degrees this morning at four-thirty when I walked cows home from the slough, and found myself drifting.

"Suit yourself. The Youngs are going to be there."

"Nora?" A burst of energy shot through me.

"Probably."

Suddenly I wasn't tired.

***

Baldhill Dam consisted of three lift stations looming over the valley. The massive structure kept the lake in its place, the valley free from flooding.

The resort stocked water equipment including paddle boats. Kevin, Charles, Harry and Hans rented paddle boats.

In the hot summer sunshine, I sat at the edge of the dock, line in the water.

"Hey Simon." Nora strolled up in a pair of cutoff shorts and a red t-shirt, smelling like strawberries.

She sat down next to me, and my heart leapt in my chest.

I tried not to stare at her long, suntanned legs.

"Do you think suicides go to hell?" she asked. "A girl in my class at school is Catholic. She said Sam Dodson is selfish and burning in hell with all the other suicides."

I pondered this a minute, then said, "Judas was damned for the ultimate betrayal. Peter, also a traitor, was forgiven. The difference, I believe, was in the heart."

Her expression brightened. "I think only God knows."

"Exactly."

"You have whiskers." She smiled.

A bundle of nerves, I'd almost blurted she'd grown breasts. Instead, I said, "You want to go swimming?"

"I don't know how."

"I can show you." I reeled my line out of the water.

"Okay. I'll be right back," Nora said, and headed for the bathhouse.

"(I've had) The Time of My Life" blared from the boom box in the sand next to the volleyball net. I made my way over to the swimming area next to the wall of rocks.

Doug trotted over when he saw me, volleyball in hand. "You birdwatching?"

"There's only seagulls."

"I mean chicks, dummy." He laughed, bouncing the ball off my head. "Did you see some of those swimsuits?"

Before I could answer, Nora emerged from the bathhouse.

Doug jabbed my side with his elbow. "She got some knockers over the summer."

Her swimming suit was pale blue. Something modest, but she filled it out in all the right places. And the top...

"Close your mouth, Simon. You're drooling."

I let it snap shut.

"Maybe if you play classical music she'll let her milk down," Doug dropped the ball and held his hands up, making squeezing motions, "Gentle, remember."

Anger whipped through me. I took a step toward him.

"Joking, bro." He took a step back and scooped up the ball. "You better play it cool. Nothing more unattractive to a bird than neediness."

Nora spotted me and made her way over.

Doug winked. "Later."

Nora strolled up to me, her gaze fixed on my torso, then trailed over my biceps.

Suddenly, I no longer felt like an ugly, lonely boy, but a man. Sticking my chest out, I stood a little straighter, and headed for the water.

She followed right behind.

I glanced back. "You know, we are a lot alike, you and me."

Nora blushed. "Told ya."

In an instant, the girl I had loved became the woman of my dreams.

35
June 8, 1991

A victory parade was held in Washington, D.C., following success in the Gulf War, and it was the Saturday before conservation camp.

The magical me looked forward to going all year, and the realistic me figured Mom would put the kibosh on it last minute.

When Ben Young showed up, I was relieved to see he brought Nora with him. Her sun-kissed blonde hair was pulled into a ponytail.

"Come with me." I lead Nora toward the south cluster of trees behind the house. Entering the trees, I made my way through the path, Nora close behind. To the east end and the clearing I made. There was a large rock covered with my old blanket. Alongside, an ice-cream pail full of super balls.

"This place is cool," she said, plopping down on the rock.

I sat down next to her. "Doug doesn't even know about this place."

"You could practice preaching here." She smiled.

"Maybe," I shrugged. "Maybe I'll be a dairy farmer."

Her eyes widened. "Really?"

"Maybe." I imagined us married, her working alongside me.

She smiled, a mixture of strawberries and vanilla wafted toward me through the gentle breeze.

Every fiber of my being wanted to kiss her. Afraid she didn't that, I said instead, "Conservation camp starts Monday. Too bad you're not in 4-H. Then you could go with me."

She frowned, "How long will you be gone?"

"Until Friday." I found myself telling her about Doug's camp experience. At the end, I said, "I doubt Mom will even let me go. The eye you know."

***

Like the flip of a switch, Mom practically pushed me out the door Monday morning. "It'll be good for you."

The station wagon had two other campers from our area. Tom, a skinny kid with black feathered hair, blue high tops, Bermuda shorts and a shirt my mom would call salmon, but I'd go with pink. Joch, an exchange student from Germany.

Neither mentioned my eyepatch.

The drive to conservation camp was long. Joch did most of the talking. I wasn't much for small talk anyway.

When we arrived, I spotted a pretty girl close to my age. Her name was Shauna. She had a full lower lip and nice long brown hair. Jordan from Cavalier said all the right things and had the right look. He stuck to her like Velcro.

There were no other cute girls.

The rest of Monday dragged on.

On my way to the dorm, the tennis court was off to the left. A cluster of trees surrounded the dormitories.

Inside the dorm assigned to me, I got the top bunk. A boy by the name of Bobby Warren took the bottom. He was a shy, skinny kid with red hair and freckles.

"Do you want to play tennis?" I asked Bobby from the top bunk.

"Sure," he said. "After lunch."

After lunch, I found Bobby with a bunch of really young girls. Arlene was the name of one. She had thick glasses, pale skin and freckles.

She wore socks with high heel shoes.

"That's tacky," said another girl with platinum blonde hair to her friend.

"Why don't you tell her it's not cool to wear socks with dress shoes?" her friend, on the pudgy side, whispered back.

She shrugged. "I don't want to hurt anybody."

There were three hours of free time to get settled. Unpacking took ten minutes. I spent the remaining two hours and fifty minutes on my bunk in a state of solitude.

Tuesday morning was hot. Breakfast was dull. Disillusioned, I sat alone at the table, a little homesick too.

Johnny Appleseed rang out through the lunch hall. *"Oh, the Lord's been good to me..."* The only thing Doug had gotten right about camp thus far.

When I finished the cold cereal and apple, my stomach growled. Lunch was some sort of hotdish, green beans, and a fruit cup. I was hungry afterward, but my stomach remained silent.

"Simon Anderson."

Bobby jabbed my side. "They're calling your name. Means you got a letter."

Must be from Mom. She said she would write. I'd told her it was only five days and she didn't need to bother. Now I was extremely glad she didn't listen.

Steve the counselor held a stack of letters. "Okay, before you lucky kids take off, how about a song? Actions too, don't forget. On the count of three," Steve said. "One, two, three..."

Embarrassed, addressees stared at the ground, and with less than enthusiastic actions, sang, *"Do your ears hang low, do they wobble to and fro, can you tie 'em in a knot, can you tie 'em in a bow..."*

After the song finished, we were handed our mail.

My heart leapt to my throat at the return address.

Nora Toogoody.

I stared for a long time before tucking it into the back of my Levis. I wasn't going to open it until I was alone during free time.

Free time finally arrived. I hurried over to an oak tree next to the sidewalk, and tore my letter open. It was one page with big writing, double-spaced.

Dear Simon,

How are you? I am fine. How's camp? Is it as fabulous as Doug bragged about? I can't believe he kissed three different girls in a matter of five short days. Then again, this is Doug we're talking about. Interesting how the kissees...

I looked up. *Kissees?*

...were from Bottineau and Cavalier. Tough to check his story. It's boring around here without you.

Nora.

Straight to the point. Like she was. I read the brief letter five more times, until I had it memorized.

Nora could write.

I was way too thrilled with the simple note, longing to go home.

***

"Simon Anderson." My name came up at mail call the next day.

After another silly song, I received my letter, glancing at the envelope.

Nora.

I tucked the letter into my back pocket and headed for the kitchen. Our cabin was on kitchen patrol.

I couldn't wait to finish the dishes.

Dear Simon,

I went to your house. I'm not sure why. I think I was hoping to go for a ride. Doug was there with Gretchen and Lisa, and I immediately regretted my decision. I can't wait until you get back. Are there pretty girls there? I can't imagine you kissing any of them. I hope you didn't.

P.S. I hope you write back.

Nora

What did she mean by she couldn't imagine me kissing any of them? And why did she hope I didn't? Could it be she loved me the way I loved her? My heart kicked up at the thought.

Hanging my head over the side of the bunk bed, I said, "Bobby, can I borrow a pen and paper?"

He reached beneath his bed, and pulled out a notebook and pen. "You can have these."

"Thanks." I propped my back against the pillow, and flipped open the notebook.

Staring at the piece of notebook paper for a long while, I gathered my thoughts.

Dear Nora,

I was thrilled to receive a letter from you. I find myself missing your smile. Your voice. You see, ever since New Year's, I can't get you out of my head.

I will never forget the day at the beach. The way the sun kissed the tips of your blonde hair. How my hands itched to touch it. The blue swimming suit you wore, your eyes, the way you had looked at me.

Like I was desirable.

I stopped and looked up from the page. Putting my feelings to words made my gut ache.

Nothing more unattractive to a bird than neediness, Doug's words wormed through my heated brain.

I reread what I wrote. *Stupid.* She might feel sorry for me. What if I'd mistaken the look in her eyes? She'd deny it and think I was pathetic.

I crumpled up the paper.

Hey Nora,
I erased it and this time,

Nora,
Camp is really great. Doug was right about all of it. There are pretty girls.

I'd taken pictures during a class where a trapper had shown us his collection of furs. One was of Shauna wearing a mink hat. When the film was developed, I'd have a picture to show Doug. Now Nora too.

One girl, from Motte.

A place in North Dakota Doug mentioned about his girls.

She's really cool. We play tennis.
I better get going. I hear them calling supper.
Simon

Staring at the few lines I'd scrawled, I was unable to come up with any more lies, and unwilling to scratch the ones I'd written. Hastily, I folded the piece of paper and shoved it in the envelope Bobby gave me.

Dear Simon,
How are you? I am fine. Thanks for writing back.
You have nice handwriting. I hope you don't come home with a girlfriend. Then we can't hang out.
There's a new pastor. He's been over at Ben's house three times.
My real dad died from hypothermia. He thought he was warm, and froze to death. He worked at Dairy Queen in Oakes when I was growing up. I don't remember him except he had large wire frame glasses and Mom hung out in the store when he was working.
It was January, thirty-five below for a week straight. He didn't show up to work, and the manager overheard the girl behind the till tell someone they found him face down in the snow in a ditch outside town... naked.
Ben said we could go to your house Saturday. See you soon.
Nora

I sat for a long while, staring at the words she'd written. Was this new pastor someone her mother was seeing? Is that why she mentioned her biological father? Regardless, it was a sad tale, and my heart ached for her.

The last night, Thursday, a dance was scheduled. The event of the week Doug had raved about. I sat on a chair by the wall. Randy Travis sang "Forever and Ever."

Arlene asked me to dance. Reluctant to make her feel bad, and also to see what the fuss was about, I found myself saying yes. We rested our hands on each other's shoulders, swaying back and forth. I stared at her socks and high heels the entire time. It was the most awkward five minutes of my life.

I sat out the next one.

Keith Whitley's "When you say nothing at all" was the finale. Couples laid their heads on each other's shoulders like they were in love.

Glancing at the clock, I counted down the minutes until it was over, daydreaming about letters learned by heart, and a friend turned woman.

Unlike what Doug bragged about or what I'd written Nora about, camp was a lonely place. The winds of homesickness made me anxious to return. I'd feigned options I didn't have, but there was only one choice for me. Simple really. No question who I would choose.

I chose Nora.

36

The tick of the clock broke the silence. The hum of a box fan on the dining room floor answered.

The atmosphere, expectant.

"Hello?" I made my way through the kitchen. "I'm home."

I checked the clock once more.

Two o'clock.

Too early for chores.

"Anybody home?" I called.

Exhausted, I headed for my room, wanting to go to bed and sleep until it was tomorrow. Lifting my arm, I sniffed and dropped to my bed. I would shower later.

"Simon!" Harry and Hans burst through the door. "When did you get back?"

"This afternoon." I folded my hands behind my head. "Where is everyone?"

They exchanged looks and shrugged in unison. The thing about the twins, they were oblivious to what was going on around them.

"Harry, Hans," Mom called, descending the stairs. "Why don't you go upstairs and clean the kitchen. I want to talk to Simon."

They scurried off.

Clean the house? The twins never did house chores. My heart began to pound, thundering in my ears. Must be something bad.

I sat up, sheepishly running a hand over my head.

Mom sat on the bed next to me and pulled a *Playboy* magazine from behind her back. "What's this?"

"I uh…" Thoughts racing, I struggled to find an explanation that didn't make me look like a total pervert.

Busted.

"I asked you a question," she said, louder this time.

"I don't know," I mumbled.

She must have gone through my stuff when I was at camp. A sudden image of her rummaging through my dresser drawers and carefully folded clothes made me ill. The magazine made me guilty.

I had no recourse and let my gaze drop.

"Shame on you." She waved the magazine in front of my face. "Do you know what this leads to?"

I had some ideas, but knew better than to answer a rhetorical question.

She stared at the wall behind me like she couldn't even look at me. "You used to be such a good boy. I didn't raise you for this trash. Next thing you know, you'll be raping women."

"Now wait a minute," I jumped to my feet, "I would never…"

She stood. "Did you just interrupt me?"

"No, ma'am."

"Because it sounded like you interrupted me."

"I'm sorry."

"Can I talk now?"

"Yes."

She gave me a disgusted look. "Why bother?"

I took a step forward. "Don't say that. Please?"

Her eyes were hard. Without a word, she went upstairs.

That explained her enthusiasm about my week away at camp. I'm sure she couldn't wait to snoop through my private things.

I marched over to Doug's door and burst into his room. "What'd you tell her for?"

He bolted straight up in bed, adjusting covers. "Ever hear of knocking?"

"You said you wouldn't say anything." I shook with rage.

"Tell who what? What are you talking about?"

"Mom came into my room and reamed me a new one about the magazines."

"I didn't tell her a thing."

"How else would she have known my hiding spot? You were the only one who knew."

"Did you tuck it beneath your mattress? The most obvious place?" He turned the page of his magazine.

"I..."

"Never admit to anything," he cut me off. "If Jesus Christ Himself came out of the sky, you tell Him you don't know what she's talking about."

I shook my head. "That's not right."

"Stop being a sissy and grow a pair." He waved me off without looking up from his magazine.

Too worked up to sleep, I shoved my camp clothes into the washer. Half hour later, showered and dressed, I made my way upstairs. I'd been working on "Walking In Memphis" by Marc Cohn before camp, and wanted to practice.

***

I reached the living room, and halted. There was a new sofa and end table and no piano.

"Mom?" I slowly turned around and headed for the kitchen, each step, filled with trepidation. "Where's the piano?"

Mom pulled a cup from the cupboard. "I gave it to the Morris'," she said with the same blasé attitude as if she'd given them a cookie or piece of bread.

My mouth dropped open. "What?"

"You know Jeffy plays the piano." She picked up the pot, pouring a cup of steaming black liquid. "Coffee?"

I stumbled back. "I do too!"

"It was Doug's piano." She set the pot back on the burner. "Besides, you should have thought of that before looking at filth."

Defeated, I sank to a chair at the breakfast table.

What now? I could ask Pastor Johnson if I could use the one at church. Once a week, and hopefully...oh what was the use? This was bad.

"I made sundaes, Simon." Mom smiled, setting two bowls, two scoops of vanilla ice cream and sliced bananas, topped strawberry, butterscotch, and chocolate syrups: a delicious trio.

"Tell me about camp." She sat down across from me. "Before I forget, Rachel Toogoody called. There's an evangelist preaching in the park Sunday. Nora will be there."

I'd been forgiven. Relief flooded me.

She was making it okay now.

It was all okay.

37
June 15, 1991

Mount Pinatubo volcano erupted in the Philippines making it the second-largest volcanic eruption on Earth of the 20th century.

"How do I look?" Mom turned away from the dining room mirror.

"Beautiful," Dad answered, scanning the *Valley City Times-Record*.

"You don't think I look fat?"

"Nope. Looks perfect." He turned the page.

"What about the color?" She turned around, eyeing her backside in the mirror.

"Yep."

"If Reverend Hall is as wonderful as everyone says he is, I can't imagine why he wants to marry Rachel Toogoody."

Dad looked up then. "Who says they're getting married?"

"I thought you said she's moving to California." Mom tore her eyes from her reflection.

"Nora's moving?" I gasped.

"Which means they're getting married," Mom told Dad.

Dad arched a brow. "You do know it's 1991 right?"

"When are they leaving?" I cut in. "Does Nora know? Where is she going to go to school?"

Mom gave me a blank stare. "By the way, I volunteered you to help prepare lunches for the outdoor service."

***

Valley City was tucked in rolling grassy hills next to the Sheyenne River Valley Scenic Byway.

Population: six thousand people.

The bank of the Sheyenne River ran high toward the west of Valley City Park's south entrance. In the east sat a large stone with the inscription:

City Park
1881
Welcome

There was limited parking space alongside the riverbank.

Attendees held signs: "Ready."

I saw people I knew from the Methodist church.

Audre Fredrick stood alongside the stage of the outdoor auditorium.

"Hello Audre. I like your dress," Mom said.

"Thank you. It's a Neiman Marcus." Audre's investigative look drifted briefly over me. "A St. John Collection."

Mom looked impressed.

Dave and Rita Bartlett were there.

Randy Morris and his wife Deanna.

"We've been watching the government screw matters up for years," Randy was telling Dave Bartlett. "Now we are ready to hear answers from a servant of the Lord."

I spotted Nora. She was talking to a guy close to our age. He had wavy blonde hair and a toothy grin.

I immediately slowed, the world around me narrowed.

Nora rushed over when she saw me. "Simon! How was camp?"

"Good."

Two inches taller than my six feet, the blonde guy smiled at Nora. "Dad needs help setting up. See ya around, Nora."

After he left, Nora turned to me. "A week seemed like forever."

"Are you moving?"

She blinked. "Where did you hear that?"

"My mom said your mom is marrying Reverend Hall and you're moving to California." The confusion in her eyes made me hopeful. If she didn't know about it, maybe it wouldn't really happen.

"That's Reverend Hall." She grabbed my arm, pointing to a man with black hair glistening in the sunlight. The sleeves of his red shirt, folded to his elbows. "Doesn't he look like a movie star?"

"Hm." I eyed his dark sunglasses.

Reverend Hall stepped up to the podium, wavy black hair glistening in the sunshine. Adjusting his black tie, he flashed the audience a devastating smile.

"Thank you all for coming," his voice boomed. The microphone screeched. "My name is Reverend Hall."

Revealing an even row of white teeth, he continued, "Before we get started, I'd like to thank the women who prepared the food, which is really the reason everyone came, am I right?"

A ripple of laughter followed.

"In these hard times, I'm honored to see you all here. With a turnout like this, we can clothe and feed half of Valley City."

Another round of applause followed his statement.

Reverend Hall waited for the applause to end before his tone turned serious, "Abraham gave God back the permission to bless the earth. Jesus had a treasury. Judas was stealing from the bag. We're made to believe Jesus was poor, and the rest of us should be too." He drew a breath and continued, "Not my will but Thine be done, He said."

How Jesus taught us to pray.

Someone cleared their throat, and I glanced over. Pastor Johnson stood off to my left, his brow furrowed. His eyes held a mixture of anger and confusion.

Apparently he wasn't buying the message either.

Alongside him, Mr. Lichte leaned over and whispered something in Pastor Johnson's ear.

"...It sounds like humility but it's really stupidity," Reverend Hall continued.

Wait. Was he saying Jesus was stupid?

I glanced over at Pastor Johnson and Mr. Lichte to gage their reaction, but they were gone. I scanned the crowd, and they were nowhere to be seen.

"It's an insult to our Heavenly Father if we have to say *Thy will be done*, then you are calling God a fool."

I noticed Taylor Hall standing at the front stage, hands lifted high.

What was he trying to prove?

"...guaranteed healing. How can you glorify God when your body doesn't even work? What makes you think the Holy Spirit wants to live in a body where the windows are dirty and you can't see out? Or your cells and limbs don't function right?" Reverend Hall was talking faster and faster. "Who wants to live in a house with a leaky roof and toilets running over and onto the floor?"

Uncomfortable laughter followed, then slow clapping.

"A rundown house, where electricity doesn't work, and wires hang out of the wall? No sir, you get it fixed. If the Holy Spirit can't see out of the body, then God's going to be limited."

If you're sick it's your own fault?

"Adam gave his rights to the serpent, the Devil. As a result, Adam got kicked out of the Garden of Eden." A pause, "Now the Devil wanders around, and God is out of the business. Out of the earthly realm. He has to have an invitation," he gave a laugh. "God doesn't have a foothold in this earth anymore, and not a thing He can do about it."

The audience pressed forward.

I stepped back, waiting for God to strike him down with lightning or show up to tell him off. Squash him with a press of His thumb.

None of which happened.

Reverend Hall went on, "...It's time to take back our rights from the Devil."

The congregation erupted in applause.

I backed away from the thick of it.

"Let it rain water from heaven to our thirsty souls," Reverend Hall shouted.

And the crowd went wild.

What would happen when people weren't healed and it didn't rain?

Everyone would feel duped.

He'd probably be gone by then. After tithes and offerings, of course. Without reason and truth, nothing good would come. His voice drifting over the crowd, truth crumbled to the ground as the Reverend delivered his message.

38

Following the service, people gathered around picnic tables.

The fragrance of juneberries, lilacs, and wild plums drifted through the breeze. A chorus of birds resonated from the cottonwoods as conversations buzzed around picnic tables, park benches, and the outdoor auditorium.

Children scampered about the play area. Adults pulled foodstuffs from coolers. Others grabbed folding chairs from the back of their vehicles.

"What are you going to do, Simon?" Nora asked.

"I have to help church ladies prepare lunches."

"Can I help?" She followed me toward the picnic area.

"If you want," I said, remembering she was moving. A jagged hole ripped through my gut. It didn't matter what Mom said, Nora was an original. There was no one like her. Maybe I could talk to Rachel. She always seemed reasonable.

"…And I drive a Rolls-Royce," Reverend Hall was telling Mom next to the table with sandwiches. "I'm following Jesus' steps. You can badmouth me all you want. It's easier to be persecuted while I'm driving a Rolls-Royce."

Mom giggled.

I strode up to the table. "What happens when it doesn't rain? Or people don't get healed?"

Reverend Hall cleared his throat. "But I will die on my terms, when I choose. God the Father cannot do anything in this realm without permission. Now again, I realize this statement is like committing adultery. It's sinful to say it from an evangelical point of view."

"It's sinful to say it from any point of view," I said.

Mom was the one to appear uncomfortable this time. "Simon is going to be a preacher after he graduates high school."

Reverend Hall gave me a jaded look. "You don't say."

"Hi sweetheart," Rachel called, making her way over to Reverend Hall.

He gave her a noisy kiss on the lips. "Watcha got to drink?"

"We have tea, coffee, or water," she said, and there were stars in her eyes.

Then I realized nothing I could say would make any difference. She wouldn't hear me over the music in her ears or see what was going on right under her nose.

Reverend Hall pressed his lips together. "I don't suppose you got any milk?"

Her eyes dropped. "I'm sorry, we don't. I can pick some up for you if you like on our way home."

"I'll wait."

Milk? Why did he ask what she had to drink if he was going to pick something unavailable?

"Simon, why don't you help Clara Sharp and Stella Richards with lunches?" Mom asked.

Cropped light brown hair, and a rather large nose for her face, Clara Sharp bagged lunches at the table set aside for the church.

In her sixties with salt and pepper hair, pinched features, pink sweatshirt with a white collar, Stella's tongue clicked, "...as it was in the days of Noah, so is the coming of the Messiah."

"For sure," Clara chirped in agreement.

A fragrance drifted toward me and I wondered if there was a scent called *Old Biddies*.

I turned to Mom and whispered, "I have to use the bathroom first."

Mom pinned me with a disapproving look. "Hurry then. Idle hands are the Devil's workshop."

In the bathroom, I gazed at my reflection. The button-down brown shirt I wore matched my copper hair and black eyepatch. A single golden eye stared back. Sinewy muscles made me think I could take Reverend Hall.

"You got mustard on your shirt," Doug said behind me in the mirror.

I jerked and whirled around. "I didn't know you were in here."

He flipped on the faucet. "If a guy woke up and saw either of those two ladies in the crook of his arm, he'd have to chew it off to get away."

I chuckled. "They're harmless."

He arched a brow. "Are they?"

I glanced in the mirror once more. Thinking of the arrogant Reverend Hall, I knew he would welcome any act of aggression on my part. I was fifteen. A stupid kid in his eyes. It wouldn't be a straight fight.

He would take Nora right out from under my nose and there was nothing I could do to stop him.

39
August 4, 1991

The French-built Greek-owned cruise ship *Oceanos* sank off the Wild Coast of South Africa. In my secret place, my hopes sank with the setting sun twinkling through leaves.

Birds chirped in the thicket.

Nora was leaving for California tomorrow morning. We sat on the ground with our backs against the rock. Mom said I could drive Nora her home. Ten o'clock was her curfew.

I didn't say anything, trepidation weighed heavy on my mind.

Her silence answered.

"I wrote a song for you," she said at last, her pretty cheeks flushed pink.

"My mom gave my piano to Jeffy Morris."

"How tragic." Her gaze met mine. "What will you do?"

"Find another piano," I said with confidence I didn't feel.

"There's a breeze in the trees bringing thoughts of you…" her voice, soft and husky, vibrated along my nerves. *"I'll think of you from now until the end of time…"*

My heart did a funny leap in my chest. "Maybe your Mom will change her mind."

"We've moved ten times in my life. I doubt it."

"What will she do for work?"

"She got a job at a 7-Eleven."

"Where will you go to school?"

"I suppose the same school as Taylor Hall."

I stiffened.

"You don't like him," she noted.

"Do you?" I asked, my heart hammering a mournful beat, almost painful in my chest.

"Not in the way you mean."

I wished I knew what she thought about me.

"You know, I never minded moving. Every time was an adventure. A new town, new people. I mean, before I met you. Of course God doesn't guarantee us happiness. I'll probably miss you." She paused. "Which will be annoying."

It was uncanny the way she read my mind. I glanced at my watch. "It's almost ten." I got up, holding my hand out to her.

She took it and stood. "I don't want to go."

Impulsively, I wrapped my arms around her, pulling her against my chest.

We stood holding each other for a long time, Nora crying softly.

"You'll write to me?" I asked against her cheek.

"Every day."

Pressing my forehead against hers, I said, "I'll write back."

"I'm going to miss you, Simon." Her voice dipped in a whisper.

"I'll miss you too."

40

Dear Simon,

How are you? I am fine. California is a beautiful place with mountains, the ocean, and sun.

What is in Aberdeen, South Dakota, Kevin and your dad go to? Anderson Bros. isn't a bad name for your farm, but like you, I don't care for abbreviations either. I'm not convinced you really want to get into the dairy business instead of preaching. What do your folks think? Of course, you have my support.

Guess what? Reverend Hall, Louis as Mom calls him, and my mother are engaged. I miss you too. More than you'll ever know.

Love, Nora

Love? A way to close out the letter. It meant nothing special. I stared at the return address.

I would write back as soon as I finished chores.

Milking cows turned out to be a messy, meaningless task, the barn echoing with Nora's absence.

Dear Simon,

How are you? I am fine. It's good to hear Kevin built a house of his own. I can't imagine the logistics. I'm glad he's only ten miles away. I can't get away from Louis Hall. He acts like my dad even though he's not married to my mom. I can't seem to get out of this gloomy funk I'm in. I know you think I don't know the meaning of the word gloomy, but it's been like this since Mom cancelled the summer trip to your place. There's so much going on,

but not much to tell. I'm rambling. Sorry. I wish you were here.
No, that I was there.

Love, Nora

Dear Simon,

How are you? I am fine. Mom said Louis (Pastor Hall) wants
to wait to get married until his trek is done. He's over at our
house all the time. Turns out his divorce isn't final yet. I wonder
what his wife thinks of him marrying my mom. I should move back
to North Dakota. I have one more year left before I graduate.
It seems forever. I can't wait to see you this Christmas!!!!

Love, Nora

Simon,

I'm sorry about my last letter. I didn't mean any of those
things I said. Anyway, something great has happened! Mom and
Louis are tying the knot Christmas! Which means we'll be spending
Christmas here. Won't be the same without snow. I'm glad you're
going to college in the fall. A physical before college is totally
normal.

Nora

Signed *Nora*, not *Love Nora*. It was so…incongruous.
Although it didn't begin with her usual greeting of *How are you,
I am fine* it was no doubt her handwriting.

I scanned the letter once more.

*I'm sorry about my last letter. I didn't mean any of those things I
said.* Was she referring to Reverend Hall? Or that she couldn't
wait to see me at Christmas?

I pulled out my notebook.

Dear Nora,

The eye doctor said I had Coat's disease as a kid. He showed me my medical chart and everything. I guess it's rare and is mainly seen in boys. I was pretty young, and the retina detached from my eye. The reason I lost it.

Mom says she told me about the Coat's disease. I heard her tell the story of how I lost my eye many times to many different people growing up, but I can't recall it being one of them. When I mentioned it to her, she said it's because I don't listen.

They all say I don't listen.

I'm going to miss you this Christmas. My folks got me a 1980 Chevy Blazer with light brown paneling and a white topper for an early graduation gift. I could come to your house the summer after graduation. I'll see if the Mattsons would do the milking.

Love, Simon

41
October 31, 1993

German unemployment hit a national record of 3.5 million, and our mailbox was empty.

Again.

Disappointment stung like the frigid January wind. The 100th day without a letter from Nora.

By day twenty, I tried to call her. Her mom said she was out shopping and she'd tell Nora to call me. When Nora didn't, I called again. Reverend Hall answered. He said Nora was too young to commit to a serious relationship.

My thoughts in a whirl, I hung up the phone. Had she met someone? Or was she with Taylor? No, he'd be like her stepbrother. Plus, she never mentioned him in her letters. The last letter she sent me played through my thoughts.

Was she embarrassed of my eye? Of me? She'd never acted like it before, but then, she'd always written me before too.

I grabbed the cow towels, slipped my boots on, and headed for the barn.

Dad drove up to the feedlot, followed by a cattle semi.

He cranked down his window when he saw me. "Selling the dairy, Simon."

"Why wasn't I told?"

"You just were." He lit a cigarette. "Oh don't give me that look. You're going to Bible school in the fall. Pastors don't milk cows." He took a drag. "I'm no good with them."

My dreams of owning a dairy farm, Nora as my wife, drove out of the yard with the last of the cows.

I turned and went into the house. In the kitchen, I grabbed a glass of water and sat down at the table. Thrusting both hands through my hair, my mind trekked down memory lane.

Your eyes look funny with those glasses.

We could go look for mud.

We're a lot alike.

Harry and Hans thundered up the stairs, bursting through the painted door into the kitchen. They spotted me, and said in unison, "Hey Simon. What's for supper?"

I leapt to my feet, sweeping my arm across the table. The water glass smashed against the far wall.

Harry and Hans' eyes widened briefly before they turned and ran back down the stairs.

I sank back down. Shoulders shaking, I wept bitterly.

There is a way that seems right to a man, but its end is the way to death.

Proverbs 14:12

42
Christmas Day 1995

The beginning of the holiday marked my first break from Trinity Bible College.

At home in the kitchen, Mom pulled a turkey from the oven with all the trimmings. Mashed potatoes on the stove, stuffing in the roaster, and pumpkin pies resting on cooling racks.

It might not look like Christmas, but it smelled like it.

We didn't need decorations to celebrate the season. Good food was the star, and the hands which prepared it, a gift from God.

Doug sat at the breakfast table. He'd gone to Jamestown College a year before he dropped out and moved back home. What he did exactly, I was never sure. He was always around when Dad, Kevin, and Charles were out running cattle. Which proved Dad still didn't trust Doug to do…anything.

Harry and Hans thundered up the basement steps. "Hi Simon," they said.

"Have a seat and I'll set the table," I told them.

Dad sat on the living room couch, coffee table littered with an array of empty whisky glasses and dirty tissues. He didn't glance away from the TV.

In clean flannel shirts and Levis, Kevin strolled in the front door, Charles behind him.

Charles plopped down at the dining room table. "Hi Simon. How's college?"

Before I could respond, Kevin took a seat next to Charles, and whistled. "Mom, you outdid yourself this year."

Mom grabbed the kettle of mashed potatoes. "The food is for Deanna Morris. She found out she has cancer."

In a state of shock, the five of us watched Doug help her load the Christmas feast into her car.

Mom returned to the kitchen one last time. "I'm sorry to have ruined Christmas," her voice broke.

I'd never seen my mom cry before.

Kevin and Charles leapt from their chairs and surrounded her. "Don't cry, Mom."

"Your father has something to tell you," she backed away, and walked out the door. We watched as her and Doug got into her car and drove out of the yard.

Charles turned to Dad. "What's the news?"

"We're getting a divorce," he mumbled.

"I'm going to my place." Kevin stormed out the back door.

"Me too," Charles said, following behind.

Hans, Harry and I sat at the dining room table set to the hilt, and no turkey.

"I'll whip something up." I stood and made my way to the kitchen. I desperately wanted answers. How long had they been planning this? Was Dad having a midlife crisis?

Dad rose from the couch and joined me in the kitchen. His eyes were bloodshot and his hands shook.

"Are you moving out or is she?" I asked, rummaging through the cupboards. There was Kraft mac 'n' cheese.

"She is. She's got a place in Jamestown." Dad rubbed his jaw, sinking down at the dining room table.

Normalcy slipping away, I searched the shelves. No noodles. No flour to make noodles. No grain to grind to make flour for homemade noodles.

Kraft dinner it was.

We ate in silence. After ten minutes, Harry mumbled, "May I be excused?"

"Me too," Hans chimed in.

"Sure." Dad stood and began to clear the table.

No, no, this was wrong. All wrong, and there was no fixing it. No making it right.

I grabbed my parka and headed out the door. The frigid winter wind matched my mood.

My stomach growled. The only thing I'd eaten was my heart out like a rotten steak. Passing the mailbox, my hand reached for the latch like a magnet to metal.

It was empty.

I braced myself for the familiar ache in my chest.

A dark void answered.

Bitterness had eased to resentment.

Resentment was easier somehow.

43
May 2, 1997

Mercury Mail announced its one millionth internet subscriber, and the pot of water on the stove began to bubble.

I glanced at the clock.

Two-thirty.

"Poker night, loser," Doug strolled into the kitchen and opened the fridge.

"Good to see you too." I scraped up the pile of cut rutabaga, and tossed it into the pot.

"We play Texas Hold 'Em in the new shop every weekend." He sniffed the milk.

I set the cutting board down and began slicing beets.

"Charles and Kevin will be there." He put the carton to his lips and began chugging.

I glanced at the clock, and then scraped the beets into the pot.

"There'll be a lot of pretty girls too. We could use a card dealer." He put the milk back and shut the fridge.

I grabbed the handle of the skillet, giving it a gentle toss. "I took the long way home through Jamestown and picked up groceries. There's this new recipe I ..."

He waved his hand at me. "Man. I think I just got dumber listening to you."

I turned back to the pot.

"Whatcha making?" Doug asked.

"Ratatouille."

He laughed. "You're going to make someone a good wife someday."

***

In the new shop, I sat down at the card table. The stereo in the corner played "The Gambler."

Doug slammed a glass of whisky down on the table in front of me.

"What's that for?" I asked.

"Empty mailboxes," Doug said.

Shuffling the deck, I looked up and my gaze locked with a woman across the room. Her eyes were an uncanny silver shimmering against the feathers dangling from her ears.

"...*For a taste of your whisky I'll give you some advice,*" Kenny Rogers droned.

Who was she? I snuck another glance at her. She wore a powdered blue shirt clinging to every curve. Long hair swept down her back in cascade after cascade of rich dark chocolate. I wanted to plunge my hands in it.

The sway of her hips sent more currents of fire through my body. When she walked toward me cards slid and burst from my hands. Blindly I gathered them up, my hands shaking.

Before I could come up with another thought, she sat down across from me. The small space became even smaller. My gaze dropped to her lips, the color of cherry wine.

I wondered what they would feel like beneath mine. My heart hammered hard in my chest. She caught my stare, a smile playing on her luscious mouth.

"I'm not very good at cards," she said.

My mind was wiped clean of all thought.

"Maybe you could teach me?" She giggled, and I didn't even care. Scooting her chair around, she was sitting close enough to see the cards. "You are positively gorgeous."

I glanced behind me, heart thundering.

"Humble too," she said in the same sultry tone.

Was she for real?

"...*know when to walk away and know when to run...*"

"You from around here?" she asked.

I thumped the edge of the cards on the table.

She giggled. "You don't talk much, do you?"

Charles plopped down, draping his arm around her. "Hey bro, how's Bible college?"

Shocked, I stammered, "G-good." She must be Charles' girlfriend.

"What do you got, another year?"

"Two."

"Aren't you going to introduce us?" the woman at his side asked.

Charles gave her a heavy lidded gaze. "This is my brother Simon. He's studying to be a preacher. Simon, Melissa Sutton."

She looked at me with a mixture of intrigue and something else I couldn't put my finger on.

Disgust.

She turned, walking her fingers up Charles' chest. "Charlie, I never get to see you."

Charlie?

"We play poker again next Saturday night," he replied.

Her lush lower lip poked out. "But that's a whole week away."

"Some things are worth waiting for." He flashed her a grin.

Then a glimpse of big blonde hair caught my eye. I looked over as Selene walked in. Doug greeted her. Together they made their way toward us.

"Hi, Simon." Selene sat down next to me.

My jaw clenched.

Doug reached for his cards. "Is there a problem?"

"No problem." I tapped the edge of the deck on the table.

"Then deal." He pushed poker chips into the middle.

I cut the deck.

44
July 1, 1997

In the early morning hours, Great Britain turned over Hong Kong back to China, and Charles announced his engagement to Melissa while I prepared supper.

"Christmas?" I tied an apron around my waist.

"Actually, Saturday the twentieth," Charles said.

I arched a brow. "Will anyone be holding a shotgun?"

"I don't know!" Charles exploded suddenly, and then more calmly, "It's not my wedding, it's hers. Melissa doesn't believe in long engagements. I've told you like ten times."

"First I've heard of it."

"Because you never listen."

I held both hands up. "Sorry. I'm …surprised. I'll be on Christmas break. Should work fine." I took a knife and scraped it across the top of the measuring cup, leveling the flour. "Where's it at?"

"Fairgrounds in Carrington. She's from there." He popped open a can of Mountain Dew.

"Speaking of the blushing bride, where is she?"

"California."

"Excuse me?"

"She flew out to see her maid of honor. They're having the bachelorette party there."

Questions began popping in my head. "The bachelor party too?" I asked.

"Nah. It'll be nothing fancy. Probably the Brass Rail in Jamestown." Charles held up his hand. "I know you don't do the bar scene."

"No, I don't."

"Just this once. You can order a pop." A pause. "Oh, and try not to be a wet blanket."

"I was planning on being a wet blanket, but since you said no…" I suppressed a smile.

"Simon…"

"All right."

"Thanks, man."

A piece of the puzzle wiggled its way into my brain. "I thought you said she's from Carrington." I wiped my hands on my apron.

"She is."

"Then what's in California?"

"Her maid of honor. I told you already."

"I thought you said her sister is the maid of honor."

"Oh. Well. I meant a bridesmaid. From Sunnydale."

"Huh."

He downed the last of his Mountain Dew, crumpling the can. "You know, you wouldn't have to ask a million questions if you would listen the first time around."

45

October 19, 1997

Harry and Hans, staying at Mom's for the weekend, made sure to call and tell me Sandy Alomar of the Cleveland Indians got the 700th World Series home run.

Which left Dad and Doug at the house, and me, the only one attending church on Sunday morning.

Breathtaking golden yellows, and deep red hues decorated the clusters of trees throughout town. Midmorning, the sun was already high, promising a short day.

Pastor Johnson's sermon was about the sheep and goats. Potluck was a place to catch up on gossip whether one wanted to or not.

Stella Richards and Clara Sharp were sitting at my table.

"It's good to see you, Simon," Clara said, taking a sip of coffee. An awkward pause followed, and I knew she wanted to inquire about my folks. "Are you going to replace Pastor Johnson?" she asked instead.

"No."

"Trinity Bible College isn't a Methodist school, Clara," Stella said, leaning forward. "Did you know Oakes hired a new police officer?"

Clara's eyes lit like an evergreen at Christmastime. "Really? Who?"

"John Golden. Originally from Park River. Moved here recently. I guess he used to work security for a firm in California."

"What's he like?" Clara asked, and before Stella could answer, she went on, "Of course, anyone will be better than Dale. Dave? Whatshisname."

"You talking about Derick Nelson?" Stella asked.

"That's him." Clara snapped her fingers. "Sheila Daltron from Oakes just got her license, and said he used to follow her around town like a stalker."

Stella's eyebrows knitted. "Lois Degner attends the Methodist church in Oakes. She says John Golden never misses a Sunday. Pretty generous donation to the suicide prevention walk too."

I glanced at the clock. "It's been nice to visit with you ladies."

"You too," Clara said, turning back to Stella. "It'll be nice having a decent police officer in Oakes. Why I..."

When I arrived home, I found Doug rooting around the kitchen cupboards. "There you are. I'm starved," he said.

I held out the crockpot. "There was potluck at church."

"You're a bro, bro." He took the pot from me, set it on the counter, and dished himself a generous helping.

"I got pulled over when I was visiting Sean Young in Oakes." Doug grabbed a glass from the cupboard. "Forgot to use my turn signal. Met the new cop, John Golden. I only got a warning."

"The church ladies were talking about the new officer."

Doug poured Jim Beam whisky over ice. "Real nice guy."

"Must be."

"Turns out he's engaged to Nora." He pushed the glass toward me.

Slowly, I sank to the chair, rubbing my forehead with a tired hand. "How do you know this?"

"Sean told me. He owns a construction place down there. I guess he's friends with Officer Golden. Nora's mom is going through a messy divorce. She left California and bought a house in Oakes. Nora's staying with her until she marries Mr. Rogers."

"You mean John Golden."

He nodded. "Who apparently doesn't believe in premarital relations."

At the image of Nora having sex, premarital or otherwise with some hero cop, I swallowed the whisky, and with it my dreams of her becoming my wife.

"Tastes like turpentine." I downed the last of it, wincing. I set the glass down. "I'll take another. No ice this time."

"Now you're talking," Doug said, pleased as a farmer during planting season.

I stared at the glass in front of me with blurry eyes, devastation threatening to choke me. There was no more waiting for her to come home. To go back to the way things used to be.

And as I downed the whisky, I knew I would never go back to being who I used to be.

46

From a dead sleep, I heard the kitchen phone ringing. I counted the rings until ten. It stopped. I started to drift off again, and then it began ringing. I rolled out of bed, and stumbled up the stairs. "Hello, Andersons, Simon speaking."

"Hi Simon Speaking."

"Who's this?"

"Melissa."

"Melissa who?"

She laughed, soft and sultry, dancing a thrill across my arms. "Is Charlie there?"

Charlie? I wished he would give his fiancée his own number rather than this one. We weren't his secretary.

"Are you there?"

"Oh yeah." I cleared my throat. "Sorry."

"Is Charlie around?"

"Not sure."

"Okay." She hung up.

I glanced at the kitchen clock.

Six.

I wandered to the living room and sank down on the couch. Where was Doug? Last thing I remembered, we were having drinks after church. And then...

There was a knock on the front door.

My eyes darted toward the door. Nora?

Doug said she was back. In Oakes, anyway. Maybe the whole thing was a misunderstanding. Could it be her? I hurried to answer it. My heart plunged into my stomach.

Melissa moved past me, strolling into the kitchen. "Holy Moly Rocky. Look at all these pastries! Your mom is quite the baker."

"I baked those."

"You didn't." Her eyes widened. "Really? Awesome." She rooted through the cupboards, and I noticed her brief t-shirt, skin like porcelain evident beneath. "You have Jim Beam?"

"My dad's."

"Will we be expecting him anytime soon?" She flicked a glance around the kitchen as she pulled the whisky from the shelf.

"Doubt it." A mixture of excitement and unease churned my gut. The sexual tension between us was palpable.

"Wait a minute," I held up a halting hand. "You belong to Charles."

"He doesn't own me." She pressed a finger against my lips. "A drink isn't a sin."

Head spinning, I retreated to the living room couch.

"I didn't know you knew Selene." Melissa sat down next to me and handed me a glass of whisky.

Every nerve in my body instantly became aware of her.

"She used to cut my hair."

Two glasses of whisky later, I found myself telling her about the haircuts and happy endings.

The sympathy I saw glittering in her eyes had me admitting the most painful part. "Worst was, she said I didn't make it last," the words slurred as they came out of my mouth.

"Good thing she's not here. I'd scratch her eyes out," Melissa's voice made its way through my foggy brain.

"Smile Simon." She held up a camera.

I turned and looked at her.

She snapped a picture. "The eyepatch is sexy. Sort of a Phantom of the Opera look."

"Thanks. I think." My hand immediately went to my bad eye. Sure enough, the eyepatch was still in place. In my alcohol-induced haze, I'd forgotten about it. "What are the pictures for?"

"To remember your gorgeous face," she purred.

More flattery. What was she after?

"Simon, are you lit?" Her relaxed and happy tone mirrored my own feelings.

I was shamefully inebriated. Cheeks flushed, I glanced over. "You know, I'm feeling pretty good."

She climbed on my lap.

"What are you d-doing?" I stammered.

Her smile dawned, slow and bright. "What does it look like I'm doing?" she asked, fusing her mouth to mine.

I kissed her back with ferocity which had us both reeling. Ravaging her mouth, a bell clanged through the haze. I broke away and stood. She fell to the floor.

The room tilted, and I dropped back on the couch.

Melissa scooted up, leaning against the side. "You drank tooooo much."

"Listen, I…"

She waved the bottle at me. "Shush. I'm going to sit here and drink," she chugged while glaring at me with cold eyes over the top, then lowered the bottle, "and you are going to sit there and shut up."

Too sloshed to contest her words, I fell into a drunken silence.

Desire cooling, I draped my arm over my forehead. My stomach rolled, and I hoped God wouldn't send me to hell for what I'd done. Charles was going to kill me.

I was in trouble.

But as for you, O man of God, flee evil. Pursue righteousness, godliness, faith, love, steadfastness, gentleness.

Paul the Apostle

47

My yesterday-self wrote a check my today-self had to cash. Regret flooding my entire being, I struggled to get out of bed. I'd gone against everything I believed. Regret, a bitter drink, chased visions of passion.

I would pretend the kiss never happened. Charles wouldn't ask about it and I wouldn't bring it up.

The back door opened.

"I made roast beef, mashed potatoes, buttered carrots, and a large garden salad," I said. "Homemade apple pie for dessert."

"Awesome, I'm starved." Melissa walked into the kitchen.

I frowned. "I thought you were Harry and Hans."

Her smile was small and cold. "I saw your car in the driveway," she said. "I thought you left for school."

I shook my head. "No classes today."

"I made you a snack." She thrust a plate of cookies at me.

"These are store-bought."

Hesitation waged war in her eyes. "Okay fine. I picked them up at the grocery store on the way over."

"Why would you pretend?"

Her eyes sparked, then quickly, the anger passed.

"To look good." She giggled, pulling two glasses from the cupboard.

I held up my hand. "None for me thanks."

"Why not?" she pouted. "I won't tell Charlie we made out if you don't."

My gut clenched. *Good, Simon. Real good.*

"Fine." I took the glass from her extended hand.

She propped her leg on the kitchen stool, her skirt high on her thigh. "Guess what?" She sucked on her finger. "I'm not wearing panties."

My body tightened with a wave of lust.

She giggled, leading me over to the table, scanning the puzzle pieces I had scattered.

"What's it supposed to be?" She took a step closer, warm puffs of air brushing my cheek.

"The Taj Mahal." My grip tightened on my glass.

"I missed you at poker night." Slowly, she reached down, grabbing the hem of her shirt, and pulled it over her head. "You ever hear of strip poker?"

A spout of laughter burst from my lips. "Sorry if I'm not comfortable with you half-naked in my dad's living room."

"I get such a charge out of you, Simon," she said, and then I noticed it. The sweet smell of incense. She was high. Her pupils were dilated.

"Wait now. This isn't… You don't…" I frowned, setting the glass of whisky on the dining room table, "I can't."

"I think that's the most I've ever heard you say." She started to run her hand up my chest.

If her hand had been a poisonous snake, I couldn't have moved away faster. "Nothing is gonna happen." *Except she'll have the munchies.* "You're engaged to my brother."

"I won't tell if you don't," she said in a sing-song voice.

Heat flooded my face, rushing to my belly and lower. "No."

Her eyes flashed fire. "You know, you didn't have to kiss me, or act excited when I took off my shirt." Her mouth was drawn tight. "And if anyone did any sinning, it was you for being a tease."

"Forget it," I said. "Not happening."

Then she smiled a brilliant, empty smile. "We'll see."

48

She wasn't leaving.

I sat in my jeep for ten minutes, waiting for her to walk out the door. Dad would be home soon, bringing Harry and Hans with him. I couldn't go back in there alone.

Maybe Kevin would know what to do. I grabbed my baseball hat off the passenger seat, and tugged it low over my brow.

I mentally kicked myself the ten miles it took to get to Kevin's house. The memory of her intoxicating kiss, poisonous. I'd performed a narrow escape.

We'll see.

The two words ran like ice through my veins. I didn't even want to think what would have happened if someone had walked in when she was topless.

I reached Kevin's ranch-style home. After three quick raps on the door, Gretchen Roth answered it, wearing a pajama top and bottoms. "Hey Simon, long time no see."

I jumped back.

She smiled. "Sorry. Didn't mean to scare you."

"I suppose there's no point in asking you if you're lost."

She giggled some more.

"Simon?" Kevin emerged from the bedroom behind her. He took a step toward me, sniffing twice. "If I didn't know any better, I'd say you've been drinking."

"One sip to appease a crazy person."

"Care to explain yourself?"

"Long story."

Kevin eyed me. "What happened to your eyepatch?"

I pulled my cap down. "Didn't feel like wearing it."

"Uh huh."

"Nora's getting married. A cop from Oakes by the name of Golden. Suppose to be a pretty good guy."

"I'm sorry, Simon," Gretchen said, her eyes soft.

Kevin's brow furrowed. "Are you okay?"

"No!" I shouted. "I mean, yes, I'm okay." No way was I going to spill my guts in front of Gretchen.

Gretchen kissed my brother. "I'm going to take a quick shower, honey."

Did I have to tell him at all? No one had to know. It would cause hard feelings.

Stupid kiss. Hopefully Melissa didn't mention it to Charles. She wouldn't. Besides, there was nothing to tell. Nothing happened other than a little kiss. One hot, little, open-mouthed, gut-wrenching kiss.

The whole thing was unsettling.

49

November 20, 1997

Iraq's Revolution Command Council formally endorsed an agreement arranged by Russia, enabling UN weapons inspection teams to resume operations in Iraq.

In the student center at Trinity Bible College, I was hunched over my Cultural Anthropology book. Fingers thrust through my hair, I stared at the pages with unseeing eyes.

I had trouble concentrating since Tuesday when classes resumed. I never told Kevin about the kiss. I couldn't tell Harry and Hans, and wouldn't tell Doug. Hopefully she didn't tell Charles.

"Hi Simon." Alexis Roseau sat down on the stuffed chair next to me. She had light brown hair pulled half-up, half-down, and was from Binford.

"Hi Alexis." I sat up. "What's new?"

"I was wondering if you wanted to go out sometime."

Before I could answer, she continued, "I know you and I haven't spent a lot of time together, but I'd like to get to know you. I've been waiting for you to ask me out since freshman orientation. When you didn't," she shrugged, "I figured I'd ask you."

Both pretty and sweet, Alexis drew attention from the men in our class. Flattered, I had no idea she was interested in me.

"I..." I started to say yes, and a corner of red caught my eye. I glanced over and saw Melissa Sutton by the door, regarding me with lazy anticipation. How could she appear so innocent?

Alexis' gaze followed mine before she glanced back at me. "You know her?"

"She's my brother's fiancée." I shut my book. "I'm sure she's here to discuss details about the groom's supper," I lied, jamming the stack of textbooks into my backpack. "I'm a groomsman at their wedding."

Alexis' smile faltered. "Oh. Maybe some other time."

"Sure." I stood and slung my backpack over my shoulder.

"Hi Simon," Melissa said as I passed her on my way out the door.

Ignoring her, I headed for the exit. The sky was overcast. A gust of icy fall wind swept up, stealing my breath.

When I reached the parked Chevy, I tossed my backpack in the back seat and shut the door. I turned around, and Melissa was right in front of me.

I jumped back. "What are you doing here?"

"My aunt lives in Ellendale. I thought I'd stop by."

I reached for the door handle.

"I'm going to marry Charles in a month, and I'm struggling with erotic thoughts about you," she said.

My mouth went dry.

She went on, "I appreciate your being religious. I want to be respectful, since you told me about Selene Tomson molesting you."

All the blood drained from my face in an instant. I stiffened, opened my mouth, but no words came out.

"Anyway, I'm glad it's out there. I'm sorry if I misread everything you told me."

I got into the Blazer and turned the key. Catching a glimpse of her in the rearview mirror, it dawned on me.

I was never going to get rid of her.

50

The last of fall leaves clung to trees, and the early afternoon sun twinkled between near naked branches.

Classes had dismissed for Thanksgiving break. Making my way toward the Blazer, I stared down at my Apologetics test in hand.

I'd never gotten a D. The lowest since school started was an A minus. Obsessed with Melissa and her unexpected visit, I'd had trouble concentrating. She was up to no good.

Nearing my Chevy Blazer, I froze. Melissa was standing next to it, fall leaves whirling around her feet and through the gutter. Ignoring her, I went straight for the driver's door handle.

"I think you have a headlight out," she said. "Do you need some help with it?"

I froze. Did she do something? Switch a good bulb out for a bad one? I got into the Blazer, started the engine, and flipped the lights on. Exiting the vehicle, I went around to the front and then back. No lights were out. I expelled an audible sigh.

I heard her high heels on the concrete behind me. "I would appreciate a chance to talk," she said.

"I'm sure you would." I turned and flicked her a quick glance. "You can't show up whenever and wherever you feel like."

Her smile was apologetic. "I told you my aunt…"

"Doesn't attend school here."

Appease her or she'll tell Charles.

"One cup of coffee." I reached over and cut the engine. "There's a gas station right over there."

She wrinkled her pert nose. "Gas station?"

I shrugged.

With Styrofoam cups of coffee, we sat on the benches in the rear of the gas station.

"What did you want to talk about?" I took a sip of coffee, remembering I didn't like coffee.

She fidgeted across from me. "I wanted to see how you were doing."

"Good. If that's all…" I started to rise.

"It's not."

I sat back down. "I figured."

"You're going to be my brother-in-law." She grinned suddenly. "I was there. You kissed me back."

I winced. I didn't hate her. Nor did I blame her, really. I was responsible for my own actions and accountable for the part I played. But she couldn't take a hint. Or wouldn't.

Never admit to anything. "No offense, Melissa, but let's not delve into the details."

"I wasn't finished," she cut in. The sharp tone caught me off guard. "I've never met anyone like you."

Oh great.

"I know I took advantage." Her face crumpling, she swiped at tears with the back of her wrist.

Imaginary tears. "Water under the bridge."

"I liked the way you looked at me poker night in the garage," she said matter-of-factly.

"I didn't know about you and Charles." I took another sip of the bitter black liquid.

She sighed loudly. "Can we be friends?"

The intimate kiss we'd shared came flooding back.

No way. "I need some time to think about it."

"Thank you."

I held my hand up. "The thing is, I forgive you, but I don't trust you."

Melissa tightened her grasp on her cup. "I love Charles. I don't want to hurt him."

"Good." I took another long swallow, wincing as it burned going down.

I stood, and she followed me out of the convenience store.

Reaching the Blazer, I felt her body brush mine. She was right behind me. I turned, my gaze narrowed in on her brown sweater dipped low, revealing generous cleavage.

She leaned close to my ear, her hot breath brushing my skin. "I've been lonely."

I whirled around, fumbling for the door handle.

The sound of her laughter echoed in my ears as I drove away.

51
Thanksgiving Day, 1997

A wreath made of fall leaves at the back door welcomed me home. I made my way inside the house, the scent of nutmeg warming the quaint kitchen space. Someone had decorated.

Melissa. Was she here?

I jumped at a knock on the door.

Deanna Morris stood holding a crockpot. "I made too much knoephla soup. I know how Harry and Hans love it." She extended it toward me.

True. I took the pot from her grasp.

She glanced behind me. "You have company?"

"Nope."

She hesitated. "I better be going. Happy Thanksgiving."

After she left, I set the pot on the counter and plugged it in. I headed toward the stairs.

Dad entered the kitchen from upstairs. Dressed in a crisp black shirt and clean blue jeans, he looked years younger.

A woman, around thirty, with strawberry blonde hair and a shy smile appeared behind him.

"Simon, I'd like you to meet Paige," he said, filling the tea kettle with water. "Paige, this is my middle son, Simon. He's going to be a preacher after he's done with Bible school."

She smiled, revealing even, white teeth.

Ah. She was the reason for the curious, gift-bearing neighbor.

"Kevin and Gretchen might stop by after dinner. Charles and Melissa are going to Carrington."

Thank goodness. I ran a hand down the back of my neck. "Are Harry and Hans around?"

"In the new shop, I think," Dad said, crossing over to the teapot. "You brought food? Paige has a turkey in the oven."

"Nope. Deanna Morris dropped it by." I slipped into my boots and headed out the door. When I reached the shop, Harry and Hans were playing dominoes at a long table next to the tractor.

"Dad has a girlfriend?" I asked.

"Hi Simon." Harry slammed a domino on the table.

"Her name is Paige Rogers," Hans said, laying his own down.

"She's real nice," Harry added, eyes on the table.

"What's Mom going to think when she gets here?"

Hans shrugged. "She's not coming."

"What do you mean, she's not coming?"

"She's spending Thanksgiving with her boyfriend in Oakes," Harry supplied.

"Frank is his name," Hans added.

I made my way back to the house, and Stella Richards pulled into the yard. Her 1983 gold Cadillac came to a halt. Stella exited, went around to the trunk, and pulled out a crockpot.

"It's green bean casserole." She handed it to me.

"Did somebody die?" I asked.

She giggled. "No. I made too much and remembered your family likes it."

I took it from her grasp. I didn't like green bean casserole or green bean anything.

Stella's eyes were on the house. My gaze followed hers. "Did you want to come in?" I asked.

"No, I've got a turkey in the oven."

After she drove out of the yard, I continued my way inside the house through the enclosed porch, crockpot in hand.

Dad and Paige were sitting at the table with cups of tea, sharing pages of *The Fargo Forum*.

"More food?" Dad asked without looking up from the paper.

"Stella Richards and her green bean casserole." I held up the crockpot.

"Uff da," Dad said. "I bet the Clemens family could use a home-cooked meal. I heard they had to go on fuel assistance."

A wave of compassion swept over me at the news. The Clemens family lived three miles south and a mile west, and had been struggling for the last ten years.

"I was going to suggest baking a fresh pan of buns for dinner," I said. "I could bake extra, and recruit Harry and Hans to make a trip over to their place."

"Good idea, Simon," Dad said.

Pulling out the mixer, I couldn't help smiling about nosy neighbors unknowingly providing a Thanksgiving meal for the more unfortunate ones.

52
December 19, 1997

The night before Charles and Melissa's wedding, the Chieftain Motel was packed with wedding guests.

Doug plopped down on the stool next to me. "Mom's moving back to the farmhouse."

Startled, I asked, "A reconciliation?"

"Nah. Dad's building a new house north of Wimbledon."

Wearing a tight black ensemble revealing every curve, Melissa caught my stare.

Heat worked its way down to my insides until I felt my entire being on fire.

She turned back to Jeff Morris, laughing at something he said.

"The little tramp has been ridden more often than the old mare Dad got at auction," Doug said.

"Not a cool thing to say about your sister-in-law." I took a drink of my Shirley Temple.

"I'll take another Gentleman Jack," Doug raised his voice to the bartender, setting his empty glass down. He turned back to me. "Sean Young knew her when he lived in Carrington. In the Biblical sense, if you get my drift."

"She doesn't seem much of a farmer's wife."

"Didn't he tell you? Charles is moving up here to Carrington. He's going to work for Sutton Construction. His soon-to-be father-in-law owns it."

Relief flooded me at once.

The further away she was from me, the better.

The ceremony was scheduled for two o'clock at Trinity Lutheran Church. It was two, and the bride was nowhere to be found. Charles paced back and forth, wearing out a path on the altar.

Whispers erupted.

She finally arrived, walking herself down the aisle.

Standing between Kevin and Doug, I checked my watch. Two-twenty.

The rest of the ceremony went without a hitch.

***

The fairgrounds' reception hall was lavishly decorated. White lights hung from the ceiling. Among the appetizers, popcorn with do-it-yourself toppings and chocolate-covered pretzels. There was a table lined with top-of-the-shelf liquor, and a bartender mixing drinks.

I expelled a breath. Gentleman Jack would go down nicely. *What are you doing? You can't drink.*

Ignoring the voice of reason, I made my way to the bar, passing the happy couple. Swaying next to Charles, Melissa was hammered, laughing uproariously.

Doug was dancing with one of the bridesmaids. He covered his mouth and coughed, making a circle around his ear with a forefinger, the universal sign for crazy.

I was on my third Jack Coke and made a beeline for the bathroom.

Washing my hands, I caught my reflection in the mirror, tuxedo with white shirt and bow tie, and black eyepatch.

"You're like Lancelot, being led around by a nose ring," I told my reflection.

The room tilted. Reaching for a paper towel, my hand connected with one warm and soft. I glanced over.

194

Wearing a sultry smile, Melissa stood next to the sink.

53

Melissa leaned in, her voluptuous body inches from mine. She was too close, the look in her eyes, too sultry, the hand brushing down my arm, too... My body tightened. I gripped her shoulders and moved her away from me.

She giggled.

I flicked a glance around.

Her hand moved to the top of her strapless gown and she began to pull.

I stopped breathing.

Soon she was reaching for my fly. A heady odor of whisky hit my nostrils. I turned and ran out of the room like Joseph from the Bible. Making my way over to the head table, I plopped down next to Kevin.

He glanced at me. "You look frazzled, Simon."

I smoothed my hair down and straightened my bow tie.

Melissa sauntered out of the men's room. She glanced over at me and winked!

I looked away.

Kevin whistled low. "You mind telling me what that's all about?"

"You wouldn't believe me."

"Try me."

In as few words as possible, I regaled the bathroom scene, reluctant to look my oldest brother in the eye.

He let out a disbelieving laugh. "She pulled her dress down and you ran out the door?"

"I said you wouldn't believe me."

"They're married now. She walks in, you leave."

Alarmed, I said, "You think I want her? I don't. I..."

He waved his hand in my direction. "I see the way you look at her."

Heat swept up the back of my neck to the tips of my ears.

Kevin took a sip of Jack Daniels. "She's a good-looking woman, but you better keep your distance."

I fell silent. No point in talking when no one was listening.

I couldn't wait to get back to school.

54
January 8, 1998

The same day Unabomber suspect Ted Kaczynski asked to act as his own lawyer, I had to report to the dean's office and plead my own case.

The dean's secretary looked up from the letter she'd been typing when I walked in. "Simon, go on in. Mr. Jenson is expecting you."

Sitting at his desk, Cliff Jenson was on the phone. He waved me over when he saw me and ended the call.

I sat down across from him, wincing at the stale taste in my mouth. What I would give for a Tic Tac.

"Everything okay, Simon?" He took off his glasses and tossed them on the desk.

"Y-yeah," I stammered, but his expression told me everything was so not okay.

***

Driving home, the meeting played over and over in my bewildered brain. I had reminded Mr. Jenson I was on the dean's list for excellent grades every semester until now. In the end, I'd begged for another chance.

Pleas that landed on deaf ears.

I arrived home in Wimbledon. Dad's home. It hadn't felt like home since they divorced. Dad's new house north of Wimbledon would be done by July. Mom was moving back August 1. Last fall, my future had been bright. Now, I faced the reality of living in my mother's basement.

What would I do in the meantime?

The front door opened and Kevin walked in. "Simon, I thought I saw your Blazer in…" He stopped short when he saw me. "What happened?"

I drew a deep breath. "You're not going to believe this, but…"

***

Kevin's little red house was tucked in a cluster of trees alongside Section Ten, ten miles from our farm growing up.

The small kitchen had a Norwegian theme.

"It's a good-sized place," Kevin said. "Two bedrooms upstairs, a large bath, and a picture window." He glanced at me. "Did I ever show you the basement?"

"Uh, no," I said, following him downstairs.

The open room had braided rugs scattered across the cement floor painted teal. There was a small bedroom with a king-sized bed, and a bathroom including a clawfoot tub plus shower.

On either side of the mirror were drawings. A boy peeing in a pond, the fish scattering. The other side had a girl with her pants around her ankles as she sat on the seat, magazines on the floor around her.

"It's nice," I said politely.

Back upstairs, the living room was a quaint space with a narrow hall. Van Gogh paintings covered the walls. The furniture was delicate and antique.

The aroma of freshly brewed coffee floated through the living room.

"Have a seat." Kevin motioned to a Victorian green sofa, curved wooden legs etched in design.

I sat down, running my hands over piping edging the arms. "This is nice."

"Gretchen bought it at a garage sale for a steal." Kevin pulled two mugs from the cupboard. "Gretchen's different now, Simon."

"Did I say anything?"

"You didn't have to." Kevin handed me a steaming cup, and sat down with his own at the stuffed chair across from me. "You're the smartest in the family. How is it you failed college?"

I took a sip to be polite, always amazed at how good coffee smelled opposed to its bitter taste.

"Long boring story." I sighed. "I was humiliated."

"Who cares what they think? Do something great. When people take notice, you can hold your head high, look them straight in the eye, and say, 'Living well is the best revenge.'" He took a sip from his own cup. "Or something like that."

"You may be right. In the meantime, I need work. Since I did the milking growing up, I don't know a lot about beef cattle, but I'm good with numbers. I could do the bookkeeping, or…"

"Gretchen does the books."

"Oh."

Kevin took a sip from his mug. "I bought the quarter around the old Hirsch and Cruff places. Going to plant corn and cut the chemical." He crossed one leg over the other. "Harry and Hans aren't going to college next year. They're working for me. Anderson Bros. is going organic."

"Really?"

"I loved the farm growing up, Simon. The wide open prairie, and running cattle. I love the pasture and the fields." He uncrossed his legs, stretching them out in front of him. "I love the land. I feel like a king every morning when I wake up and have a cup of coffee on the deck with a chorus of birds in the background."

He took a sip. "This is your place if you want it."

"What do you mean?" I set my cup down.

"I upgraded. Moved a five-bedroom house from Valley City two miles north of Cruff's old place last fall. Gretchen is pregnant."

This was about Gretchen. She probably insisted he get a bigger place.

"We're going to be calving before you know it. Then I'll need to put up new fencing. I could use you. You can live here for a fraction of the cost of rent in Jamestown. You'll need to make room when Hans and Harry graduate." He smiled. "Don't think they want to live in Mom's basement either."

"Not a problem."

"Didn't think it would be." He downed the last of his coffee.

55
May 4, 1998

A federal judge in Sacramento, Calif., gave Unabomber Ted Kaczynski four life sentences plus thirty years.

Passing a magazine rack in Jamestown County Market and a magazine covered in blue, my own conscience convicted me of shoplifting nine years ago.

Give no opportunity to the devil. Let the thief no longer steal, but rather let him labor.

The past five months of fencing and running cattle had been grueling work. Head held high, I walked past the *Playboy* in the rack.

***

Across the vast prairie land, the sun shone brightly overhead.

A crow cawed.

Kevin was in the tractor with the posthole digger.

I followed behind, picking up wooden posts and sliding them into designated holes.

Following behind me, Hans set the level against the post. Harry kicked a little dirt into the hole. Together, they tamped fresh soil down with the handle.

The magazine I hadn't bought came to mind along with the blonde centerfold above the blacked-out area. Like a secret lover, the temptation to sample beckoned.

***

The sun dipped low by the time I arrived home. Nearing the house, I saw a gray Ford F150 parked in front of the house.

Inside, Doug was rooting around in the fridge. "There's no good food in here. What is wrong with you?"

A blonde woman with striking features moved further behind him. Her appearance, a baggy sweatshirt, blue jeans and no makeup, did not detract from her wholesome beauty. What was she doing with Doug?

"Nice pickup." I glanced away, pulling my hat low.

"It belongs to Alice," Doug said, closing the fridge. "I guess we're going to Bonanza." On his way out the door, Alice trailing behind, he called, "By the way, I left you a little something in your room."

The knowledge created an odd little tingle in my belly. I hurried downstairs to my room.

A magazine was on my bed.

No longer innocent or naïve, I reached for it with shaky fingers, laid down, and flipped to the centerfold.

Calvin Klein created the big new flap in women's underwear. The Playmate of the Month was wearing them.

"Men the world over have been trying to find out what comes between Kim and her Calvin's. For more on this unfolding story, turn to..."

I turned the page.

Across the room, the closet door was open. I couldn't shake the feeling I was being watched.

56
September 11, 2001

I would always remember the sunrise being one of the most beautiful I'd experienced, but the least I enjoyed.

In my kitchen, I sliced two pieces of bread and popped them into the toaster. I flipped on the TV.

A plane flew into the South Tower of the World Trade Center in New York City.

The toast popped up, my gaze glued to the screen as the second plane crashed into the south tower.

The clock said eight-oh-three.

The newscaster's voice went soft. My mind heard over and over again the plane crashing and never landing. I would never hear another plane's descent and not think of today.

The phone rang and I picked it up. "Hello?"

"Simon. Are you seeing this?" Doug's voice was astonished.

"Yeah."

"What are you doing today?"

"Gonna get a load of fence posts from Aberdeen."

"I'll stop by around seven. I've got some news."

"I should be back by then." I hung up, mentally preparing a meal for three people.

***

On my way home, a red Mazda pickup was pulled to the side of the road with its hazards flashing. From a distance, I saw a woman crouched next to the front left tire. I neared and my heart gave two hard kicks in my chest.

Nora.

Heart thudding in my ears, I pulled up behind her and got out.

Glancing back, Nora quickly stood. Sweaty blonde tendrils clinging to her forehead, cheeks rosy with heat, she was pregnant.

"This is a busy highway." I wiped sweaty palms on the front of my jeans, and took the tire iron from her grasp.

She stepped back, glancing toward the truck. "John's feeling sick, and I…"

Suddenly, the passenger door opened, and a man got out. He made his way around the front of the grille, holding his gut.

"I'm John Golden," he said. Blonde hair feathered and a bit too long, he looked like the movie star who played Bo Duke.

Nora looked uneasy. "Simon stopped to help."

"Simon?" John Golden glanced at me, then at Nora. "Simon Anderson?"

She had talked about me? A thrill shot up my spine, and I gave myself a swift mental kick. By the stars in her eyes, I knew it was too late.

"Yes." A pearl of sweat trickled down her forehead.

"You sure you're not too tired?" John Golden asked Nora.

"A little."

"Why don't you sit in the car, darlin'?" He chuckled. "Let the men handle this."

She got in the pickup and shut the door.

I let the jack down, readjusted it, and then jacked the truck back up. Grabbing the tire iron, I set it to a rusted bolt.

"Halloween is a ways off. What's with the eyepatch?" John was bent over, holding his gut.

I gritted my teeth, my ego taking a hit. I'd lost Nora, my Nora, to this tool.

"Lost my eye in an accident when I was a baby." *Too much information, Simon.*

He was watching me. "You catch the news?"

"Yeah." He didn't look sick.

"A third plane hit the Pentagon."

I pulled the old tire off, lining up the new one.

"I wonder what will happen now."

I began tightening bolts.

"You grew up around Nora," he continued. "You still live around here then?"

"Wimbledon."

His eyes narrowed. "Kinda far from home."

I tightened the last bolt.

"What are you doing down this far?"

"Hauling fence posts." I straightened. "Your other front tire is bald."

"I got it from here. Thanks." He took the jack and tire iron from my grasp.

Pulling away from the shoulder, Golden watched me through the truck's rearview mirror.

I saluted him.

57

Cooking and drinking.

There was a fine line between a creative buzz and the point of no return. Making seafood casserole, I explored the edge. I found a bottle of cooking sherry behind a sticky bag of rotted potatoes in the cluttered pantry.

The first forbidden taste was chalky, a bit bitter, and after a few more swallows the buzz reached out, took hold, and I anticipated the next illicit sip.

And the next.

He who finds a wife finds what is good and receives favor from the Lord.

John something, cop and do-gooder, had won the favor.

He was her husband. I was her…no one.

I prepared the side salad, a side of jealousy, swift and punishing.

I took a sip of sherry and deveined shrimp.

Downing another, I carefully set the table.

I gave myself another mental kick, worried I'd gotten Nora into trouble with the salute.

No, she'd been in trouble long before the flat tire. I figured Nora had been in trouble since the day she said "I do."

Sick or not, he'd used his pretty boy looks and smooth talk to sit in the truck while his wife struggled to change a tire on the highway. But it was him she chose.

He wasn't sick. I scanned the recipe.

Stir until smooth. *Take a drink.*

Salt and pepper. *And another.*

Stir in the sherry. *A sip first.*

After gently folding the seafood, I poured the mixture into a buttered casserole dish. And, of course, took a sip.

After topping it with cheese, I slid it into the preheated oven. Waiting for the guests to arrive, I slumped down at the table and gulped the last of the sherry.

"Like she's so perfect," I told the glass.

There was a commotion outside the front door before it burst open, and Doug stepped inside, followed by Mom and Alice.

"How was Aberdeen?" Doug leaned toward me and sniffed. "Are you drunk?"

"Yep." I poured Mom a glass of wine.

Mom sat down at the table. Doug sat across from her. He rested both elbows on the table and I didn't even care.

In an oversized green sweater and leggings, Alice took the chair next to him. I was once again stunned by her beauty.

"Changed a flat today," I said.

"Oh yeah?" Mom took a sip from her glass.

"It was Nora and her husband. Did I mention she's pregnant? Oh, and his name is Golden." I snorted. "Doesn't it just figure?"

"Simon's high school girlfriend married John Golden," Doug told Alice, and then glanced at me. "Alice is from Oakes."

I set a pitcher of water on the table.

"Supposedly Goldens are tight with swingers from Forman," Doug continued mercilessly. "Their parents used to go to key parties in the eighties."

Key parties? I set a bowl of hot rice at the table.

"Back then, couples would go to each other's houses, and put their keys in a dish," Mom supplied, taking a sip of her wine. "Then they would make a blind grab on the way out. Whoever's keys they drew they would go home with."

Doug reached for the casserole. "Who even knows if Golden is the father?"

An image of Nora, swollen with another man's baby, was a knife to my gut. Time to get off the subject. "You said you had something to tell me."

Doug grinned. "Alice and I are getting married this Christmas."

"Congratulations." I glanced at her. "I don't even know your last name."

"Wilson," she said, glancing away.

Mom set her glass down. "I hate to say it, but I told you Nora wasn't an original."

And we're back.

"An original whore, maybe." Doug snickered.

"Oh Doug," Mom giggled.

Alice looked down at her plate.

And I, feeling humiliated, had to look up to see hell.

58

From my crouched position in the slough, I knew the end was drawing near, and sensed the hellhound did too—powerful and skilled in the art of violence.

The flames from a campfire licked the starry night sky. Next to it, the hellhound poked tinder with a stick.

The crackling of embers chorused with the hoot of an owl.

The much quieter thump of a human heart across the warmth from the fire was loud as a drum, and sweet music to the creature's ears.

The sound of salvation.

Voracious and tenacious, the creature rounded up souls leashed. Until it learned a common trick used by demons: possessing bodies of the damned. Successful after a few botched attempts, the hellhound became quickly addicted to humans' lust of flesh and pride of life.

The hellhound fetched the damned for no one, sniffing out souls for the mere thrill of owning them.

Hopeful and hopeless souls, delightful in each respect.

The hunter's eyes were on the creature.

***

I woke in a cold sweat. The room spun around me. My head pounding, bits and pieces of last night came flooding back. I'd never gotten drunk in front of my family before. I hoped I hadn't said anything stupid.

I couldn't shake the nightmare.

One thing was for sure.

I had an enemy.

Part II

Adversity toughens manhood, and the characteristic of the good or the great man is not that he has been exempt from the evils of life, but that he has surmounted them.

Patrick Henry

59
Thanksgiving Day, 2013

Kevin provided his extravagant house for the Thanksgiving meal. I provided the meal. Outside, pumpkins adorned the steps going in. Inside, leaves, turkeys, and pilgrims decorated four long tables.

"Hi Uncle Simon," Trey, their oldest, rushed me. "Want to work on a puzzle?"

"Sure. After lunch."

Sarah, the next in line came up and grabbed the roaster from my grasp. "Hi Uncle Simon. Thanks for coming."

Then the following younger ones, Thomas, Darcy, Rosie, and Rachel came tearing in. "Hi Uncle Simon!" they said in unison.

Kevin emerged from the kitchen. "You finish checking the fences yesterday?"

"Yeah. I have a place to fix over by the south slough. It'll hold until Saturday."

"Hi Simon. Set up wherever you like." Pregnant again, Gretchen's cheeks were flushed, a smile on her lips. "The kitchen is all yours."

"If you two have any more kids I'm going to have to buy personalized t-shirts with their names so I know who's who."

Sarah laughed. "You're funny, Uncle Simon."

Carrying casserole dishes from my truck, Harry and Hans made their way inside.

They married sisters from Valley City.

Harry married the oldest, Trista, and Hans the younger, Mary. Harry built a house at Cruff's and Hans at Hirsch's.

Mom and her new boyfriend, Richard, arrived with a kettle of stuffing.

Dad was having Thanksgiving in Minot with Paige's family.

Charles came alone. I wondered where Melissa was, but didn't ask.

Doug and Alice arrived late. Alice caked on the makeup as she often did lately, and wore a yellow sweater two sizes too small. Her jeans were skin tight. Compliments of Doug's influence, I was certain.

When Alice excused herself to the bathroom, Doug pulled out his phone. "Check this out."

On the screen, two topless women were kissing.

I felt a surge of lust straight to my groin and handed his phone back. "Dude. Don't show me that."

"Did you hear Andy Kaufman faked his death?" Doug tucked his phone back in his pocket, following me around the kitchen.

"No."

"In 1999, Michael Kaufman was given instructions to meet his brother at a restaurant on Christmas Eve. Michael said he went to the restaurant, met a man he didn't know, and was handed a note from Andy."

"Wait. He didn't meet Andy himself?" I sampled the mashed potatoes.

"In the note, Andy said 'everything was great' in his life. It explained his disappearance this way: he simply 'wanted to get away from being Andy Kaufman.'"

"Huh."

Alice returned from the bathroom, and reached for a piece of banana bread.

"Is bread on your diet?" Doug asked.

She glared at him and put it back.

"I'll eat it if you don't want it." He grabbed the slice.

"Alice said the Noonan House in Oakes is for sale," Doug said through a bite. "Used to be House of 29."

I'd toured the Noonan House once at Christmastime during an open house, and it left an impression.

I sliced the turkey. "You know, the Mattsons lived there in the seventies and eighties."

"The Mattsons and Sims are a cult, Simon." Doug filled a glass of water, his voice dipping low, "Kevin used to serve better drinks before he got religion."

Gretchen scorned God when I held Bible study. Now Kevin started going to church, and suddenly she followed Jesus like a pied piper.

Like you used to.

A longing to return to my faith was swift and overwhelming. The basement magazines, a reminder I couldn't.

Ignoring the inner voice, I focused on the Noonan House, a four-story landmark in Oakes. The used-to-be hospital had four floors. Several chimneys supplied three fireplaces, one in the basement, one in the living room, and one in the den. It had an apartment above the garage in back.

"I wonder how it is to heat," I mused.

"The last owner switched out the furnaces and changed the three wood fireplaces to gas," Alice spoke at last.

"Hmm," I said, the wheels began to turn.

***

I served the meal buffet style. The kids sat at tables in the dining room, the adults by the glass doors leading to the deck.

Kevin gave thanks for the meal.

Lively conversation and laughter filled the room full of diners.

"You outdid yourself, Simon." Kevin leaned back in his chair, sticking out his gut. "The banana bread was the best I've ever had."

214

"The apple dessert is marvelous," Mary praised through a mouthful.

"Coffee strong enough to get up and walk," Trista added.

I held up both hands in surrender. "Gretchen made the coffee."

"Simon always cooked better than he did anything else," Mom sighed.

It wasn't meant to be a compliment, but I took it as one anyway. Taking a bite of banana bread, an idea was born.

***

"Pull!" Hans shouted.

Harry pulled the target thrower, and three clay pigeons sailed into the air. Hans pointed the 12 gauge, firing three shots. Two clay pigeons exploded.

The hard ground was dusted with snow, the temperature was 28 degrees. I balled cold hands in the pockets of my jeans, shivering beneath my Carhartt jacket. The women and children went Black Friday shopping and the men went outdoors to shoot clay targets. Doug and Alice went home.

I wasn't good with a gun, but wasn't much for shopping either. Plus I wanted to talk to Kevin, Charles, and the twins about the Noonan House.

"They were asking three hundred thousand, but I think they went down to two fifty." I stamped my cold feet.

"A down payment on two hundred and fifty thousand dollars in this area is steep." Kevin loaded his shotgun.

"I have it."

Kevin flicked me an astonished look.

"I invest." I shrugged. "I told you I was good with numbers."

"Yeah, but in Oakes?" Kevin dug in the box, grabbing another three clay targets.

Empty casings flew as Hans racked his shotgun. "I hear Nora Toogoody's getting divorced. Sounds like she and their two boys are moving back to California."

The wind whipped across the prairie and into my right ear. I pulled my sweatshirt over my head.

An odd emptiness settled in my gut. I ignored it. At least I wouldn't have to see her, him, or their kids. "I could buy Anderson beef and make the place an organic restaurant."

Kevin tossed three clay pigeons in the air, shooting one. "I like this idea. What about wheat for buns and baked goods?"

Harry jumped in. "We could plant wheat at the section over by my place."

"Make it a steak and burger joint," Hans said.

Charles grabbed the shotgun. "Not just a steak and burger joint. A place where you can enjoy a juicy steak and feel good about it. Melt-in-your mouth made-from-scratch desserts."

"Let's not get ahead of ourselves," I said. "Charles, you and I should check the place out to see how expensive it'll be to update the kitchen. I'll need a walk-in cooler and a bar counter."

"I ain't cheap." Charles shot two of the three clay pigeons.

"Didn't think you were."

"The mind is its own place and in itself can make a heaven of Hell, a hell of Heaven..."

John Milton, Paradise Lost, Book I

60
June 25, 2015

"Opening day is the fifth of August." In the kitchen of my new restaurant with the phone to my ear, I sharpened knives.

"Of course," Mom said on the other line. "I can't wait."

"You need a ride?" I picked up a knife from the storage block and slid the blade over the sharpener.

She giggled. "Ride for what?"

"Opening night." I sighed. I could hear a man's voice in the background. What were they doing? *Don't ask...*

"Stop it," she said, laughter in her voice.

"What?"

"I was talking to Dorian. I promised Dorian I'd watch his dog. He's having surgery. Dorian is, I mean."

Right. "I suppose there's no one else who could possibly watch his dog?"

"Simon. What a thing to say."

She was right. "I'm sorry. It was rude of me to ask."

"Besides, when you were over at my house last week, I was sure you told me your thing was on Friday."

My thing? "No. I told you it was August fifth. I watched you write it down."

"I'll be at the next one." She sounded chipper.

"Next one? I won't have two openings."

"The one where you celebrate your success. Probably in Paris." She giggled.

Feeling two inches tall, I said, "Okay."

"Did you get your license for the alcohol?"

"Yes." Thanks to Charles who reminded me I needed one. The old dining room was a perfect spot for the counter and bar area. A separation between the rooms made it legal. "I'll open at eleven in the morning, and pull the divider at five for supper."

"Now smile so I can hang up," she said.

"I'm smiling."

"Don't act like that."

"Like what?"

"Like you're upset." Her laughter was cold and cruel.

"I'm not upset," I lied.

"I'd better go."

"Okay." I hung up.

In the breakfast nook facing three kitchen windows, I sat down at the table. Pulling out my laptop, I opened QuickBooks.

I'd hired three waitresses. Bella Clemens was a graduate of Oakes High School and planned to attend UND in the fall. Jill Brown, a former stay-at-home mom whose last kid graduated, and Sheila Daltron who had been working at the gas station.

I hadn't hired a bartender yet, but Doug agreed to fill in. Mixed drinks and bottled or canned beer would be available.

Nothing on tap.

Kitchen appliances were upgraded. The north door led to the main floor bathroom and the basement. At one time, an apartment, the basement was now an area for extra food storage and the walk-in cooler.

I closed out QuickBooks and clicked on favorites. Glancing around, my heart hammered two hard strokes.

A video popped up.

Naughty Farm Girls. Palms sweaty, I picked up my laptop, started to head upstairs to my room, and caught a glimpse outside the window.

It was a cop car. *Police City of Oakes* on the side in silver.

The driver's door opened and John Golden got out. In full uniform, he hiked up his utility belt.

I snapped the laptop shut and set it back down on the table.

What does he want? I crossed over to the back door, waiting for him to knock.

He didn't knock, instead turned the handle and stepped into the enclosed entry.

I opened the inside door.

"I wasn't sure if I should knock." He chuckled.

"You should." I glanced down at his boots. "You should also take your boots off."

"Oh I'm not coming in," he said, even as he took a step forward. "I heard you bought the place." He glanced around the kitchen, eyeing the knife storage block. "Got a lot of knives."

I glanced at the blades I'd been sharpening.

"Knives are alright for close combat, but this works in most situations," he patted the gun in his holster.

"This is a restaurant." *Okay, Simon. No need for sarcasm.*

"Your pickup?" He pointed at my truck parked outside.

"Yes sir."

"It's got expired tabs."

"I've got thirty days."

He gave me a hard stare. "Technically."

"What's that supposed to mean?"

"It means make sure you aren't driving with expired tabs." He turned around. I started to close the door between us, and his hand shot out.

"Congratulations on the restaurant."

61
Simon's place
Opening Night
Oakes, North Dakota

"The Noonan House changed hands so many times, I lost track," I said, putting my feet up on the chair at the table next to us.

Kevin, Charles, and I sat on the deck at the once-Noonan House-now Simon's Place.

Charles smoked a cigar and nursed his Jack Daniels.

Kevin drank coffee.

I drank the leftover wine from the open house straight from the bottle.

"The night was a huge success," Charles took a sip of whisky. "I got to admit, Simon, I didn't think you'd pull it off."

"People love this house," I said. "A lot of them came to see what we did to the place."

"To Simon." Kevin held up his cup. "May your future be an even bigger success."

I held up the bottle of wine. "To Charles, for his construction talent."

"To brothers." Charles joined in with his glass.

Kevin's phone buzzed. He held the screen up. "Avery."

"She's cute," I said. "How old now?"

"Just turned 15 months." Kevin set his phone back on the table. "Gretchen is pregnant again."

Charles tapped ash on the tray. "You know when God said in the Bible 'be fruitful and multiply' He wasn't talking about just you, right?"

"I had to make up for you two guys." Kevin leaned back in his chair.

Charles took a puff of his cigar. "Melissa wanted to visit her friend in California. I started to make arrangements for two. She said it was a girls' trip, then ghosted me the whole week."

My gut churned. Did Melissa tell him about me and her? Not that there was a me and her. There had never been a me and her.

"I was devastated," he said, his voice sorrow-filled. "I was sure she was missing me as much as I missed her, and called her phone. A man answered."

"Who was it?" I sipped my wine.

"She said it was her cousin."

Kevin gave a nod. "So that's how it is in their family."

"I got served divorce papers." Charles took a drink of whisky.

"You told her it's a family farm," I said, guilt turning to anger in my gut. "She can get alimony like every other divorcee. Not like you have kids."

Charles downed the last of his whisky. "I called Ben Klinkineckt."

Ben was the family lawyer.

"Probably a good thing," Kevin said. "It'll never be over with her."

"You opened the door to a crazy person." I set the bottle of wine down on the table with a clunk.

"Simon." Kevin said, a travesty of a smile forming on his lips. "About your eye…"

"I know," I cut him off. "The doctor told me I had Coat's disease." I took a pull from the bottle. "Clever story about the tomcat."

Kevin and Charles exchanged glances.

Kevin said, "Doug bit you."

"When you were a baby." Charles tapped his cigar against the ashtray.

Unable to find my voice, I felt all the blood drain from my face.

Kevin leaned forward, resting his elbows on the table. "We were sworn to secrecy."

My mind flew in a dozen different directions. At last, I managed, "You shouldn't put your elbows on the table."

Kevin sat back. "Sure. Sorry."

My stomach rolled, and I felt like vomiting. "Did Mom and Dad know?" I asked.

Kevin said, "They weren't there. Just us and the babysitter. We told Mom when she got home."

"She always told the story of the tomcat. Then later, it was Coat's disease," I said in a small voice. "Was Dad ever told?"

Kevin shook his head. "Not that I know of."

It was Charles who spoke next. "I didn't know which was more disturbing, Doug biting you, or the silence demanded from us afterward."

Kevin crossed his legs. "Now you know Melissa isn't the first crazy person in this family."

My phone buzzed.

I knew who it was even as I picked it up off the table.

Mom: I could use your help cleaning the house tomorrow. I have investors coming over.

I tucked my phone in my back pocket.

"Mom?" Charles tamped out his cigar.

"Who else?" My pocket buzzed.

My pocket vibrated again. And again. By the fourth time, I was beyond irritated and snagged it. Still Mom.

Are you there?

Hello? Honoring your mother is one of the Ten Commandments.

"Still Mom?" Charles asked.

"Yep." I took a sip of wine. "She couldn't even stop by for five minutes."

"I'm sure she had a good reason," Kevin said.

"Yeah, she had to watch her new boy toy's dog." I winced at the bitterness in my voice.

Suddenly, Mom came tearing by in her Prius, pulling into the back alley.

"I better go see what she wants." I stood. "Otherwise, she'll start..." Suddenly the horn began blaring, "Honking the horn."

Mom got out of the car and slammed the door. She was wearing her brown coat and a scowl.

"Hey Mom, you're late." I fixed my gaze on the hedge behind her.

"Why aren't you answering your phone?" Her voice was panicked. "Are you drunk? You drink too much. You know..."

Fear twisted my gut. "What's wrong?"

"Doug called. He's on the balcony. He's threatening to jump."

62

On the other side of the metal gate surrounding the two-story balcony at Simon's Place, Doug held onto the railing, eyes wild.

"Simon?" he asked.

We all agreed only one of us should talk Doug down off the balcony. I drew the short straw. "How long have you been up here?" I asked.

Doug shrugged. "A while."

I frowned. "I didn't even hear you come in."

"I parked over by the church, and came in through the back door. There was no one around, and everything was shut down."

"That's because it's almost midnight."

"I came up here to think."

"Mom showed me the texts you sent her." I rubbed my jaw. "Probably won't kill yourself if you jump. You'll just get maimed."

"Alice left me."

"It's all right to yell, swear. Crying's okay too." I gave a small smile. "But don't jump off balconies."

Etched with horror and pain, his bloodshot eyes met mine. He was overwhelmed to the point of breaking. Something I understood. My hand snaked out and grabbed his arm. "You have been drinking."

"Maybe." He rubbed his eyes, fighting against the torrent. "I was perfectly fine three days ago. She said I drank too much."

"Get on this side of the railing and we'll talk about it."

"Did you know the easiest people to kill are those who are expected to die?" he asked.

"Death comes for us all eventually."

"Do you think Andy Kaufman got away with his greatest stunt? I mean, evading his own death."

"The comedian? Doubt it." I gazed out at the stars. "What was with wrestling women in nightclubs?"

"There's Andy for you." He laughed loudly.

The look in his eyes made me doubt he'd ever been depressed or suicidal. The gleam, near maniacal. There was no Doug in there.

Had I ever known the real Doug? All these years. This was not my brother. My brothers looked out for me. They would never cause me intentional harm, toddler or not.

He took my hand, stepping back over the rail.

"Doug?"

"Yeah?"

"Whenever you think about what happened here, remember...It was a really big deal."

Police sirens echoed in the distance followed by flashing lights. A cop car pulled into the back alley below the balcony.

"This is Police Officer Golden. Stay where you are. I'm coming up there," he said through the car microphone.

"Who called the cops?" Doug asked.

"My guess is Mom." The same who covered up what really happened to my eye. Why did she hide the truth? For Doug? My jaw clenched at her betrayal.

Officer Golden called, "Simon?"

"Yes sir."

"Who's up there with you?"

"My brother, Doug."

"I'm coming up. Don't move."

Soon, the door opened and Officer Golden stepped out onto the balcony. He held a flashlight against the darkness. "Mind telling me what's going on?"

Squinting against the light, I gave Officer Golden a short version of events.

"No one has to know about this," Officer Golden said.

Relief flooded Doug's face. "Thank you, sir."

Officer Golden clamped his hand on Doug's shoulder. "Not a problem. Looks like you've got family looking out for you. What happens in the family, stays in the family."

"Yes sir," Doug said with a happy chuckle.

Officer Golden followed him into the house, stopping inside the doorway. "From down there it looked like you were the one about to jump," he said for my ears only.

I noticed he still had his boots on.

"Does anyone give you grief about your eyepatch?" he asked.

"Not to my face." I stepped inside, flicking a look back at the clear night sky before shutting the door.

It was a cold moon.

63

After cleanup following the supper crowd, I sat down in the breakfast nook. "Who's Cheatin' Who" by Alan Jackson played on the kitchen radio.

"I see you hired Sheila Daltron." Doug opened the fridge. "I tapped that."

"Ugh. Doug…" My stomach rolled at the callous way he objectified women.

Oh yeah? And those videos you watch don't paint women as objects?

"Want a beer?" Doug grabbed two bottles of Corona.

Give the message straight to the horse. Or was it straight from the horse's mouth? "Doug, you need to go to rehab."

"You want me to go to rehab, I say no, no no…"

"I'm serious."

He waved a bottle at me as though I were a pesky fly, and sat down. "I promise to limit myself. There will be no repeat of last week." He handed me a beer.

"Next time you pull a stunt where Golden ends up in my place, you're fired." I took a swallow.

"At least he was nice." Doug crossed his legs in front of him.

"He didn't even take his boots off."

Doug laughed. "He's a cop, Simon. They go into people's houses all the time with their boots on."

"Maybe, but I asked him to take them off the first time he was here."

"He didn't have time." Doug shrugged. "For all he knew I was plunging to my death."

I arched my brow. "From a two-story balcony?"

"I agree it was stupid," Doug said, "I should have known. Alice always tried to cut me down. She was pretty cold-hearted."

"Funny. I always thought she was quiet." I took a pull from my bottle.

"All an act."

Or was it the other way around? A sudden image of him as a toddler, biting his baby brother's eye, flashed through my head. Should I tell him I knew what he did to me?

He sighed. "I guess I thought I could always go back. No consequences too dire."

He wasn't reasonable. He probably didn't even remember it, being only three years old. "Time to suck it up," I replied.

Doug's eyes narrowed. "Went to Sean's New Year's party a while back. Quite the bash."

"All Sean's parties were wild."

"Saw Nora and John Golden." He took a swallow of beer. "Back when they were married. She was looking fine, sweater enhanced her finest assets."

I hated the thought of him checked her out, but mentioning it would do nothing other than give him fuel. So I said nothing.

"Luke Doric, you know the electrician in town, said he hit a deer one night coming home from the bar drunk. Golden gave him a ride home."

It sounded like a different cop than the one at my doorstep last week lecturing about expired tabs on my parked vehicle.

And the way he talked about the knives.

"Guess who was in the car with Doric?" he asked.

By the glee in his tone, I guessed no one good.

"Melissa." His voice was triumphant.

"Charles' Melissa?" I was unprepared for the shock.

"You know any other Melissa?"

Something inside started to give. I mentally replaced it with indifference. It was a cold, empty sensation.

64
Simon's Place
March 13, 2018

Luke Doric pounded cans of Budweiser and shot eye daggers at Jeff Morris.

Jeff wore a black crew neck shirt to show off his gym time.

Word on the street was Luke caught Melissa, used to be Mrs. Charles Anderson, and Jeff in his pickup. Since then, Luke hadn't let Melissa out of his sight. Thankfully, Melissa pretended she didn't know me.

"If I were you, I'd keep an eye on your wife too," Jeff uttered beneath his breath.

Luke smashed his empty can down and stood. "Don't talk about her like she's fresh meat."

Jeff wiped crumbs from his mouth with his napkin. "You're the one stalking her."

I couldn't blame Luke for wanting to kill him, but I couldn't have a brawl in my restaurant. Why couldn't Luke ignore Melissa like Charles had? I caught Melissa several times stroking Luke's arm. It seemed to be riling him up more than calming him down.

I stepped between the tables. "Gentlemen, let's behave like gentleman."

Luke sat back down and waved me over. "I got one for you: what do snowmobiles and women have in common?"

I managed a tight smile. "What."

"You work on them for an hour for a five-minute ride." He peered up at me with glazed eyes. "Get it? You work…"

"I get it," I said in a quiet voice.

"I'll take another one of these." He held up his beer can.

"Maybe it's time to call it a night."

Luke staggered to his feet, hesitated, and then swayed toward me. "Wait a minute. Wait just a minute."

Sweat tickled the back of my neck, and I held my hand up. "I mean it." The restaurant fell silent, all eyes fixed on me.

Had I really shouted?

I searched for something to say, and White Stripes began "Blue Orchid." "...*You got a reaction, didn't you?*"

Whether it was the song or the atmosphere, diners returned their attention to their food.

Bella hurried over. "How was everything?" she asked, bringing them their tab.

Luke reached in his pocket for his wallet.

After Bella rushed off to run his credit card, Melissa caught my eye, a sultry smile forming on her lips. "Good to see you, Simon," she purred.

Bella returned with his receipt.

"Make sure you drive," I told Melissa, unable to keep the irritation from my voice. The last thing I needed was for the cops to show up.

The remainder of the evening dragged on.

Closing time couldn't come fast enough.

The waitresses turned in the cash from the till.

Once alone, I shut the lights off, locked the doors, and retreated to my room and laptop.

Don't do it, Simon. Walk away.

Afterward, I was alone with my thoughts.

You don't make it last long enough.

Next thing you know, you'll be raping women.

This had control over my life. I had mindlessly sat down and watched.

If your hand causes you to sin, cut it off.

I looked at my hand, the back of it, and my palm. He really didn't mean I should cut off my hand. Did He?

I had become a slave to my impulses.

But what was to be done?

Stand true to your calling to be a man. Real women will always be relieved and grateful when men are willing to be men.

Elisabeth Elliott

Part III

65
Thanksgiving Day, 2019

In New York City at Macy's Thanksgiving Day parade, 46-feet tall and five New York taxis wide, the new Green Eggs and Ham balloon took 90 people to hold its ropes.

At Kevin's house decorated fall festive, Gretchen and his girls, Sarah, Darcy, Rosie, Rachel, and Avery made the meal.

Harry and Trista were there and their girl Suzy.

Hans and Mary and little Anna went to their in-laws in Valley City.

Kevin's boys, Trey, Thomas, and Seth shot clay targets with us Black Friday.

Mom was in New York and made sure to text several selfies a day to remind me of the fact.

Dad and Paige were at her son, David's place.

Charles had a new woman and stayed in Oakes.

Kevin told Doug he could join the men outside, but wouldn't let him have a shotgun.

Doug politely refused.

On his way out the door, Doug said, "Did you know there's a new gal working at Sweets 'N Stories?"

Sweets 'N Stories, the espresso bar, eatery, and bookstore was a unique treat in Oakes.

Kevin leaned in the archway leading to the kitchen. "It's creepy when old dudes like you hit on women."

He chuckled. "Nora is not my type."

Nora? My heart kicked up.

"Nora is working at Sweets 'N Stories?" Kevin pushed himself off the doorframe.

Doug nodded. "Looked real..." he paused, catching Kevin's stare. "I guess I better be going."

After he left, Kevin turned to me. "Well?"

"Well what?"

"You might need a book." He scrubbed his jaw. "I hear they got pretty good fudge too."

"She's married to the cop."

"Was married."

"Right. Divorced, which means she doesn't want a man."

"She doesn't want *that* man."

"He'll go postal. Besides," I said, even as a shot of adrenalin rushed through my veins, "I haven't seen or spoken to her for years. She might be fat. Old by now…"

"Ugly probably."

A laugh burst from my lips. "She could never be ugly."

Kevin's brow arched. "One way to find out."

66
Sweets 'N Stories
Oakes, North Dakota

I pulled up to the front of Sweets 'N Stories.

White and black checkered flooring could be seen through the glass front. Wire chairs with heart-shaped backs were pulled up to round tables.

I stepped inside.

Next to bookshelves were black couches lined with silver studs. Each adorned with white and black checkered pillows. There was a separate shelf for children's books.

Reading quotes decked the walls.

I perused George RR Martin tomes and chose two.

Pink pinstriped wallpaper gave it a candy store feel. A flying fish kite and a winged dragon kite for sale brought me back to 1985.

A half wall of wooden white pillars complemented the trek to the old-fashioned cash register.

There were platters of fudge with pinstriped curtains on the display case. Ahead, a display cooler full of various flavors of hard ice-cream.

I studied the cashier while pretending I was studying the chalkboard menu.

Nora looked good. More than good, she looked vivacious and wholesome at the same time. A soft brown sweater and blue jeans made her appear approachable. Her blond hair was pulled back in a ponytail, making her look like the girl I once knew.

She was talking to an older lady about a book. A smile touched her lips. Her eyes, the color of whisky, were happy.

My heart tripped, fell.

"Always good to see you, Mrs. Otto," she was saying, her voice, soft and lilting.

"Pastor George will be expecting you Sunday," Mrs. Otto said.

"You know I never miss a Sunday."

"He doesn't want to bring people to church. He wants to bring them to Jesus."

"Yes, he's…" Nora's golden gaze shifted and caught mine.

Mrs. Otto turned and saw me. "Oh. I didn't mean to hold up the line."

I smiled, too nervous to say anything.

Mrs. Otto eyed the stack of novels in my hands. "Oh! *A Feast for Crows* was such a good book. George RR Martin is a fantastic writer," she said.

"I didn't take you for a fan." It was out of my mouth before I could pull it back.

"It's the gray hair." Mrs. Otto laughed and turned to Nora. "I best be going, dear."

"Thanks for stopping in," Nora said. "See you next week."

After Mrs. Otto left, I set my books on the checkout counter.

Nora smiled. "How have you been?"

"Good. Heard you're back in town."

The flush in her cheeks deepened. "Yes, just."

My heart stopped, then kicked up and pounded hard in my ears, dimming the room around me. "I heard you have kids now."

She rang up my books. "Dane got a job as the assistant manager at Pizza Ranch in Valley City. He met Olivia his wife in California where we lived. Jordan is sixteen. He'd like to work as a cook."

"Have him stop by Simon's Place. I could use another chef." I picked up my purchases, reluctant to leave.

"Thanks." She eyed my stack of books. "Would you like a bag for those?"

"I'm good."

There was an array of Jelly Belly jars of candy with silver lids on shelves, from buttered popcorn to coconut. Soda pop shop and everything in between. I saw Nerds and Pop Rocks. Bob Rott's Happy Little Tree Mints with a cardboard cutout of the painter himself.

Real Scorpion Suckers.

"Do you think that's true?" I pointed at the box.

"They look real."

"I'll take your word for it." I grabbed one and brought it up to the till.

She rang it up. "One ninety-five."

I pulled out my wallet and handed her two ones. I turned and started walking out. Passing Bob Rott's Happy Little Tree Mints, I grabbed one.

Nora rang it up. "Seventy-five cents."

I dug in my pocket and pulled out three quarters. I made it another three steps, and reached for a handful of Nerds.

"Three twenty-five."

I pulled a five from my wallet and handed it to her.

She gave me the change. "You sure you don't want a bag, Simon?"

"Maybe I'd better."

She handed me a plastic bag. I slipped my books and candy inside. This time I made it to the door.

"Simon," she called.

I turned around, and she hurried up to me.

"You forgot this." She held up the Real Scorpion Sucker.

"Thanks." I dropped it in my bag, catching her scent of fresh flowers. "Would you have dinner with me Sunday?"

Her eyes widened. "At Simon's Place?"

The tips of my ears grew warm. "Yeah. We're not open Sunday, and I wanted to cook for you."

"I'd love to." Her golden eyes sparkled.

Relief flooded me at once. "Is five-thirty too early?"

"Five-thirty sounds perfect." She smiled, showing her dimples.

"I best be getting back. I've got to check on an order arriving this afternoon." I turned to leave and stopped once more. "Nora?"

"More candy?" Her breathless reply stole mine.

I'm not letting you go this time. When you're ready, I plan to make you mine. What I actually said was, "See you Sunday."

"See you." Her smile reached out and grabbed hold of my heart.

67
December 8, 2019

Low in the west, the early afternoon sun twinkled through skeletal branches. The smell of wood smoke lingered in the air.

Nora pulled into the back alley at five thirty-three.

I saw her from the kitchen windows and hurried to greet her at the back door.

Her cheeks rosy with the cold, she wore a red wool coat.

"Come on in," I said.

She stomped snow from her boots. Kicking them off, she set them on the shoe rack in the small entry, and entered the kitchen.

"Smells heavenly. What are we having?" she asked.

"Flank steak with balsamic roasted eggplant, herbed potatoes and tomatoes." I helped her with her coat. "For dessert, peach cobbler." The white sweater she wore underneath was soft and clingy, making my palms ache to touch her.

"Have a seat here," I motioned to the kitchen nook. "Can I get you something to drink? I have beer, wine, water, milk…"

"A glass of wine sounds nice."

I poured her the red liquid. "How was your day?"

"Good. Church was nice. Pastor George gave a sermon about the lost sheep of Israel, and Brent Degner fell asleep."

I chuckled.

"His wife Lois spent five minutes jabbing his side."

"Compliments of Anderson Bro.'s all-organic wheat." I set a loaf of homemade bread and serving of honey butter in front of her, and popped a slice into my mouth. "I like fresh bread plain."

"I remember." She spread the honey butter across her piece.

"I canned these last fall." I picked up the jar of peaches off the end of the counter and sat across from her.

I had so many questions, but I was alone in my own place with Nora. For a sliver of time, everything was good and right with the world.

Unmindful of the sticky syrup encasing them, I popped one in my mouth and set the jar on the table in front of us.

She fished one out. "Yum," she said through a mouthful.

Peaches.

An indication life was good again.

***

I pulled out items for tea. The fireplace in the den was warm. The loveseat I'd pulled out earlier faced the hearth.

Nora ran a hand over the piano in the corner of the dining room. "Dinner music too?"

"Came with the place. Needs to be tuned," I said. "Shall I make popcorn?"

"I couldn't eat another bite." She patted her tummy.

"You want me to show you the rest of the house?"

Her face broke into a grin. "I thought you'd never ask."

I set my hand on the curved banister, and mounted the first staircase. Nora followed. Straight ahead in the large hallway, my red velvet loveseat.

"Oh, I love this," she hurried over and sat down.

"My mom gave it to me when I bought the place. I put it here to relax on since the living room and den have been turned into dining areas."

242

"Too bad there isn't a fireplace up here."

I led her through the laundry room and out to the balcony. "Doug threatened to jump opening day," I told her, gazing out at the treetops.

"Ouch."

I showed her the three bedrooms and the bathroom with the stained glass window dating back to the seventies.

Then, my room.

She stepped inside, making the scene intimate. To keep from imagining her laying upon my bed, blonde hair splayed across the coverlet, I said, "Rosemarie Mattson said my room was hers growing up."

"I don't remember Rosemarie."

"She was homeschooled."

"Like you."

"Sort of. I did schoolwork at the dining room table when my brothers attended in Wimbledon. Rosemarie's whole family along with another family attended in a one-room schoolhouse they moved to their farm."

"A modern-day Little House on the Prairie."

I thought of what Doug said about them being a cult. I'd always liked Darwin Mattson, and bit my tongue from speaking ill about the families.

***

Back downstairs, we sat before the fire in the old den. Warmth from the hearth, relaxing.

At last, Nora spoke, her voice like velvet, matching the magic of the atmosphere. "I was surprised to see you in Sweets 'N Stories."

I chuckled. "I can probably start a candy store with all I bought."

She laughed and then sobered quickly. "What happened to you becoming a preacher?"

I gave her the short version of events, including Dad selling the dairy, bad grades in college, and hearing about the sale of the Noonan House while living at Section Ten.

"Then this place came up for sale." I stretched my arms, resting them on the back of the sofa.

Flames from the fireplace reflected in her eyes, "I don't see you in church on Sundays."

"Probably because I don't go."

She blinked. "Want to come next Sunday?"

"I see no point in warming a pew every Sunday morning. God knows my heart."

"God saved me, Simon." I could see it in her eyes, hear it in her voice. She had peace. I was jealous of that peace.

"From your husband?" I asked.

She hesitated. "Mostly from myself."

"I always thought you were a good kid. You were always nice to me." I caught her gaze.

Nora looked away. "It's getting late."

I felt the wall between us, insurmountable. I glanced at my watch.

Eight-thirty.

She stood. "I guess I should be going. Thank you for inviting me."

What was this? *Stop her, you fool.*

In awkward silence, we headed for the door.

I held her coat up for her, too scared to ask her what was on her mind. I already knew. "Good night," I said.

"Good night." She walked out.

A blast of winter air slapped my face.

There never was yet a truly great man that was not at the same time truly virtuous.

Benjamin Franklin

68

The hellhound smoothed edges of the blood-stained red flannel shirt he wore, stifling the impulse to bay at the first sign of fear in its prey.

I watched the clever creature mimic common behavior seen in people; scratching his nose, smoothing a waning scalp, rubbing his jaw.

It would wait until whimpering, sobbing, and begging commenced. Like a cat toying with a mouse, the hellhound played its victim.

"You said you don't hunt." Shadows from the firelight danced across the hunter's bearded features as he eyed the creature.

He had one eye.

I opened my mouth, tried to scream, only no sound came out. *Run!* But he couldn't hear my thoughts. *Help yourself,* but my limbs were lead.

69

December 15, 2019

In Nairobi, Kenya, food security held a special place among Russia's priorities in its efforts to achieve sustainable development globally.

Simon's Place was filled with the excitement of the holiday season. A Christmas tree sat outside the front door of the restaurant on the veranda. Inside, white lights and garland lined the fireplaces. Soft instrumental Christmas music played.

At the bar, my new employee, Jenna Lund from Forman, wore a bright red Christmas sweater with a reindeer on the front. Trees dangled from her ears.

In a non-holiday green sweater, Bella was in the kitchen showing Jordan Golden, Nora's son, how to make salads.

A red bandana on his head, Jordan hadn't said more than two words since I hired him.

Officer Golden and two county deputies sat in the dining area, each with a burger and homemade fries. All uniformed, full utility belts with handcuffs, Tasers, and pistols.

And I was in a fog. Last night's dream clung like bad odor.

The pounding of my head was no nightmare.

An emotional breakdown was out of the question.

Instead, I pulled my phone from my pocket and searched up the meaning of dreams about demons.

"Hey, Simon I'll take another round," Jeff Morris called from the end of the bar. Next to him sat a perky blonde, not Melissa Doric, thank goodness.

I grabbed two Heinekens from the fridge.

On my way back to the kitchen, I stopped short.

The waitresses were speaking in hushed tones.

"He's never been married," Bella was saying.

"Why not? Is he gay?" Jenna's response.

A spurt of laughter from Bella. "No."

"No girlfriends?"

"Nothing serious."

"How long have you been working for him?"

"Almost five years. Since opening day."

"And you don't think he's hot?" Jenna sounded incredulous. Jenna Lund was divorced and in her mid-thirties, a kid in junior high. She was attractive, but also part of my staff.

And Bella's response, "No. Gross. He's way too old for me."

I entered the kitchen.

Laughter halted and they scattered.

I returned to my Google search about demon nightmares.

1. You're surrounded by malevolent people. The danger surrounding you could be real and from people who are close to you.

2. You could be sinning. If you are very religious but somehow doing something which goes against your religion...

"Officer Golden tipped twenty dollars on a thirty-dollar bill," Bella said, crossing over to the cash register behind the swinging doors in the old pantry. "By the way, he wants you outside at the front."

"Why?" I returned my phone to my pocket.

She shrugged. "I didn't ask."

Outside, lanterns on either side of the front door lit the night sky. Officer Golden was waiting on the wraparound deck, puffs of air emerging from his mouth.

"Busy night," he said.

"I'm a law-abiding citizen."

"You and everyone else." His eyes gleamed in the moonlight.

I shoved my cold hands in my pockets.

"I know about you having dinner with Nora Sunday."

Had she told him? Or had he driven by and saw her vehicle out back? Either option was unsettling.

"Nora can make up her own mind." *Shut up, Simon.*

Officer Golden pulled his pistol from his holster. "Know what this is?"

"A gun."

"Not just any gun, but a Glock 19." He turned it over in his hand. "In a salon in California, a guy walked in and shot eight people after a fight with his ex-wife."

A chill raced up my spine.

He returned his gun to his holster. "You're not in high school anymore."

"I need to get back to work," I said, wishing for the first time in my life I had a gun.

He turned to leave. "By the way, the Juicy Lucy wasn't bad. Maybe a little more cheese next time."

I turned around and hurried inside.

His deep chuckle followed me through the night.

70

The hellhound's groin itched. It was bothersome, and it slid his hand down the pants as it had seen others do. Scratching, it nearly groaned in relief. A large chunk of flesh separated from the scrotum. The creature cupped something soft, round, and warm beneath the surface of the skin.

Testicles.

The hellhound removed the hand, wiping it on the side of the pants. Now there would be no time to play. It couldn't comprehend how a race could tolerate such flimsy and fragile flesh.

The creature's head came up abruptly. Dark thoughts were on the slough.

I ducked further in the cattails.

The hellhound stood. "Thanks for letting me use your fire to warm up."

The other Simon said nothing, reaching for the rifle next to him.

***

I bolted up in bed, heart slamming in my chest. I couldn't shake the feeling the creature from hell and the hunter sharing a campfire were real.

The nightmare lingered long into the night.

***

Pulling into the yard at my dad's place north of Wimbledon, I rubbed my tired eye.

Deep snow covered the prairie. Scattered stars adorned the clear sky between the two-story farmhouse and a red barn in the east, giving light to the wee hours of the morning.

John Golden was crazy.

And showing up to your dad's place at five in the morning for the first time isn't?

I pushed the thought aside. It was time to take action.

My life depended on it.

The moon lit the snowy tundra. An owl hooted, breaking the winter silence.

I drew a breath and rang the doorbell.

Minutes later, Dad opened it wearing pajamas. A shadow of nearly all white whiskers covered his face. His white hair in a wild array.

I didn't smell whisky or cigarettes.

My mouth opened, and before I could utter a word, he pulled me into a rough embrace, awkwardly patting me on the back. Tension vibrated beneath his cold exterior.

I pulled away and took a step back. "I need a gun."

He moved to the side. "Would you like to come in?"

I walked past, steeling myself against welling compassion.

"Can I get you something to drink?" he asked, opening the fridge. "I have orange juice, milk, water…"

"Orange juice is fine."

I'll put the tea on," Dad said. "Should be ready in a few minutes."

He was the only one who knew I preferred tea. "Nice house."

"Thanks. At first, when your mother insisted on my old house, I was furious." He chuckled. "Of course, everything she did back then ticked me off."

For the first time in my life, I considered how it had been for my father having to live with my mother.

"Don't know why she needed it so badly. She's never even there," I said.

"To irritate me. Doesn't matter. I love it here." He sat down across from me. "Is the restaurant a lucrative business?"

"I do alright."

"I don't suppose you want to tell me what you need with a gun." Dad stretched his legs out in front of him.

"No." I scratched the back of my head. "You quit drinking?"

"Yep. Smoking too. Turns out it's hazardous to your health." He grinned.

Never stopped him before. I wondered if his dad had been a smoker. "What was your dad like?" I asked. "You've never talked about him."

"He was a cold, bitter man." His mouth twisted. "Couldn't stand the sight of me."

"Because Grandma died in childbirth?"

He shrugged. "My Uncle Bernard took me in when I was fifteen, and never saw him again."

"What happened to Bernard?"

"He was killed in a rollover accident." A pause. "My dad didn't even attend the funeral."

"I didn't know," I mumbled.

"It was a long time ago. I don't think about it anymore." Dad laced his fingers behind his head. "So you want a gun. Have you ever shot one? Or a better question, will a gun solve your problems?"

I shrugged.

"You'll need ammo too," Dad continued relentlessly.

"Look, are you going to help me or not?"

The tea kettle began to whistle.

Dad stood. "There's my cue."

He returned with a tray containing two cups of tea, a teapot and container of sugar cubes, and set it on the breakfast table in front of me.

I picked up a delicate cup laced with intricate flowers, and eyed him over the top. "Fancy."

Dad gave me a sheepish look. "Paige thought since I like tea, I should be the one to use her mother's china. I don't have room for things I don't use. On special occasions, I get them out."

"What's the special occasion?" I eyed the beautiful teacup.

He grinned wide. "You showing up at my doorstep."

***

Bill's Gun Shop in Fargo had an indoor range.

"Bill's a friend of mine," Dad said on the way inside.

Bill provided ear and eye protection and let us pick whatever gun we wanted to use for practice.

I stared at the wall of pistols, only able to distinguish automatics compared to revolvers. Black versus silver.

Dad picked one out, racking the chamber. He handed it to me, chamber open. "Walther PPK .380. I think you'll like it."

My hand shook as I took it from him.

Dad clamped his hand on my shoulder. "Let's go have some fun."

Afterward, he said, "You are quite the shot."

"Probably my one eye." I stood a little straighter. "Has to do the work of two." I thought about revealing the eye incident and cover up, and quickly discarded the idea. After all, Dad didn't really need another reason to hate my mother.

I purchased the Walther PPK .380.

On the way out of the store, Dad said, "It's about Nora isn't it? The reason you need a gun."

I halted.

He gave me a wistful glance. "You've always loved her."

Shooting was fun, but I wasn't about to talk personal with him.

***

Upstairs in my room above the restaurant, my thoughts reeled. It was a good day with Dad, but did I really need a gun? John Golden was a cop. Would he really shoot me?

Unsettled, I reached for the computer and clicked on the favorites, scrolling through videos.

If your eye causes you to sin, pluck it out.

Okay, gouge my eye out? What kind of message was this? *Cast it from you.*

Instead, I clicked on the latest video.

Long afterward in a pool of shame, I sat up in bed, wishing for stairs to count.

I wasn't winning the battle.

There was no fight, really, in mindlessly watching debauches. Each, a little more perverse. Needing more to be stimulated with every scene I consumed.

I reached for the wine on the nightstand and returned the glass without taking a sip.

More than another drink, sexual experience, or even a gun, I needed an exodus in my soul from the bondage of sin.

71

The hellhound ripped from the current host, the body crumbling to the ground like a deflated human balloon.

It's finally over.

Suddenly, crippling fear crossed the other Simon's terrified expression when in a blur, the hellhound was upon him. Unable to see the creature's true form, I could only imagine its visage by the look of sheer terror on my replica's face.

Horrified, I couldn't tear my gaze away.

Screams echoed across the Dakota prairie as my heart pumped its last, the creature's heart pumping anew.

***

I bolted up in bed, gasping for breath. Understanding flooded my sleep-laden brain. The meaning of the dream, illuminated by the morning light. I had become a slave to my impulses and my mind, a living hell.

It is more profitable for you that one of your members perish, than for your whole body to be cast into hell.

The nightmare disappearing with the dawn pouring through my bedroom window, I knew what to do.

***

"Thanks for coming early, Bella."

Sitting at the table in the breakfast nook, she tucked her hands beneath her. "Am I in trouble?"

"No."

"Is this about Jenna asking if you were gay? You know, it wouldn't hurt you to date. Then people wouldn't think you're living in the closet."

"People think I'm gay?"

She blushed. "I…"

I held up my hand. "It doesn't matter. Why didn't you ever go to college?"

"I told you."

"Humor me."

"I like working for you." Her cheeks flushed. "Not in a romantic way. It's just you're a really good boss and I like waiting on people."

"You mean it."

"Yes."

I drew a breath. "You are really good with people."

"I'm not bad." She straightened her shoulders.

"I could use a manager. I mean, someone to work the books and hire and fire as needed." I pulled out my smartphone and handed it to her. "You'll need a work phone."

Her eyes widened. "Me? You never seemed to care much for handing the reins over. No offense."

"None taken. I'll provide the laptop. You won't have to work weekends or holidays. The apartment above the garage is available. You want it?"

"I'd love it."

"It's yours, boss." I smiled.

"What will you do?"

"What I do best. Cook."

72
March 14, 2020

Saturday morning, brunch was ready at nine forty-five.

The staff was scheduled to come at ten.

I pushed the long dining room table next to the bar counter, and covered it with my finest tablecloth. Each place was set with silverware on green cloth napkins.

In the center, glass pitchers of orange juice and milk. Keurig for coffee. Hot water for tea. Caramel rolls on platters. Grapes, strawberries, and blackberries in separate dishes.

Jordan arrived five minutes early. "Hi Simon. You wanted…" he stopped short at the feast on the table. "What's with all the food?"

I motioned to a chair. "Have a seat."

He glanced over the spread and sat down. "Pie too?"

"Ham quiche actually. Try it. There's also scrambled eggs in the red and white crock. And if homemade sausage doesn't do it for you, I'll make you a steak to order. Do you drink coffee?" I asked.

Just then, Jenna and Bella walked through the door wearing long faces and carrying a dozen doughnuts.

Jenna handed me the box. "So you don't fire Bella."

I arched a brow. "You bring store-bought doughnuts, and don't expect her to be fired?"

Bella pushed her. "I told you he wouldn't like it."

"Who's gonna fire you after doughnuts?" Jenna blinked.

"No one is getting fired."

"Not even demoted?" Bella asked.

"The shutdown concerns us all, and as the owner, it's my place to provide comfort food." I set a platter of scones in the center. "The schools are closed."

"I love these." Bella grabbed a warm one.

"We're closing for sure?" Jenna asked.

"For two weeks," I said, sitting down.

"Is all this for us?" Jordan asked.

"Yep," I smiled.

Jordan reached for the kettle of scrambled eggs. "Better get started."

***

"I tried calling you and Bella answered." Mom barged past me into the kitchen. "They're shutting the schools down."

"Good thing I don't go," I chuckled.

"It's a total lockdown, Simon." Mom gave me a frosty glare. "I shouldn't have to call your landline."

"It's the only way to get a hold of me. I gave the cell to Bella. I'm guessing she told you we're closed temporarily."

"Are you seeing her?"

"Bella?"

"What's with moving off the grid? You turn Posse Comitatus or something?"

"No. You know me and technology." I gave her my widest grin. "Bella has my computer too."

Mom looked at me like my eye had grown back. "How will you breathe without your computer?"

I shrugged. "Inhale, exhale."

"She doesn't even have a degree. All she's ever done is work as a waitress for you."

"Which makes her perfect for the position."

"What if there's an emergency? How's she supposed to get a hold of you?"

"I'm sure she can handle whatever. If it's an emergency, you know the number to the restaurant."

Mom glared at me. "Have you lost your mind?"

"Probably." I shrugged, and drew a breath. Now was my chance to confront her about the tomcat lie. "Mom, did I lose my eye from Coat's disease as a kid?"

She sat down at the breakfast nook. "Yes. You were too young to complain you couldn't see out of it. I noticed one day it was glazed over, and I took you to the eye doctor." She offered a sad smile. "He said the retina had detached and it was too late to save it."

Recalling all I'd learned about Coat's disease versus getting an infection in your eye from an injury, this was the most plausible explanation. Still, why lie about it? I started to ask and realized the likely truth was terrifying.

Instead, I said, "I made lunch. Beef roast with baby potatoes, peas, and rhubarb cake for dessert."

She frowned, "You know I don't care for roast."

"I could make you lobster mac 'n' cheese."

"I suppose." She sighed. "Don't put too much cheese in it."

She ate two servings.

Afterward, I asked, "How was it?"

"Oh, it was alright. Not as good as The Lunchbox in Fort Ransom."

I opened my mouth to tell her she could go to The Lunchbox next time, remembered I had to honor my mother, and snapped it shut.

It is not the situation which makes the man, but the man who makes the situation.

Frederick William Robertson

73
June 1, 2020

Tchaikovsky playing over the sound system at Simon's Place, I was in the process of major housecleaning when Jordan walked in the front door. "Simon?"

"Coming." I descended the main staircase.

There was another man with him who appeared to be in his early twenties with a blonde beard, and sunglasses parked on his baseball cap. The woman with a messy blonde ponytail appeared around the same age.

Jordan shuffled forward. "This is my, uh, brother, Dane and Olivia his wife."

"Nice to meet you Dane." I thrust out my hand.

He shook it. "You too."

The brothers exchanged glances.

It was Jordan who spoke. "Dane was laid off two months ago from Pizza Ranch."

"Was only supposed to be two weeks," Dane added.

"Not good."

They exchanged another covert glance.

"Olivia was working at the Kirin House and she was laid off too," Jordan said.

I tossed my cleaning rag over my shoulder. "Does your mom know you're here?"

"No sir." Dane's face reddened.

I arched a brow. "Your dad?"

"No sir." Dane tugged his cap down.

"Follow me." I turned and headed back up the stairs.

"Sir?" Dane asked.

"Call me Simon." I reached the landing, turned, and mounted the next staircase.

"Okay, sir...Simon," Dane said behind me.

***

Sitting on the sofa in the middle of the fourth-floor living room, Olivia said, "The shower and tub in the bathroom is nice."

"Three bedrooms too," Dane said. "The tunnel is cool."

"You like it?" I sat in the stuffed chair alongside them. "I heard back in the day this was the floor where they delivered babies. This used to be a hospital."

"Cool," Olivia said.

"I can't give you a job, Dane. However, the place is yours if you want." I stretched my legs out. "The furniture stays. Unless you three want to haul stuff up and down three flights of stairs."

Dane's eyes widened.

Olivia's were fixed on her lap.

"All I ask is you fix what you break, and don't help yourselves to the refrigerator downstairs."

Olivia said, "Of course not."

"I'm handy when it comes to fixing things," Dane added.

"Then we should get along fine." I scrubbed my jaw. "Someone gonna tell your mom?"

Dane held up a hand. "I will."

"Good." I gave a nod. "Welcome home."

74

The setting sun twinkled through oak trees. I was parked in the back alley next to the hedge of bushes, the scent of wood smoke lingering in the air.

The heavy atmosphere from lockdown had me eating my dinner Sunday evening on the tailgate of my black Chevy pickup.

Nora's Dodge Intrepid pulled up and she got out.

My heart leapt in my chest, pounding until I was dizzy. I hadn't seen her since our Sunday night date. I'd avoided Sweets 'N Stories after the unspoken message between us.

In a yellow sundress and tan cowboy boots, she strolled over, welcome as a fresh summer evening.

"What are you doing out here?" she asked.

"Eating my dinner." I caught her gaze. "How about you?"

She rubbed her hands together. "Long story."

"If you don't mind my eating in front of you," I shifted on the cool metal surface of the truck bed, motioning to the space next to me, "Have a seat."

She jumped up. "I hate to bother you."

"It's no bother."

"I tried to call."

"I'll give you the house number."

"You don't have a cell phone?"

"Uh no. Just a landline." I recited the digits and she put them in her phone.

"Thanks." She set her phone on the bed next to her.

"Can I get you something to drink?" I asked.

"I'm good."

I took bites of my burger.

She swung her legs back and forth.

Lost in our own thoughts, neither of us spoke.

"Taylor Hall used to come into my room at night and do things to me while I slept." She broke the silence.

My jaw clenched with the blow of her confession.

"When I woke up one night, I tried to tell Mom." Her eyes took on a haunted look. "She was different after she married Louis Hall. She said I shouldn't provoke Taylor."

I couldn't find the words to respond.

Nora stared straight ahead. "I wasn't brave either. I cowered under the slightest threat." A pause. "Louis confiscated our letters. He edited the ones I wrote to you."

"Now I know why your last letter was so confusing."

"Fake, really," she said.

"The empty mailboxes were a kick in the gut." I took a swig of Pepsi.

She glanced over, her whisky-colored eyes, cloudy. "I didn't know what to say that wasn't horrible."

I held her gaze. "Even horrible would have been something."

"Then I met John," she said.

I downed the last of my Pepsi and shook the can.

"It was at the local coffee shop I frequented. He was a surfer slash cop. Tan, muscular, funny, and my ticket out away from the Halls."

I didn't speak for fear she would retreat back behind the wall she built around herself.

She swallowed visibly. "I know what people say about the couples we were friends with. It was all true."

I felt like I'd been kicked in the chest.

"We were married for thirteen years. For most of those, I couldn't leave. For some...I didn't. I can't explain why."

But I could. *Hamlet.*

"I got custody of the kids and a job offer at the coffee shop in California. It was a fresh start for us."

"Why come back here?" I held my breath, dreading the word *reconcile*, needing to hear she was over him.

"My mother was admitted to Good Samaritan nursing home. I couldn't keep her grandsons away from her. Not while she's dying."

"I suppose not."

"Now you know. I'm not the good girl you thought I was." She looked down.

I crumpled the aluminum foil into a ball.

"I wanted to tell you the night we had dinner at your place, but I was happy to be with you, and... "

"You were happy to be with me," I said slowly.

"Yes. Weren't you happy to be with me?"

"Yes."

"Like spending time with a sister?" It was a question.

I smiled. "Nothing like a sister."

75
June 15, 2020

Dane and I carried a stuffed green chair up the second flight of stairs to the fourth floor at Simon's Place.

"Ready, Simon?" he said. "On three we'll set it right across from the couch. One, two, three." We set the chair in the middle of the room.

I took a step back.

"Anything else, Olivia?" Dane kneed the chair into place.

"No. Sadly, it's the only piece of furniture I own."

"You guys want tea or anything?" I smoothed my hands over my shirt.

Dane nodded. "Sure."

I served tea and scones on the table in front of the fireplace in the old living room.

Olivia took a sip. "You're the only man I know who serves tea on a platter."

"My dad was hardly ever around when I was growing up, but when he was, he'd always serve tea on special china."

"You're lucky. My dad was always around." Dane took a bite of his scone. "Except when we needed him."

"Dane," Olivia admonished.

I bit my tongue to keep from asking how it was between his father and mother, and instead said, "I learned how to be a man from my father. Be alert, stand firm in the faith, act like a man, and be strong."

"Sounds like Paul the Apostle," Olivia said.

I smiled. "You know your Bible."

Dane's head came up. "I thought you said your dad was never around."

"You can learn a lot from watching a man to find out what not to do. Especially when you see results over a long period of time." Not to mention my mother, the way she hid the truth, and the burden it must have been on my dad.

"Is he the reason you never married?" Olivia asked.

"I guess I never met the right woman."

"Is it because of my mom?" Dane wiped his mouth with a napkin. "She told me you two knew each other growing up. Then she married my dad and you married no one."

Reluctant to tell the truth and look like a love sick fool, I didn't respond.

Olivia glanced at her phone. "It's almost three."

Dane stood. "I got an interview at Bobcat in Gwinner."

"Oh I almost forgot." I hurried to the kitchen and returned with a plate of homemade chocolate chip cookies. "A housewarming gift."

Dane took the plate from me.

"Good luck on the interview." I gave a nod.

He paused at the front door. "My mom is lucky to have you."

Lucky to have me?

After they left, my brain was flooded with questions. Did she want me? Had she discussed it with Dane?

At the thought, I picked up the tea platter and headed for the kitchen, whistling Bobby McFerrin's "Don't Worry, Be Happy."

76
June 30, 2020

The Food and Drug Administration took action to help facilitate timely development of safe and effective vaccines to prevent COVID-19.

For the first time since lockdown, the doors were open at Simon's Place. John Golden was waiting outside the door in street clothes.

"Good evening, Officer Golden," I said amicably.

He brushed past me. "Twenty five percent capacity is the maximum for eating establishments."

I bit back a retort and returned to the kitchen, slicing the roast for sandwiches.

Jenna walked through the back door, tying her apron. "I didn't know you were cooking tonight, Simon."

"Jordan wanted the night off to go fishing. Supposed to be biting at Lake LaMoure."

"I'm glad, actually. I was wondering if you wanted to go out with me sometime. My treat."

I looked up. "I'm flattered, but no."

She frowned. "Is it Nora?"

"I don't date my staff."

"If I quit, would you go out with me?"

"No." I returned my attention to carving the roast. "Don't quit."

She slipped past the barrier and into the bar.

I gave a sigh of relief.

By the time the roast was sliced, I could hear conversation buzzing behind the kitchen barrier. I peeked around the barricade.

Officer Golden sat in the bar area, drumming idle fingers on the tabletop, humming "Farmer in the dell" while Jenna took his order.

Jenna giggled at something he said.

The real reason I would never date Jenna.

Wearing a red farmer's cap with the inscription, "Mannlake: We know bees," Luke Doric sat at the bar and ordered a Ranger. Melissa wasn't with him. I hoped a good thing, but nothing was ever good between them.

All I needed was to have Luke Doric make a scene with Golden to witness it. I ducked back behind the barricade, and grabbed a potato.

Bella arrived for work. "Hi Simon."

"We got customers," I motioned to the dining room.

"I'm on it." She disappeared, and was back minutes later. "Officer Golden wants to know if we serve regular fries."

"We don't."

"Exactly what I told him. He says he doesn't like homemade fries."

I looked up. "Do you need me to talk to him?"

"No, I got it. Just wanted you to know." She took the tray of salads and returned to the dining room.

Officer Golden was a regular customer at Simon's Place. He'd complained to Jenna we didn't serve tap beer. He'd complained to Jordan he undercooked the burgers. To the waitresses, he tipped poorly.

I reached for an onion.

Bella walked in and grabbed a bottle of Guinness from the fridge. "Nora's here."

I put the knife down, and wiped my hands on my apron, rounding the corner.

In a lavender dress and brown cowboy boots, Nora sat down at the bar. She glanced over, smiling when she saw me.

Ignoring eye daggers Golden shot in my direction, I approached her. "Hi," I said, breathless.

She blushed. "Hi Simon."

"I'm cooking, and I don't have time to talk," I said, feeling Officer Golden's stare burning holes through me. "If you need anything, tell Bella."

"Thanks."

Closing time, Nora was still at the bar.

I reached for her hand. "Don't go. I'm about to eat my dinner."

"Okay," she said, her eyes shining.

Kitchen clean, I removed my apron and grabbed two bottles of Guinness from the fridge.

Sheila and Jenna retired for the evening.

Bella retreated to her apartment above the garage.

I handed Nora a beer. "How was your day?"

She smiled. "Good."

"The ex behave himself?" I sat down, taking a pull from my beer.

"He left right after he ate."

"Good."

"You have the right to refuse service to anyone for any reason, you know."

"It's tricky. He already patrols Simon's Place every weekend at closing time." I took a bite of my burger.

"To keep people from driving drunk. John is a lot of things, but people love him as a cop. He's fair, and doesn't play favorites."

"He doesn't patrol The Angry Beaver," I said, knowing embarrassing John Golden meant trouble for Simon's Place.

"I could write him a strongly worded letter." She smiled.

"Better yet, don't write a letter at all, and break the poor guy's heart." It was out of my mouth before I could stop it.

Silence.

Then, "I did not break your heart."

I held the bottle to my lips and glanced over at her. "It was a long time ago. Who cares?"

She appeared shaken. "I wanted to thank you for giving Dane and Olivia a place to stay."

"I couldn't say no."

"You could."

"They're good kids." I wiped my mouth with a napkin.

***

"Hey there. Long time no see." Officer Golden got out of his cop car as I was emptying the evening's trash.

I didn't have to check my watch to know it was after one in the morning. I'd gotten off the phone with Nora to make sure she'd arrived home okay.

"Did I do something wrong?" I opened the dumpster lid and threw the garbage bag inside.

His dead eyes stared back at me. "I don't know, did you?"

My mouth opened, but no words came out. At last, I managed, "Was your food alright?"

"It was there."

"Good night." I turned to go inside.

"You remind me more of a preacher than a cook."

I halted. "Chef."

"First you give Jordan a job. Then it's free rent for Dane and Olivia." Officer Golden's gaze narrowed sharply. "I can imagine what you give the ex-wife."

"She has a name." Anger burst in my chest, swift and overwhelming.

John shook his head at me. "You can have my leftovers when it comes to my wife. My boys, on the other hand, are my boys."

I held my ground.

His expression turned thoughtful. "You're more like a TV evangelist than a preacher. Shaking babies, kissing hands," he joked, and then in a more serious tone, "Nora's had quite a few hobbies in the past. The religion thing is a phase."

I didn't respond.

"Make sure you lock the place up at night, Simon." He turned to leave, and then glanced back. "A lot of break-ins in town since the riots started in Minneapolis. I suppose you could fire a few rounds in the air to scare the perp."

You'd like that, wouldn't you? Then he could arrest me for firing shots in town. "I'll think about it."

"Gotta roll. Lots of time, so little to do." He snickered, turned, and headed for the cop car. "Whatcha going to do? Whatcha gonna do when they come for you, bad boys, bad boys..." the laughter was of a desperate man.

I felt the fine hairs rise on the back of my neck.

77
Simon's Place
Thanksgiving, 2020

The mantle of the dining room area was decked with pilgrims and gobblers.

There was a turkey warm in the oven, and a fire blazing on the hearth. Sides of stuffing, mashed potatoes, and green beans with mushroom sauce topped with shoestring onions. Cranberry sauce for Charles and Gretchen. They were the only two who ate the stuff.

For dessert, pie: Pecan, pumpkin, and apple. Heavy cream to top them off I whipped myself.

Suddenly I was nostalgic for the dairy.

"Tell me again why we buy organic milk," I said to Kevin who sat in the breakfast nook.

"Nobody wants to be married to the cows, Simon." He leaned back in his chair. "Not even single guys like you."

I thought of Nora and the intimacy growing between us since she opened up about her past. She was coming for dinner.

"Doug's hauling a truck load this coming Monday, Simon," Kevin said, pushing an invoice across the table. "Look it over and let me know if you have any changes."

"I'll make sure Bella looks at it and sends a check."

"Oh right. How's living in the Stone Age?"

"I'm not the one tethered to the phone." I took a bite of cheese and crackers.

He laughed, setting his phone face down on the tabletop.

The wall phone rang and I answered it. "Hello?"

271

"Should I make knoephla? I know Harry and Hans prefer mine to yours."

"Hi Mom. I got plenty of food. Just come."

She laughed. "Too late. I already made it."

Then why ask? "I'll see you later."

I hung up as Hans walked in the door. "I thought COVID would never go away. All our vehicles make it look like you invited half the town to Thanksgiving."

Behind him, Mary, Anna, and little Grace.

Harry mounted stairs with suitcases in each hand. "Happy Thanksgiving, Simon."

Harry's Trista and Suzy trailed behind followed by their youngest, Frank.

"How's the law enforcement here?" Hans asked.

"So far so good. The cops have stayed out of it, thanks to Bella," I said. "Golden likes to work with her rather than me directly."

Charles' truck pulled in shortly afterward. "Kevin and his family are going to put us over the top this Thanksgiving. We're already over capacity." He chuckled.

"Twenty-five people all together, give or take five," I said.

Everyone poured into the dining area.

Dane descended the stairs, Olivia ducking behind him. I'd been waiting for them. My large family was often overwhelming to outsiders. "Come on down, guys," I said with a wave of my hand.

"It's nice enough to sit outside," Olivia said, scrolling through her phone.

Trey, Thomas, and Seth came over.

"We're Simon's nephews," Thomas said.

Trey asked, "Do you want to come downstairs with us? We brought my Nintendo Switch."

Dane's eyes lit. All of them thundered down the stairs. Except for Kevin's girls. They set the tables I'd covered with brown and gold tablecloths.

Jordan and Nora arrived a half hour before lunch.

Nora was wearing a gray cable sweater dress and winter boots. She removed her boots in the entrance. Her blonde hair fell about her shoulders in waves.

"Kids are downstairs playing video games, Jordan," I told him.

He kicked off his shoes and hurried away.

Nora flashed her dimples. "Looks like quite the crowd."

"Come on. I'll help you get reacquainted with my family before lunch." I took her hand.

After making the rounds, Nora turned to me. "It was easier to remember the names of the kids who aren't Kevin's."

I threw my head back and laughed.

In the kitchen, she helped with finishing touches on the meal. I carved the turkey, turned around, and accidently bumped into her. The kitchen space I'd become familiar with, now intimate and thrilling.

For the next four hours, she followed me around, chatting away like when we were kids. She was the perfect height, only a few inches shorter than me. Her presence was welcoming. She seemed to warm the entire room.

***

After dinner, games were downstairs. The adults drank tea and coffee around tables. I took Nora's hand, and we slipped out to the back alley.

The November evening was unusually balmy, nearly sixty degrees at sunset. The sun turned the western sky an array of soft colors, glimmering through skeletal branches.

I flipped the tailgate down, and helped Nora up.

"I had a good day," she said. "Remember when we were kids in our secret place."

I glanced over at her. "After you left, I used to go there and read comic books alone."

Her eyes glittered in the moonlight. "This tailgate can be our new secret place."

"Or not so secret," I said, watching the alley as the cop car pulled up.

Nora stiffened alongside me. "Oh great. What does he want?"

The car came to a halt and Officer Golden stepped out, hiking up his utility belt.

"Is there a problem, Officer?" I asked.

"I got a call you have cars lined up on the street out front and in the back."

"I reckon I do."

"Need I remind you you're supposed to be at twenty-five percent capacity or less?"

"Simon's Place is closed for the holidays. Far as I know I'm not breaking any laws."

His arrogant gaze gleamed. "You see, there's where you're wrong. Family gatherings are supposed to follow social distancing and be immediate family only." He flicked Nora a glance.

"What are you going to do about it?" *Shut up, Simon.*

"I'm a reasonable guy. I don't want to spoil anyone's fun." He chuckled. "Just a friendly reminder to keep your distance."

What did he mean exactly? I opened my mouth to ask, and Nora laid her hand on mine. "We will. Thanks John."

He scowled at Nora's hand on mine, turned, and got back in his car. After he drove away, I turned to her. "He's sure got a bee in his bonnet." I hopped off the tailgate.

Nora got down. "He always does."

I pulled her into my arms, resting my chin on the top of her head.

"This isn't exactly social distancing," she said, even as her arms slipped around my waist.

"Let me hold you for a little while," I whispered against her hair.

The air around us was a bit chilly, but the woman in my arms warmed me to the core. Holding Nora in the twilight, her arms around me, a perfect ending to a perfect day.

Lost in the moment, I barely heard the vehicle pull up until Mom's sharp voice came up from behind me, "What are you doing?"

Nora jumped away.

Wearing masks, both my mom and Doug emerged from the car.

"Hi Mrs. Anderson. Hi Doug," Nora said.

"The crockpot is in the trunk," Mom said. "I can teach you how to make knoephla one of these days. I made bars too."

"I got them." Nora took the pan from her.

Doug hurried up the steps. "Let me get the door for you, Nora."

I grabbed the knoephla.

Mom shut the trunk. "The ride here was impossibly long."

"Didn't Doug drive?"

"Yes, but there was no cell service. YouTube froze right in the middle of my TED talk."

"How tragic," I murmured, thinking of how good Nora felt in my arms.

She flicked me a glance. "You know they're swingers."

"You know she's divorced," I said, aware of the direction the conversation was taking.

"They were inseparable with the Thompsons."

"Be nice to her, Mom." I turned and went inside. Feeling intense disgust, I set the crockpot on the counter. Putting a face on nameless men was more than I could take. Jake Thompson was the absolute worst.

Anger boiling, I turned around, accidently brushing against Nora. I stiffened and took a step back.

She frowned, "What's wrong?"

"Nothing."

"Is it something your mother said?"

"Forget it."

For the next hour, I couldn't shake the images of Nora with unknown men. Nora went home early, and I breathed an audible sigh of relief.

The visions haunted my dreams.

78
December 15, 2020

"This is the last one." Dane set the box of Christmas decorations in the middle of the dining area.

"This is a lot of decorations," Olivia said.

"Thanks for helping me decorate." I set the tea tray on the table in the den. "We'll tackle the job after tea. Have either of you seen a Walmart bag? It was on the table."

"It's in your room," Dane said. "I thought it was the decorations you asked me to put there. I'll go get it."

"Wait. Take these with you." I handed him the plain bag of decorations.

He headed upstairs.

"May I pour the tea?" Olivia asked.

"Sure."

"I feel fancy, drinking tea, and decorating such a mansion for Christmas."

"The tea is a habit I acquired from my dad. The rare occasion I saw him in the kitchen, he would be preparing tea. He never did anything half way, and tea was no exception."

"Was he the one who liked to decorate?"

I chuckled. "No, I was. Ever since I can remember, my mom allowed me to do all the decorating. There's nothing at her house Christmassy now."

"Sad. We should go to your old house and decorate for her like when you were little."

"Yeah, we should." What was taking Dane so long?

277

I headed for the stairs as he was coming down. "Can we go shooting sometime, Simon?" he asked.

The Walther was in his hand.

"What are you doing?" A sliver of fear raced up my spine.

He blinked. "It was in your nightstand, and I..."

The slide wasn't open. "Did you check the chamber?"

"What do you mean?"

"Come, I'll show you." I climbed the stairs, and held my hand out. He set the pistol on my palm.

"Rule number one, when you pick up a gun, check to see if it's loaded." I pushed the slide release, and racked the slide back. A bullet popped out.

I slid the magazine back in. "If you pull the trigger, it won't shoot, because there isn't a bullet in the chamber. You have to rack the slide back to load it."

I racked the slide back and flipped the safety on. "Some pistols don't have a safety on them." I tapped Dane's temple with my index finger. "Safety's up here."

Olivia joined us. "Will you take us target shooting sometime?"

I returned the pistol to the nightstand. "Didn't your dad ever take you shooting, Dane?" Grabbing the bag with sugar cubes, I headed for the stairs.

Dane followed in silence, Olivia trailing behind.

Sitting in the den in front of the fireplace, teacup in hand, Dane spoke at last.

"Some days my dad would come home from work, sit in front of the TV and demand to be waited on. If we didn't ask how high when he ordered us to jump, he'd break things."

"What things?" And what did this have to do with target practice?

Dane shrugged. "Jars or whatever. Plates. Dishes. If we jumped or got startled, he'd laugh."

My stomach churned. "What did your mom do?"

"My mom never raised her voice or freaked out. She always held it together, waiting on him and picking up his messes whenever he had a whim."

"I noticed her long fuse when we were kids."

"I've never even seen my mom cry. She always held it together." He pinned me with a look. "My mom would never go to the range with my dad."

A shiver rolled through me at the implication. "Jordan is cooking Saturday. I have to go to Fargo for some supplies. I'll take you both to Bill's Gun Shop."

Their expressions lit. "Thanks, Simon."

I hadn't seen Nora since Thanksgiving. Several times I reached for the phone to call her, and changed my mind at the last second. Mom had to paint a picture.

Who cares whose fault it is? You fix it.

"What do you need a gun for anyway?" Dane asked, downing the last of his tea.

"Long story." I handed him a string of lights.

"We should decorate our apartment," Olivia told Dane.

"I'm not helping haul a Christmas tree to the fourth floor." I chuckled. "You'll have to settle for a Charlie Brown tree."

They exchanged glances.

"Don't tell me you don't know what a Charlie Brown tree is."

"Okay, we won't." Olivia smiled.

"Kids these days." I sighed. "Will you be at your dad's this Christmas?"

Dane said, "Dad doesn't celebrate Christmas. He believes in God, but says Christmas is too commercial."

"It would be cool if you wanted to have Christmas here." I picked up a string of lights. "I was thinking of inviting your mom and Jordan too."

"Sure," Dane said.

"We'd love to." Olivia worked on the string of lights in her hand. "I hadn't even done my Christmas shopping."

"You don't need to bring presents."

Working at the tangles in a string of white lights, Dane rolled his eyes. "Simon, you can't invite someone over for Christmas and tell them not to bring gifts."

"Fair enough. We'll do a gift exchange and keep the cost low," I said.

Now to invite Nora. I should go to Sweets 'N Stories instead of calling. The obsession with her past was real, but I owed it to her to try.

"Uh, Dane?" I said tentatively.

He looked up from the string of lights.

"What does your mom want for Christmas?"

Fill your house with stacks of books. To all the little crannies and all the nooks.

Dr. Seuss

79

Sweets 'N Stories was quiet.

White and pink pinstriped wallpaper greeted me. The chalkboard menu was decorated with candy canes.

There was no lack of fudge.

A completed Ravensburger puzzle adorned the concrete wall between brown pillars. There was a rack with puzzles for kids.

There was an old-fashioned white stove with a kettle on top. Also on the stovetop, black mugs, plastic wrap, aluminum foil dispensers, and cookbooks.

Working up my nerve to approach the cash register, I read a George RR Martin quote on the wall above the black fireplace *A reader lives a thousand lives before he dies…the man who never reads lives only one.*

I grabbed a bottle of lemon syrup and Dean Koontz's latest, and plopped down on a black chair.

I mentally rehearsed what I would say. All my anger had faded, and I couldn't even remember why I was mad. I mean, I knew it was because of the past, but it somehow didn't seem to hold weight anymore.

What I really wanted to know was if she noticed I hadn't called. Or if she had a good time Thanksgiving. At least, up until my mother opened her mouth. Where our relationship stood. Not like it was a relationship, anyway, just a day.

One incredible day.

***

"Simon," Nora's voice made its way through my dreams. "Simon. We're about to close."

I sat up and blinked. "I must have fallen asleep."

"I'm locking up. You have ten minutes to finish browsing."

"I'm ready." I stood, my thoughts in a whirl. I had no news of good tidings. I just needed the forgiveness of the season. Didn't I? I hadn't done anything. Not really. Should I tell her I knew about the Thompsons?

No, don't make it about the past. It wasn't going to be easy. "I didn't see your car," I said.

"I walked."

"Can I take you home?"

"Yes." She gave me a tremulous smile.

"Sorry about falling asleep. I didn't do anything embarrassing, like snore, or drool..." My shoulder struck someone. I turned and offered, "Sorry."

In blue jeans and a cable sweater, John Golden somehow appeared more intimidating than in uniform.

"Hi John," Nora said.

He glanced at me. "You're parked illegally. I had to give you a ticket."

My jaw clenched. "I am not."

"Fifteen minute parking only."

He wasn't even in uniform.

"I can give you a ride home in my pickup, Nora." He drawled.

282

"No, thank you." Nora laid her hand on my arm. "I'm ready, Simon."

John cut me a hard look.

"I'm closing up, John."

"Sure." He chuckled. "We'll see you now."

After he left, Nora shut the lights off.

"I don't know why he hates me," I said as she locked the doors.

"He hates everybody."

Golden pulled away from the curb. Jenna was in his pickup. She waved when she saw me. I wished she wouldn't date John Golden. I preferred to avoid drama wherever possible.

"Would have been an awkward ride home." I opened the passenger door for Nora.

Nora laughed as she got in. "He's always up to something."

I rounded the front of the grille to the driver side, and got in. "Seems strange to be this close to Christmas and not have snow."

"I agree. I wish it would snow."

I pulled out of the parking space, searching for the words to tell her how foolish I'd been, but my mind went blank.

She sat rubbing her hands.

In five short blocks, I pulled up to her house. "Here we are."

Nora glanced over. "Would you like to come in?"

"Maybe for a minute."

I cut the engine and followed her inside. *Say it. Stop being a chicken.* "Look Nora, I..."

"Simon, it isn't..."

We shared a laugh. Nora said, "You first."

"Would you like to spend Christmas with me? Jordan too of course. Dane and Olivia will be there."

"Yes."

"There will be more food and drinks than the whole town can consume. My family...you will?"

She nodded. "It's lockdown at the nursing home this Christmas. The only thing I planned was a phone call."

I looked at Nora, imploring a silent plea of forgiveness, for not calling, for judging the sliver in her eye when I couldn't see past the log in my own.

Then at last she came into my arms and I felt the world was right again.

80

The sun peeked through the skeletal cottonwoods alongside my house the next morning. Earthy smells of mud and grit suggested spring.

However, the ringing of Christmas bells meant winter in Oakes, North Dakota, had begun.

It was a welcome sight when Nora's car pulled into the back alley at five-thirty in the morning. She got out. Wearing a black leather jacket, she bounded up the back steps.

I opened the door as she reached for the handle.

Her cheeks flushed. "Merry Christmas."

"You too. I mean, Merry Christmas." I helped her with her coat. Her sweater was red minus the ugly Christmas part. "I forgot to tell you what time to come."

"Is Santa late?" she whispered. "Should I go home and come back?"

"He just left." My faded blue jeans and black crew neck shirt revealed none of the holiday's clichés.

"I hope you left one chimney unlit."

"Of course. He knows to use the den. Why are we whispering?"

"Because it's early." She laughed. "What can I help you prepare?"

"Do you want to make mini cheese balls?"

"I'd love to." She washed her hands.

"On the menu, we have cheddar seafood chowder, mashed potatoes, green beans with bacon, crisp caraway bread, and for dessert, eggnog crème brûlée, and old fashioned gingerbread cake."

She rolled a ball of cheese in sesame seeds. "All this for us?"

"I figured the boys will eat a lot. I also have Tupperware for leftovers you might want to take home."

She poked a chip in a cheese ball. "I told Jordan to call me when he wakes up, and I'll go get him."

"Perfect." I pulled the gingerbread cake from the oven.

***

The hearth was cold, our drinks were hot, and we sat around the Christmas tree. It was eight when Nora brought Jordan over. Stockings were hung by the old living room fireplace.

Dane rushed over like a little kid. "It's got my name on."

Olivia drew up alongside him. "We didn't help decorate these."

"Santa must have left them." I winked at Nora, handing her the stocking with her name on it.

Nora arched a fine brow. "Santa got you one?"

"Of course. He knows I need deodorant and socks," I chuckled.

"Do you hear that?" Nora asked.

I cocked my ear. "I don't hear anything. What about you, Dane?"

"Nope." He unpacked his stocking.

"I swear I can hear…It's coming from over there," she pointed at the presents under the tree.

"I hear it too," Jordan said.

"I must need to get my hearing checked." I put my finger in my ear, wringing it.

Nora stood, crossing over to the tree. "Simon, it's right..." She stopped at the present with the holes on top of a wrapped box and separate lid.

She lifted the lid. "A kitten!"

Jordan leapt to his feet and hurried over. "It's adorable." He took the black kitten with a white chin from her grasp. "Is it a boy or girl?"

Nora held the tail up. "A boy?"

"Yep," I grinned.

"Who's it for?" Jordan asked, picking up the lid. "Mom, it's for you! It says 'To: Nora From: Simon.'"

Nora walked on her knees over to me. "Really?"

"Really," I said, feeling myself growing warm beneath my collar. I flicked Dane a glance for affirmation. He looked at me and shrugged.

"A kitten?" Nora didn't squeak, but almost.

"I knew I should have put from Santa on the card. Then you..."

She threw her arms around my neck. "Thank you."

"You're welcome." I slid my arms around her.

"Get a room," Dane said with a grin.

***

Gusts whipped through the trees. The wind had taken the plastic dumpster to the other side of the alley. I went to retrieve it. On my way back, a pair of headlights entered the alley.

City police.

Officer Golden pulled up alongside me and stepped out of his car. "Merry Christmas," he began to sing, "I'm dreaming of a brown Christmas..."

"I haven't broken any laws today, Golden."

"You have a merry Christmas?" he asked.

"Very."

"My ex is like a little kid at Christmas." He chuckled. "She's a little...eccentric."

"I'm going in now."

He got in my face. "You know what? You need to be smarter than a tree."

I took a step back.

"Think you can?" he asked, his eyes, wild with hatred.

A few more steps back, and I felt my back against the old oak tree. I stepped away.

"You see this tree right here?" He patted the trunk. "You only need to be smarter than this tree."

Then he took a step back. "I'm off. I don't have any plans tonight, seeing my family is all with you. Well, not quite. My evening plans consist of a pizza while watching the only true Christmas movie there is." A pause. "Die Hard."

***

Before I crawled into bed, I folded my sweater and set it on the top shelf in my closet. The shelf was barely out of reach, and the magazines Doug brought Thanksgiving came crashing down.

The cover from the one on top blurred.

Everyone who drinks of this water will be thirsty again, but whoever drinks of the water that I will give him will never be thirsty again, Jesus' words to the woman at the well floated through my head.

Afterward, staring numbly at the wine glass in hand, it was Lot's wife from the Bible on my mind. She just had to look back.

I wondered if I was going to turn into salt.

81
February 14, 2021

I woke with a start, rolled over, and checked the clock. Three-fifteen.

I lie awake, staring at the ceiling.

The house was quiet.

Flipping to my side, I sighed loudly and attempted to return to sleep. When would I see Nora again?

Another sigh.

I was worse than a little kid. The clock on the nightstand read four. I rolled out of bed and headed for the kitchen.

The busyness of a booked Valentine's Day weighed me down. I wouldn't see her until tomorrow. Probably okay too. Never attractive appearing too eager.

I picked up the phone.

When she answered, I said, "I was wondering if you wanted to do something tonight. Not for Valentine's Day," I cleared my throat, "I mean, it is Valentine's Day, but you don't have to be my Valentine." I picked up the pencil off the table to give my hands something to do. "I'm going to play the piano. A couple songs. Would you sing?"

Wow Simon. Not eager at all.

"Simon?"

"Did I call too early?" I wrapped the phone cord around the pencil.

"No. I was up."

Silence on the other end.

"Are you still there?"

"Yeah I'm here. What songs?"

"Norah Jones 'Come Away With Me.'"

"Okay. But only because you never ask me for anything."

Relief flowed through me. "Dinner's served at five. Steak or shrimp are the two choices. Can you be here by four?"

"I'll do my best."

***

It was unusually balmy for February, reaching close to 60 degrees. Without a puff of wind, warm enough for tables outside. The propane lamp lit, stars twinkling, the atmosphere held an expectant tone.

I checked over the sound system.

"I set up a microphone for Nora. See?" Bella strolled over. "Bluetooth capability. The speaker is on the piano."

Inside, the tables were decked in red and black.

"The new waitress has the hots for you," Bella said. "I heard her and Jenna talking about how you look like Timothy Olyphant."

"More like Dan Crenshaw." I set the microphone down.

Her voice dipped low. "Jenna seems to think the eyepatch is a ruse."

I snorted.

"Is it?"

Suddenly, the loss of my eye and how it really went down no longer mattered. I would always have one eye and a mother who didn't have my best interests at heart. Might as well let it go. I looked at Bella and flipped up the patch. "Boo."

Her eyes widened and she jumped back.

I laughed, putting the patch back down into place.

"It's not that bad," she said.

"Right."

"You're a really handsome man." She drew a breath. "Remember it when I tell you the problem."

"What problem?"

"We're booked."

"I suppose it doesn't take long to be at twenty-five percent capacity."

"We're at full capacity."

I frowned, "I thought I said…"

"I took some reservations and Jenna made some. Next thing you know, we were full. I couldn't cancel on one couple without cancelling on them all."

"It is what it is." I swallowed my fear and pride in one long gulp. Maybe this wasn't such a good idea. A thousand dollar fine wouldn't be the end of the world. But what if I was arrested? I hadn't heard of anyone around here getting arrested, but they were in Canada. They were even shutting down businesses.

"The Angry Beaver is always packed. The government says twenty-five percent, but no one really cares around here," Bella said.

"I sure hope so."

"You look good, Simon." She eyed my red turtleneck sweater and tailored gray slacks. "Nora's going to drool."

Heat crept up my neck. "Just tell me you ordered enough filet mignons."

She rolled her eyes. "Of course. What do you take me for?"

***

Four–oh-five. Nora hadn't arrived.

I glanced at my watch. What could be keeping her? I said four o'clock, I was sure of it. I'd planned on starting half past four but wanted to discuss a few more song choices.

Another glance at my watch: four-twenty.

291

A burst of fury shot through me. Where was she? Better yet, who was she with? I wasn't important enough to her to be on time.

Maybe she got into an accident. All anger drained from me. What if something happened to her? I checked my watch.

Four twenty-seven.

By four-thirty, I sat down at the piano, feeling dozens of pairs of diners' eyes on my back. I'm sure she had a good reason for being late.

Resigned, I lifted the lid and drew a deep breath.

And then she entered.

Her relaxed honey blonde ringlets reached below her shoulders. She wore a full-length red velvet dress with a sweetheart neckline and spaghetti straps tied at each shoulder.

Some things were definitely worth waiting for.

I stood, unable to tear my gaze away as she walked over to me. Her mouth was the color of rubies, and when she smiled, her dimples reached out and grabbed hold of my heart.

Speechless, I took her hand, drew it to my lips, kissing her fingers. *What are you doing, fool?*

She blushed, a tremulous smile touching her beautiful lips. "I'm sorry I'm late."

"You're here now." I sat down at the piano.

She stood next to me, then gave me a slight nod.

I began to play "Come Away with Me."

Eyes closed, Nora hummed the tune. Her smoky voice soon filled the air, richer than Norah Jones, but suiting the song.

My hands floated over the keys, keenly aware of Nora, leaning on the piano next to me, her sultry voice enchanting.

"…Falling on a tin roof while I'm safe there in your arms…"

I looked up and caught her eyes, hardly believing she was in my dining room, singing. I hoped, just for me.

All too soon, it ended.

The room erupted in applause.

I stood, took Nora's hand, and bowed. She curtsied alongside me.

Bella crossed over to us, raising her voice over the applause, "The cop's outside. He wants to talk to you."

Jolted back to reality, I dragged a deep breath.

"What is it?" Nora asked, studying my face.

"Don't worry," I squeezed her hand and walked out.

Officer Golden stood at the bottom of the veranda steps. "Chilly night."

"It's February."

"Lots of guests."

"It's Valentine's Day."

Silence.

"Quite the show in there." He motioned toward the large picture window. "I didn't know you could play the piano."

"Yep," I said, irritated at the idea of his peeping.

He pulled a pen from his pocket. "Looks like you're more than twenty-five percent capacity."

"What are you going to do about it?"

He pinned me with a hard look. "You know, I was going to wish you a good evening, but I'm watching, and I see you've got people singing. It's crowded and no social distancing."

"It's a free country," I clenched my fists.

He began writing. "It's a thousand dollar fine."

"You're joking." Anger shot through me, hot and volatile. This wasn't about any fine. It was about me and Nora, a red dress and a song. I took a step toward him.

His eyes held a challenge.

"Simon?" Nora's voice came from behind me. "They're waiting for an encore."

"I was finishing up here." Officer Golden closed his ticket book. "I'm going to give you a warning this time. Have a good evening."

Nora touched my hand. "Do hurry. The food is about done." She glanced at Golden. "Good night, John. Drive safe."

John tipped his hat, turned around, and hopped down the steps.

"Can you believe him?" I gritted. "Smug as a cat who took down a rabbit."

"You're hardly a rabbit." Her gaze searched mine. "I can't see a rabbit opening his restaurant in spite of fines or being shut down."

My face grew warm. "I wouldn't say I was unafraid."

"You didn't let it stop you," she continued, her eyes shining in such a way my heart kicked into a gallop. "Does a rabbit kiss a woman's fingertips like a gallant hero in a storybook? Make her heart pound loud enough for all to hear." She held out her hand.

I took it, laying it on my chest. "Feel what you do to mine."

She smiled then.

The early spring evening echoed with a few people clapping. Then I remembered the two tables of guests sitting out on the veranda.

"Okay, show's over," I said gruffly.

Nora gazed at me beneath heavy lids. "Shall we?"

"Indeed." I led her back inside, sailing on a cloud.

82

The sun shone above us even as a chilly breeze followed
along the sidewalk. The crunch of dry leaves beneath my feet
were like mini explosions in my ears. "I should have raked last
fall. Who would have thought we'd have such a warm winter?"

"I had a good time last night." Nora strolled alongside me.
"I did too."

"I'm sorry I was late. I know you are picky about time."

"Ouch." I laid a hand on my chest. "I'm not picky."

"You're always glancing at your watch."

"Sorry," I chuckled. "A bit of a reflex, I guess."

She gave a smile which failed to reach her eyes.

"What is it?" I asked, thrusting my hands into my pockets.
"You have a dragon for me to slay? A puzzle to defeat? Oh I
know. A gourmet meal to master."

"He knew things he couldn't possibly have known. It scared
me." She trembled.

"I take it we're talking about Golden."

She nodded. "Remember Eddie Van Halen?"

"Good dog."

"When I was first met John, we would talk for hours. I told
him everything about my mom. About you, and how I used to
help you milk cows.

"He took my hand and studied my palm. Then he described
Eddie Van Halen's death." She caught my gaze. "He said he
saw the four of us praying over his grave. Even how old we
were. Then he described what Eddie Van Halen looked like."

Parlor tricks? A chill raised the hairs on my arms. "He could have found out somehow."

"I swear to you I told him nothing about your dog." She pressed her lips together.

"No need to swear. I believe you."

"Then he said something I'll never forget. He said lasting love was possible for me, but someone would have to die."

I stopped. "He threatened you?"

"You don't understand."

"Explain it to me then." I gritted.

"He was a good guy and a…monster. One minute he would shower us with love and gifts, and the next he'd be holding a gun to his head." A pause. "He's partners with Satan."

I arched a brow. "If the milk curdles, you know it's not the Devil playing tricks, right?"

She glanced over at me. "It's the only way I can explain the way he knew things. How he took delight in hurting us."

"Sounds to me like your darling husband doesn't need any help from Satan." I balled my fists in my pockets. "He's a snake all on his own."

"I'm not saying we shouldn't own our selfishness and pride. But if you're awake sixteen hours of the day, you're in a battle sixteen hours of the day. It's why you need the full armor of God."

I thought about telling her the demon dream, but I couldn't. Then I would end up telling her about the porn. My ears burned thinking of her discovering the truth.

***

A police officer was on the wraparound porch by the front door at Simon's Place when we returned from our walk. He was writing in his ticket book.

"Are you Simon?" he asked me as I mounted the steps.

"Yes sir."

"I'm Officer Rick Pendleton. I'll take a few minutes of your time."

What was this about?

John Golden.

What if he confiscated my work computer? It was at factory settings when I gave it to Bella. Besides, there was nothing illegal about watching porn.

The man who sins is a slave to sin.

But I didn't put it past him to embarrass me in front of Nora. Imagining the look on her face if she found out…

"Go inside, Nora."

"But…"

"I'll be right there."

Reluctantly, she turned and slipped inside.

"You must be new," I said.

"Yep." He pulled out his ticket book and began writing.

I glanced over his shoulder. "A thousand dollars?"

He looked uncomfortable. "Officer Golden said you knew."

"He said I was getting a warning," I sputtered.

Officer Pendleton ripped the ticket from the ticket book and handed it to me. "If you disagree you can tell the judge in court. There's a date on the ticket."

He turned around and bounded down the steps.

I clenched my fist and crumpled the ticket, shoving it in my pocket.

Nora stepped out. "What did he want?"

Without a word, I pulled her into my arms. I stroked through her windblown hair, my fingers buried in the tangled strands. I felt the heat of her breath against my face.

At once, I was kissing her. She responded as desperate, as needy. For a dizzying eternity, I was swimming in sensations, the scent of her, strawberries and vanilla.

The wind swept gusts around us, threatening to be a dry spring.

83
June 13, 2021

The sun was shining hot and bright, without a cloud in the sky. The land was dry in most parts of the state.

The Methodist church was a quaint brick building with large stained glass windows. There was a card table next to paraphernalia from the church and stacks of New Testament Bibles.

I peaked in the sanctuary, and saw The Cross against a red lectern cloth. The pulpit, adorned with a purple scarf etched with gold.

A rotund man in his sixties with balding hair and round glasses approached me. "Nice to have you join us today. I'm Pastor George." He thrust out his hand.

I shook it. "Simon Anderson." A pastor not afraid of germs. I liked him already.

"You from around here?" he asked.

"I own Simon's Place."

"Oh yes, I've heard you cook a mean steak."

"I've heard that too." I smiled.

A light came on in his eyes. "Wait. Do you know Pastor Johnson from the Methodist church in Wimbledon?"

"Yeah."

"He talked about you. Said you were going to be a preacher."

"That's when I was a kid."

"You know he's close to retiring," Pastor George said. "They'll need a good pastor soon."

"I never finished school. I…" …glanced over, and saw Nora. Dressed in a teal sundress, she lit up the sanctuary. "Excuse me," I murmured, and headed in her direction.

Nora spotted me and rushed over. "Simon. I can't believe you came." Sunshine in her eyes. "I thought you said you weren't going to do any pew warming."

"I guess your weekly invitation got under my skin."

"I'm glad." She glanced around, and whispered, "I wish I brought candy or something. My mouth tastes stale."

I dug in my pocket and pulled out a package of Pop Rocks. "Compliments of Sweets 'N Stories."

Her eyes widened as she took the candy. "I don't know, these might be pretty exciting for church."

"All the better." I smiled, motioning to the sanctuary with a tilt of my head. "Shall we?"

***

"For our struggle is not against flesh and blood, but against the rulers, against the authorities, against the powers of this dark world and against the spiritual forces of evil in the heavenly realms," Pastor George read from the Bible.

All heads bowed and eyes closed, he then prayed for the church, the community, the country, and rain.

Pastor George summarized the scripture reading, "The enemies are the Devil, your flesh, and being born children of wrath."

***

Afterward, a lady in her sixties with wire glasses and a constant smiled regaled stories of her house of cats and her Harold, who had been gone for five years.

I smiled, nodding at the appropriate places while ignoring the hollow ache of hunger creeping inside me.

She laid a hand on my arm. "After church, a few of us go to Donna's Diner for lunch. You're welcome to join us."

"Thanks, but I've got dinner in the oven." I couldn't help but wonder if the lack of social distancing drove John Golden nuts.

"Oh yes, Simon's Place?"

"Yes ma'am."

"Do you live there?"

"Yes."

She stepped closer. "Sure is a big house. Are you married? Do you have a family?"

I started to answer, and Nora cut in, "It was good seeing you, Bea, but we better get going."

"Thanks," I said for Nora's ears only as we made our way to our vehicles.

"No problem."

"I noticed Golden didn't show," I said, reaching my truck. There was a ticket beneath the windshield wiper. I snatched it. "What the…"

"Is it John?"

"Nope. Officer Pendleton." My jaw clenched. "Says 'For being parked too close to an intersection.'"

"I don't know Officer Pendleton."

"He's new."

"Oh." She walked the distance to the curb. "Doesn't look close to me. I wonder if he used a measuring tape."

Or Golden gave him the make, model, and license plate of my pickup.

She took the ticket from me and glanced at it. "It's only twenty dollars."

Only twenty dollars? It was a lot more. It was sleepless nights and dreams about demons.

I shook my head, unable to find my voice. At last, I said, "You know, suddenly I'm not hungry."

She frowned, "Over a parking ticket?"

I sighed loudly in frustration.

"You'll call me later?" she asked hesitantly.

"Sure."

***

On the way home, I went out of my way to drive past the police station. The squad car was parked out front. Officer Pendleton was in his office.

"Can I help you?" he asked when I walked in.

I held up the ticket. "I wanted to talk to you about this."

"Be happy to help, although the court date is on there."

"It's not about the ticket." I scratched my head with four quick fingers. "John Golden has it out for me."

Officer Pendleton's expression remained blank.

"Look. Just tell me if Golden told you to keep an eye on me."

He shifted in his chair. "It's not personal."

"Isn't it? He gave me a parking ticket outside Sweets 'N Stories because I was parked there five minutes after nine."

"You can talk to the chief if you want. He'll be in tomorrow."

"I'll think about it." I blew a long breath.

84
June 15, 2021

Charles came over to help install new shelving for food storage in the basement. Kevin hauled a load of beef and wheat for the restaurant. The three of us finished out the day with drinks on the wraparound deck.

Charles puffed his cigar. "This reminds me of opening day."

"Yeah," I said, sipping my Shirley Temple. I couldn't stop thinking about the Methodist church in Wimbledon and a chance to become a pastor. It seemed a pipe dream. Even so, I wasn't taking any chances.

"I went to church yesterday," I told them.

"Nice Prodigal," Kevin said. "Pastor George is quite the guy."

"The Methodist church is real strict. Him being in the bar and all, perked my interest too." Charles puffed his cigar.

"In the bar?" I asked.

"Preaching," Kevin corrected. "He's been known to hold adult Men's Bible Study there. Occasionally, he'll have a beer with the after-work crowd."

A seed of hope started to bloom like a kernel of wheat in my gut. Perhaps I didn't need to be perfect to preach. "Doug still haul for Anderson Bros.?" I asked.

"When he feels like it," Kevin took a sip of his coffee. "I should really fire him, but then I'd have to deal with Mom."

"Yeah. I've had my share of crazy people," I said, wishing to retract the words as they emerged from my mouth.

"Oh yeah?" Charles' eyes lit with interest.

I found myself telling them about John Golden, from the day I ran into them on the highway with a flat, until church yesterday.

"Talk to the chief." Charles blew a smoke ring. "Dell is his last name. I helped him with some remodeling on the police station last year. Seemed like a stand-up guy."

"You know him?" Hope burst inside me. "I don't suppose you'd be willing to go with me to talk to him. You see, John Golden is a pretty big deal in town. Even Nora thinks he's a good cop even if he was a not-so-good husband."

"You tell her about the harassment, Simon?" Kevin asked. "She was married to the jerk. I'll be she saw the not-so-sunny side of him."

"No. Although she was there when Pendleton gave me the tickets."

"I thought you two were pretty serious." Kevin leaned back.

"I'm not going to tattle to her about every little thing happening in my day."

Kevin smiled. "Why not? Women love it when you do. I know Gretchen does. Then she kisses me to make it better."

Charles chuckled. "Tell Nora. The kiss will be worth it even if she dozes off listening to you."

I downed the last swallow of my drink.

Charles tapped ash on the tray. "Women accrue a much higher stake in the game of love. Like pregnancy, feelings, and emotions."

"Wow, Charles. Well put," I said.

"Simon, about John Golden…," Kevin fingered the handle of his mug. "Life is like a spider web of choices, one leading to another. Choices we make can't be undone. If you ever get the opportunity to pardon someone, including yourself, don't wait."

"When did you two become philosophers?" I sighed. "I'll talk to her."

85

Eight-thirty.

I bounded up the steps, whistling the theme to The Andy Griffith Show. Reaching the top, the door burst open, and Nora came tumbling out.

I raised two Styrofoam cups of coffee in the air. "Whoa, Nora."

"Look in the dryer." She groaned.

"What?"

"Follow me," she turned around, and I trailed behind.

"Look." She was shaking.

I caught a glimpse of black fur laying amidst damp laundry

In a quick, smooth motion, I set the coffee on the dryer, and ducked my head into the open drum. Pulling Boris from the dryer, steam rose from his damp fur.

"I killed him," Nora said over and over, clutching the sides of her head.

"Nora," I said sharply.

She gave me a blank stare.

"Do you have a fan?"

"In my closet."

"We'll need it." I made my way to the kitchen and filled a glass with water. Kneeling down, I splashed water on the steamed kitten. "Plug the fan in and point it in his direction."

"I heard the clunking and thought it was a shoe." She turned the fan on, soon the breeze reached Boris. "I killed him."

"Not yet you haven't." I continued to splash water on Boris' steaming fur.

Nora knelt down next to me. "He's still alive?"

I stroked his fur. "Seems to be."

Boris rolled to his side, stood, and flopped back down.

"Will he be okay?" Nora hiccuped sobs.

"He's overheated." I looked up. "How long was he in there?"

Nora wiped her forearm across her dripping nose. "Probably twenty minutes?" She covered her mouth.

"Hey." My voice was sharp in my ears. "Breathe."

Nora drew a breath and shuddered.

I turned the fan to low and grabbed the box of Kleenex on the counter and handed it to her.

She blew her nose. "Thanks."

A few moments passed where I worked on cooling Boris.

Nora searched "drying my cat" on her phone.

Boris worked on rising and falling until he was able to take a few steps across the floor, and vomited.

Nora grabbed the paper towels, and proceeded to clean the barf. "I guess drying your cat isn't uncommon. This one girl dried her cat for ten minutes, then freaked out and put him in the freezer. The vet gave the kitty something for shock and inflammation."

"What happened to it?"

"It lived, apparently."

I watched Boris weave around the linoleum floor. "Seems to be trying to walk. A good sign."

"It was the last load of laundry. He must have been playing in the clothes. I guess I was daydreaming when I filled the dryer." Nora grabbed a towel from the basket of clothes.

I set Boris in the nest I made in front of the fan. "He's a tough one. Don't they say cats have nine lives? If he makes it, you should call him 'DK' for Dryer Kitty."

"Ha ha."

"I'll finish the laundry," I said.

"I won't argue with you."

Boris was asleep and Nora was relaxing on the couch when I returned. "Coffee's cold," I held up the cups. "You know what's worse than coffee?"

"What?"

"Cold coffee." I set the cups on the kitchen counter.

"If you don't like coffee, why do you drink it?"

"Because everyone drinks it." I flipped on the faucet, and scrubbed my hands. "I put the clothes back in the washer. In case Boris was dizzy in the dryer and puked on them."

"Poor thing."

I glanced over my shoulder. "What do you expect after a twenty-minute tumble in the dryer?"

Nora handed me a towel. "Thanks for bringing me morning coffee, saving my cat, and…waiting for me."

"No problem. Glad I was here." I wiped my hands. "The back door was open."

"What?"

"When I went to do the laundry, I saw the door was open a crack."

"I didn't leave it open."

"Huh."

"You don't think someone came in and put Boris in the dryer."

I shrugged. "You'd have to be crazy."

"Yeah you would."

But I couldn't shake the feeling something was off.

"Everything okay?" she asked.

"I want to talk to you about something." I rubbed the back of my neck. "Do you have stuff for tea?"

"Yes."

86

Nora set her teacup on the end table next to her. "You don't know how happy it makes me to hear what a jerk he's been to you."

"What?" I laughed.

"Everyone in town says he's the best cop. Everyone at church loves him. Even Pastor George."

"Strange. I think of Pastor George as a smart guy."

"John's good at being nice when it suits him. He only shows the dark side to a select few."

I rested my arm on the back of the loveseat. "Why did you stay with him so long?"

"John didn't attend church before we got married. Afterward, he took to it like a bee to honey, diving in, and delivering meals to shut-ins. He is the special music part of the service. He sings like an angel.

"The day we were married, he told me what to wear, what to say, who I could talk to. What to think. If I didn't do everything just so, he would lose his mind." She swallowed visibly.

"I did wonder how you got away from him."

"I…" she looked down at her lap, "…Felt sorry for him."

I held a tight grip on my cup to keep from reaching for her.

"Every now and then, there would be a week where John would lavish attention on me. I lapped it up like a starving dog. Then he would ignore me for weeks on end," she said, her eyes, haunted.

"I thought it was sweet when he bought me clothes, even while being embarrassed by the attention the outfits drew from men. Then bit by bit, I looked forward to seeing appreciation in their eyes."

Lust. "I'm the last person who should point fingers."

"John was real subtle. I didn't notice the changes until one day I looked in the mirror and didn't recognize the woman staring back at me."

"Did he...?" I searched for the right words. "...Coerce you into...hanging out with the swingers?"

She nodded, averting her gaze. "At first, I thought he was merely open to the lifestyle. After the first time, I stood up to him and told him no more. He was..." She shivered. "...very convincing."

My jaw clenched. "He hurt you?"

"Not physically." Her eyes shadowed with fear. "At least, in the beginning."

"Did you tell anyone?"

She shook her head. "Who would I tell? John had a lot of friends. Fellow cops were like brothers. Besides, what would I say? He had a clean history, and never did anything criminal," She sighed. "Nothing he could get arrested for anyway."

"He brainwashed you, Nora. He managed three things, desensitizing, jamming, and conversion." I removed my arm and sat forward, glancing back at her. "You were lucky to escape. How did you do it?"

"John moved to Park River, and I refused to go with him. When he begged me to reconsider, I realized how weak of a man he really was, and stood up to him." She flushed pink. "It's embarrassing to remember how he ran like a dog with his tail between his legs. He talked a big game, but when it came down to it, he was a coward. And I was..."

"The bravest woman I know." I gave her a tender smile.

The color in her cheeks deepened. "I was going to say silly, but I'll take it. Me and the boys moved to California, and bam," She snapped her fingers, "It didn't matter if he ever saw us again."

"It sure matters to him now."

A humorless laugh burst from her lips. "Not because he loves me. I doubt he ever did. He's afraid someone stole his favorite toy."

"I know I have no right to say this, but I want you to stay as far away from John Golden as you can."

Oh yeah? What are you going to do?

"You don't think he had anything to do with Boris being in the dryer."

I shrugged. "I mean it. He shows up at your work, call me. He shows up at church, call me. He shows up at your house…"

She held up a halting hand. "Let me guess, call you?"

My heart took flight at the look in her eyes.

87
August 13, 2021

The Taliban overran three key cities in Afghanistan, inching government closer to collapse in the final days of the U.S. withdrawal.

I cleaned the house, top to bottom, and made myself a peanut butter and jelly sandwich I ate standing in the kitchen. Cup of tea in hand, I made my way upstairs, and sat on the loveseat in the large hallway outside my room. I drank my tea, and glanced at the clock: Ten minutes after three. I had all afternoon and a whole evening ahead of me.

***

"Simon. Wake up." Charles stood over me.

"Huh?" I cracked my eye open, and wiped my mouth with the back of my hand. "Charles? What are you doing here?"

He flicked a photograph at me.

"What's this?"

"You tell me."

I picked it up and glanced at it briefly. My stomach took a dive. The picture was of Melissa and me on the living room couch at my house growing up. I remembered her taking a picture of me, but hadn't realized she'd taken one with me and her. We were both dressed, but clearly drunk, and the worst of it, together.

"I can explain," I said, pushing to my feet.

"You got her drunk," Charles accused, his eyes bloodshot. "This looks like it was taken about the time we were engaged." His nostrils flared.

"Can I get you a drink?" I asked, heading for the stairs.

"Seriously?" His voice shook with rage. "No I don't want a drink." He swore.

When we reached the foot of the stairs, he grabbed my arm. "You just going to walk away?"

"No." I cleared my throat. "Doug and I got drunk," I said matter-of-factly. "I passed out. Doug disappeared. She called and asked for you and I told her you weren't there. The next thing I knew, she was over at the house, making drinks."

"Did you have sex?"

"No," I said emphatically, a little too emphatically. I sounded horribly guilty.

"She said you kissed her." He cut me a hard stare. "Did you? Don't lie to me."

The room around me grew smaller, and I swallowed hard. "Yes, but it didn't mean anything."

"It didn't mean anything," he echoed, anger vibrated through his voice. "You made out with my wife and it didn't mean anything."

"She wasn't your wife then." I ran a shaky hand through my hair.

"My fiancée. I introduced you." Another slew of expletives flew from his lips.

Indignation boiled inside me. "Now wait a minute. What are you mad at me for? She's the one who came over when I had too much to drink."

"She's nothing to me, Simon. I'm even embarrassed to call her my ex-wife. To me, she's just somebody I used to know. But you, you're my brother," his voice cracked, pain flooding his face. "I trusted you."

He turned to leave, stopped, and turned around. Then he hauled back. His fist crashed into my temple. An explosion of pain ripped through my eye.

The hurt in his eyes made me wish I was dead.

Then, with a look of disgust, he turned and walked out the door.

"What happened?" Nora passed Charles coming in the front door.

"A picture from the past." Charles stalked out.

Nora left the room and came back with a frozen bag of peas. "Can I see the picture?" She touched the bag to my temple.

I winced, pulling slightly back. "He got my good eye too."

"Hold still." Once again the frozen bag was against my eye. I stiffened, but didn't move.

"Is it...pornography?"

"No."

"But it must be bad, or he wouldn't have punched you."

Might as well show her. Charles wasn't ever going to speak to me again, and he was the only one who believed me about John Golden besides Nora.

I handed her the picture.

"I know it looks bad," I mumbled, continuing through her silence. "She took it to blackmail me."

She cleared her throat. "You're saying she took a picture over twenty years ago to cause a fight?"

"I knew you wouldn't believe me."

"I believe you."

My gaze met hers and I winced. "Shouldn't move my head so fast."

"Don't forget I was married to John. Would you like to tell me about it?"

"Yes," I said, eagerly regaling poker night, and the ones after. The bad grades, up until the opening day of Simon's Place. Guilt lifted, and I felt clean for the first time in decades.

Nora's eyes filled with compassion. "What a horrible person she was. If anything, you should be commended for getting away from her."

"I tried to tell Kevin at the wedding, but at the time, he found the story unbelievable. Can't say I blame him."

"She's the reason you never married," Nora said, her voice lifted with recognition.

"Nah." I smiled, flinching at the pain. "You were."

88
August 16, 2021

The Taliban seized control of Afghanistan after three short days of President Biden's decision to withdraw U.S. troops.

"You need a barn to milk them, a milkhouse," Kevin mused when I told him my idea of going organic with the dairy.

I nodded. "And a feedlot and pasture."

"The section south of Section Ten could work," he said. "The house is still there too."

"Really? I thought Trey would have claimed it by now."

"Naw. He and Trina are moving to Oakes. He's going to work for Charles."

"Thanks Kevin." I hung up the phone and tried Charles' number, a sad ache working its way inside me. He hadn't talked to me since the blowup. I tried calling, but he wouldn't answer. I left a voicemail. He didn't answer. I showed up to his house, his girlfriend Beth said he wouldn't talk to me.

After the sixth ring, I gave up and called Pastor Johnson.

"Hello?"

"Pastor Johnson? This is Simon Anderson. I don't know if you remember me, but I used to attend church in Wimbledon back when you were a new pastor."

"I remember you, Simon." There was a smile in his voice. "How have you been? How's the restaurant business?"

"Real good."

"I was sorry when you didn't become a pastor."

"I might be doing a little farming up there. Twenty milk cows. Nothing serious. Pastor George says you might be retiring?"

"Yes. In a year or two is my plan."

Silence on the other end.

Then, "Are you considering the position?"

"I'd like to." I tucked the phone in the crook of my neck. "I don't know what I'm qualified for, but I'm willing to do whatever it takes."

"There's practicum you could do. If you are available, you could work under me while you're finishing your courses. We should really discuss this in person. What are you doing Sunday after church?"

"I don't have plans as of yet."

"Come to church, and we'll have lunch at the Café. It's in the old Red Owl now, you know, instead of where it used to be by the post office."

"I'll be there." I hung up.

The idea both terrified me and thrilled me. I was over the porn addiction. I could be a pastor now.

The silverware clock said it was eight-thirty. I started to walk out the back door, and my eye caught the open laptop on the breakfast table. The work space clutter looked eerily familiar. Bella must have forgotten it.

Was this some kind of test?

I hadn't been on a site since Bella became manager. What would one video hurt? A mild one. I flicked a glance around.

No one will know.

I sat down at the computer, my blood pounding hot through my veins.

But each person is tempted when he is lured and enticed by his own desire.

I slammed the laptop down, stood, and paced the small kitchen space. I returned to my chair, and lifted the screen.

318

Then desire when it has conceived gives birth to sin, and sin when it is fully grown brings forth death.

Intoxicated by my own raw desire, I instinctively knew this wasn't merely a bad idea, but a fatal one.

89
August 18, 2021

"What's the special?" Bella asked, tying her apron as she strolled into the kitchen.

"Prime rib sandwich with choice of side, and boneless wings, anyway you like them." Jordan set a frying pan on the stove.

Bella slipped out to the dining room.

"How's Boris doing?" I asked.

Before Jordan could answer, Bella burst into the kitchen. "Luke Doric is in the dining room. He says last time he ate here, his burger wasn't cooked."

Jordan's face turned two shades of red, and his eyes dropped to his tennis shoes.

I clamped my hand on his shoulder. "Wash your hands and I'll show you how to cook a burger."

"I'll never be able to do it like you do," he mumbled.

"Nonsense. Let's give it one more try."

He appeared unconvinced. In fact, he looked like he was going to be sick.

"Don't you want to see the expression on Luke Doric's face when he tastes the burger, knowing you were behind the magic?"

Jordan flipped on the faucet. "Making burgers isn't magic."

I grabbed a stick of butter from the fridge. "It could be."

***

Jenna strolled out to the dining room with Luke Doric's burger basket. I hurried over to the barricade, motioning Jordan over. I opened it a crack in time to hear Jenna ask, "Can I get you anything else?"

Luke poked his burger with a fork. He took a taste, his eyes growing wide in surprise. Taking two more quick bites, he praised through a mouthful, "Fantastic."

I glanced over at Jordan. "What'd I tell you?" Stepping back from the divider I saw Nora at the bar. Her eyes brimming with unshed tears, she turned and hurried out of the restaurant.

I flicked a glance at Golden. He took a bite of his burger, looking nonchalant.

I turned around and slipped out the back door. Nora was parked on the street south. I ran toward her. "Nora."

Struggling with her keys, she wouldn't look at me.

"What's wrong?" I asked, reaching her.

"Nothing." Her voice wobbled.

I took her hand. "Come back inside."

"But you're busy…"

"Come with me," I said, leading her inside, through the kitchen, and to the basement. "I wanted to make sure we aren't overheard." I turned to her. "What did he do?"

"It doesn't matter. I'm fine."

"It matters to me."

She pressed her lips together and I saw the fear in her eyes.

Dropping her gaze, Nora murmured, "I shouldn't have let him get under my skin." She wrapped her arms around herself. "He didn't do anything. Anyway, it's not like I don't deserve it. After we got divorced, I knew I should buy more modest clothing, but…"

"Nora," I put my finger beneath her chin, lifting her gaze.

The tears spilled over. My jaw clenched. At the sight of her tears, my mind was wiped clean of logic. I turned around and headed for the stairs.

"What are you going to do?" She rushed up behind me.

And after you have done everything, to stand. "Something I should have done a long time ago."

"He'll get mad and blame me. Everyone knows I'm oversensitive. Anyway, I'm just as bad. He always said I cave whenever..."

I stopped and turned around, gripping her shoulders. The fear in her eyes ripped me apart. The Nora I remembered wasn't afraid of anything. "It is not your fault," I said, putting emphasis on each word. "He's a predator."

Fury rising, threatening to boil over, I marched into the dining room. Drawing the attention of every diner there, I walked up to John Golden. "I'd like you to leave."

His eyes rounded. "I haven't finished my dinner."

Mine narrowed. "You're finished."

He wiped his hands on his jeans, pushed away from the table, and stood. "Fine. Food sucks here anyway." He reached for his wallet.

"Be sure you leave a tip," I gritted.

"I don't need you to escort me." His gaze hardened.

I smiled slowly. "It would be my pleasure."

90
August 20, 2021

In the news, Maine's oldest lobster trapper had no plans to retire at 101. In my kitchen, Nora was eating peanut butter cups at six in the morning.

"We're a lot alike." Nora handed me another peanut butter cup.

"Sounds familiar." I said good-naturedly.

"You stuck up for me," she said. "Right in front of everyone, you told him to leave."

"I was running on adrenalin more than logic. I suppose I should be ready for him to double down." I tore open the peanut butter cup.

"Brace yourself, Simon."

I paused, the chocolate halfway to my mouth.

"John resigned."

My mouth gaped. "What? Really? Why? Who told you?"

She laughed, a happy sounding one. "Chief Dell wouldn't share the details with me. He came into Sweets 'N Stories for a latte. He always orders a latte every morning we are open.

"Anyway, this morning, on his way out, he said, 'Oh by the way, John resigned from his position. He's moving to McHenry and is going to be a deputy for the county,' and walked out."

Too easy. John Golden was just going to go away? Leave behind his ex-wife and two sons?

He had to.

"I wonder why?" I mused.

"Who cares? As long as it's not here."

"What about you and the kids?"

"Jordan's going to culinary school and Dane and Olivia have their own lives." She crumpled the wrapper. "I'll stay where I'm at. I like working at Sweets 'N Stories."

"His timing could have been better." I chuckled. "I plan to move out to the farm, and he decides…"

Nora's eyes widened. "You're moving?"

I nodded. "I sufficiently fazed myself out of Simon's Place. Bella manages the staff and does the ordering. I'll come once a week to see how things are going." I ran a shaky hand over my hair. "Dane and Olivia will stay at the house."

"I thought you like cooking."

"I've always wanted to preach. You could…" …*marry me*. But she couldn't. She would have to quit Sweets 'N Stories. And would I really come back once a week between milking? Suddenly, the memory of the demand of dairy hit me. "Pastor Johnson said I could help at the church. Maybe even take over one day."

Silence followed.

"Have you thought this through? I mean, about being a pastor? It wasn't too long ago you didn't even want to warm a church pew because God knew your heart."

Every word she spoke was like a flaming knife to my gut. She'd always known what was going on inside me. At one time endearing, now infuriated me.

"You know what? Forget it." I slapped my hands against the sides of my jeans in wild frustration. "I don't know why I even told you."

"You don't need to go back and fix things." Her tender gaze met mine. "Anyway, you can't."

"I don't know what you're talking about." I'd always known I wasn't good enough for her. Apparently, she knew it too.

"You made choices, I made choices. Neither of us can go back. You chose a restaurant over milking cows or being a pastor."

"And now I'm choosing to become the pastor I was always supposed to be," I insisted, even as I sank beneath the weight of her words.

"People depend on you here. Bella, for one. You put her in charge, but she needs you around for advice. Like it or not, Dane looks up to you. Olivia can't wait until you take them shooting again. And don't get me started on Jordan. He actually looks me in the eye now."

"What about you?"

"What about me?"

"Do you...depend on me?"

She pressed her lips together. "Can I depend on you?"

"You better not," I bit out. "I'm leaving. I'm moving to my old place in the country, and I will be a pastor." I turned around and stormed out the door.

You seek the heights of manhood when you seek the depths of God.

Edwin Louis Cole

91
August 26, 2021

It was dark in the wee hours of the morning. I glanced at the glowing digits of the clock.

Three-thirty.

In the distance, thunder rolled. A flicker of lightning flashed outside my bedroom window.

I rolled out of bed and dressed in the moonlight. Stepping out the back door, hot wind whipped through the alley. Lightning lit the sky as far as I could see. Thunder shook around me.

I climbed into my pickup. I'd gone to bed angry and frustrated, but this morning, I was thankful I hadn't given in to temptation.

I held my head up.

The atmosphere was charged, electrifying.

I started the pickup and made my way out of town.

Giant raindrops began to fall on the dry earth around me, hitting the windshield. I drove north.

It took seven minutes of holding my head high before my forehead wrinkled in frustration and my mouth tightened. Nora's words pounded over me like the rain on the roof.

Can I depend on you? Depend on me for what exactly? Her life was perfect. John Golden was leaving, so what did she need me for? She never once told me she loved me or asked me to stay.

You were the one who chose to eat poison.

Despair unlike I had ever known crashed over me in a wave, pinning me beneath. I struggled to rise above, but couldn't get on top.

Flashes of light burst through the darkness, rain hammering on the roof, thundering around me. The windshield wipers raced back and forth.

I gripped the wheel. I was nearly on the vehicle ahead before I saw the glowing red lights. I pressed the brakes. The pedal went to the floor. The truck barely decreased in speed. My heart did a funny thump in my chest. Stomping the brakes, I held a white-knuckled fist on the wheel, and the truck didn't slow down.

A shot of adrenalin slammed me.

Stay calm.

No one adds a day to his life by panicking.

I reached down and hit the hazards.

Think! I cut the engine, and lost all power steering.

Pumping the brakes, I careened through the darkness, and prayed, "Our Father, who art in heaven…" I trailed off. "I know I haven't…spoken to you in a while, but if you're there, and if you're listening…" I stopped. "If you still care, I need help. Please answer me quickly, for I'm in trouble."

Lightning flashed, illuminating the interior. I glanced over and a woman with blonde hair, dressed in white and bright as the sun, was in the passenger seat.

"Am I going to die?" I asked her.

She began to sing, a sweet heavenly tune. I saw my own death on the gloomy horizon.

Felt it when the wheel hit the ditch.

Saw the world turn over and over.

With peace like a river flowing over me, the angel of death sang next to me.

***

In the early morning light, I blinked up at the sky. I was lying on my back in a soybean field, rain pouring down on me.

"He's over here," I heard someone shout. It sounded like Chief Dell.

Then Charles stood over me, looking haggard, his eyes were red. I must be dead. Charles never cried.

"How did…" Was there mud in my throat?

"He's trying to say something," Charles told Chief Dell.

"It's a miracle he's alive," Dell said. "He wasn't wearing his seatbelt."

Thirsty Ground

92

Mom's car pulled into the back alley right before noon. She exited the Prius, Doug in tow. I opened the back door as she reached for the handle.

"This is why you need a cell phone," she said, barreling past me.

"Hello to you too, Mother."

Doug came in behind her, holding up a crock pot. "Knoephla."

"Thanks, Mom," I said, taking the soup from Doug. "Can I get you something to drink?"

"A glass of wine, please," she said, plopping down at the breakfast nook. "Doug won't be having anything alcoholic."

I arched a brow at Doug. He shrugged.

I poured Mom a glass of red wine and opened the fridge. "Doug, I've got milk, water, pineapple juice..."

"He'll take pineapple juice," Mom said. "I want to hear all about it. When Kevin called and told me, I knew I was right about you giving up your phone."

"I can't recall a whole lot, but Charles said Chief Dell called him when he found my truck in the ditch," I said, handing Doug the glass of juice. Then I told them what I'd learned of the events.

Doug took a sip of his juice. "November of last year, I was on I-29 going north from Fargo to Grand Forks. It was foggy. Didn't think anything of it until I went to pass a car doing thirty-five. I hit a patch of black ice and spun into the ditch, ending up in oncoming traffic."

Mom's eyes widened. "You never told me."

He shrugged. "No big deal."

"I remember now!" Mom's face lit up. "Jeffy Morris got into a fender bender that same day. It was around two when…"

They regaled tales of near misses, and I found myself reevaluating the choices I'd made.

***

The moon hung like an omen in the late afternoon sky, its large craters forming a mocking smile. Sitting on the veranda, the horror of events created a mood as foul as the dairy barn on a hot summer day.

Like the moon, my future was cold and ominous.

Nora's Dodge Intrepid pulled along the side street. She got out and glanced toward me. I stood and waved her over.

"How are you doing?" I asked.

"How am I doing?" she echoed, mounting the steps. "I should be asking how you are doing."

"Still alive. Want to sit down? I have hot cocoa and an extra blanket." I held it up. "Are you hungry? My mom brought knoephla."

"I'm good," she said, sitting down.

I sat across from her. "Did you know drivers who are thrown from a vehicle during a crash are twenty-five times more likely to die than those who were wearing seatbelts."

"You don't say." She caught my gaze. "Charles said the cab was completely crushed and you shouldn't be alive. Said it took them a half hour to find you."

"I guess I shut the engine off at one point. You'd think I would remember something. Freaks me out how it's totally blank." I fingered the handle of my mug. "Did Charles tell you someone cut my brakes?"

Her mouth dropped open. "You don't think… I mean, I can't imagine John doing that. He would lose his job, and John would die first."

"The police are looking into it." I took a sip from my mug. "What are you nervous about?"

"I'm not nervous."

"You're playing with your hands."

She folded them on her lap. "I'm thankful you're alive and okay."

"I don't remember much. It's like bits and pieces of a dream. I remember laying in a dark field and rain."

She flicked me a haunted look. "When Charles called me, he sounded…let's just say, he thought you were dead."

"He said I told him I saw an angel and she was singing to me. I don't remember or even telling him about it."

"Are you still going to the farm?" She pressed her lips together.

"Yeah. Kevin said he'll meet me out there in the morning." Truth was, I had no idea what to do. Could I really decide in a blink of an eye to give up a lifelong dream? For what? The most important words seemed to be the hardest.

"Well." We both said it at exactly the same time.

"I need to see if being there will shed some light on a few things." I reached over and put my hand on hers. "Can I call you when I get back?"

"I'd like that."

After she left, I called Dane. He answered after the first ring. "Hey Simon. Did you get my rent check?"

"Yeah."

"I meant to back pay, but…"

"No back pay. I appreciate the offer, but monthly payments from here on out is sufficient." I drew a breath. "I need to ask you something about your mom."

93

Charles insisted on driving me to Section Ten the next morning, and waited in the pickup while I got out and roamed my old haunt.

Surrounded by cottonwoods, the silhouette of the house outlined the pale pink eastern skyline. Grazing cattle beneath the peaceful rise of the morning sun, a bittersweet memory.

Inside the house, empty walls held no promise of the past. Walking upstairs and down, memories lingered.

Nora came to mind. *For this reason a man leaves his father and mother.* I walked outside the house, the dream of becoming a pastor disappearing in the morning sunshine.

I tilted my head toward heaven and thanked the Lord for my life.

Kevin's pickup pulled up. He got out and waved. Making his way toward me, he called, "Makes you nostalgic, doesn't it?"

"A bit," I said. "Kevin, I can't go back to milking. I don't even want to. I'm sorry, I don't know why it was important for so long."

"I figured."

"You did?"

He shoved his hands into his pockets. "Sure. Who wants to be married to the dairy when you could be with Nora running your restaurant?"

"I don't want to preach either." I scratched the back of my neck.

"Who says you have to be a preacher to spread the Good News? Take me and Gretchen, for instance."

"I'll leave the repopulating of the planet to you two."

He laughed. "I mean in the little things in life. Letting your light shine. Sharing your faith." He chucked my shoulder. "Standing firm."

I didn't know what my future held, or if Nora wanted me. But I would not die, I would live, and shine my light for all to see.

Death comes for us all eventually.

But not today.

94

"...Police say Anderson lost control of his vehicle, careened into the ditch, where his vehicle hit an approach. Police say Simon Anderson, who was not restrained at the time of the collision, was ejected from his vehicle and was transported to the Medical Center in Jamestown where he was treated for minor injuries."

We ate a late lunch with Kevin's family. After taking turns shooting clay targets, it was almost six by the time we headed back.

Charles reached over and turned down the radio. "Mom's moving to Rapid City. She's been seeing her attorney, Daren Kliche. That's where he's from."

"South Dakota? What's she going to do there?"

He shrugged. "Spend his money. Supposedly he comes from family money, and a lot of it."

"I can't imagine Doug living at the farm alone."

He glanced over at me. "He's moving to Rapid City too."

"Now that I can imagine." I tapped a knuckle against the window. "Mom selling the farm then?"

"Doubt it. Then she wouldn't have anything to hold over Dad."

Silence.

Charles said, "You really don't remember seeing an angel?"

"Nope."

"You were thrown pretty far. Took us a half hour to find you. I gotta tell you, I was pretty sure we wouldn't find you alive."

"I don't remember much about it, thank goodness."

"Do you have any idea who might have cut your brake line?"

"Officer John Golden would be at the top of my list."

He slammed his fist against the wheel. "I told Chief Dell about him."

I held my hand up. "It might not have been him who cut the brakes."

"Who else would have done it?" Charles asked.

A tremor rolled through me. Who else indeed?

His phone buzzed. Charles answered, "Hi Chief Dell." He glanced over at me. "What? Black and white you say? I'll ask him. Sure. Okay thanks for calling."

"What did he say?"

"Do you own a black cat?"

"Nora does. I gave it to her for Christmas." My stomach clenched. "Why?"

"Apparently, there was black fur and blood smeared all over the engine of your truck."

95

The sun hung low in the west behind her house when Nora answered the door. "Simon. I was wondering when…"

"Charles dropped me off. Is Boris…?"

Just then, Boris strolled over, rubbing himself against her legs.

My knees wobbled with relief. "Oh, thank goodness."

She stepped to the side, her brow furrowed in concern. "Would you like to come in? Supper's about done."

I kicked my shoes off in the entrance, the savory aroma of cooked carrots, onions, chicken and celery wafted toward me. "Smells good. What is it?"

"Pot pie."

Boris brushed himself against my leg. I sat down. "How was Sweets 'N Stories?" I removed my cap and set it on the chair on the right.

"Good. Mrs. Otto was there. She said to tell Pastor George to pray for you in church." She removed the pie from the oven and set it in the center of the table on hot pads.

Sitting down across from me, she took her oven mitts off and set them on the chair next to her. "Would you like to say the blessing?" She held her hand out.

I slipped my hand in hers, and bowed my head. "Dear Lord, we thank you for this food and the woman whose hands prepared it."

"What did you want to talk to me about?" She poured two glasses of water.

I took a sip from mine. "You know how when you turn on a switch, the light doesn't change what's in the room? It only shows the way things really are.

"My old house at Section Ten was like a light switch, and I was able to see who I really am."

"A pastor? Dairy farmer?"

"Forgiven." I caught her gaze. "I realized there was no point of a house unless it was home. There's no home without you."

"Simon." Her eyes shined with the brilliance of a thousand suns.

The way she said my name brought me to my knees in front of her. Her eyes growing wide, she pushed away from the table as I fumbled in my pocket for the ring. I pulled the red velvet box out and popped it open. "Will you marry me? I know I don't deserve you, but I…"

"Yes."

My hands were shaking so badly, I blew a sigh of relief when it finally slid it into place. Then her arms were around me, her face against my neck.

At last, she pulled back slightly. "You knew you were going to ask me even before you went out to meet Kevin."

I smiled. "Yeah, I knew."

"And the ring," questions flickered in her eyes. "How did you know what size to get? It fits perfectly."

"I called Dane."

Her eyes widened. "Dane knew my ring size?"

"No, but he asked Jordan. Turns out Jordan has a keen eye for that sort of thing."

She nodded. "He might not be a chatterbox, but not much gets past him."

My ears grew warm. "He may have given some tips on the style you would like."

338

"If the boys know and you have a ring…" Her forehead crinkled. "How long have you known you were going to ask me to marry you? I mean, when did you decide?"

I scrubbed my jaw. "When I was nine."

***

After supper and dishes, we watched the brilliant colors of the sunset in her back yard.

Nora turned and laid her hands on my chest. "I am the luckiest woman in the world."

I lifted my head, my gaze locked with hers. "And I'm the luckiest man." I pulled her into my arms.

My future was still a cloud. John Golden's departure didn't make me feel better. My gut said he killed the cat. Which meant he wasn't really gone. What had John Golden done he had to skip town practically overnight?

The scent of lavender in my nostrils, I set my lips to hers. Her arms found their way around my shoulders. My hat tipped beneath her fingertips, falling to the ground.

I would not worry what I would do.

I would simply stand.

96
September 25, 2021

The air on our wedding night was winter chilly. For the reception, propane lamps were scattered about the veranda. I danced with my bride. She wore her red winter coat over ivory and lace, looking quite the Midwestern bride.

In a tux and no coat, I held Nora close, relishing the warmth radiating from her body. "When You Say Nothing At All" played in the background.

Mr. Lichte from Wimbledon was in attendance.

Bella and Jenna too.

Nora's mom attended the ceremony and left before the reception. Frail and thin, Rachel Toogoody was a shadow of the woman I remembered. She smiled, laying a hand on my arm, and said, "Simon. I'm happy it's come to this."

I smiled back. "Me too."

Mom went to Paris with Daren Kliche. Doug went too. The only two not in attendance from my family, making for a total of fifty-five family members in attendance.

The sun set a little after seven.

Alongside us, Olivia and Dane swayed to the music.

Jordan tentatively drew up next to me.

The song ended, and I stepped back. "Hey Jordan. How's school?" Jordan was in his first week of culinary school at Moorhead State University.

"Lame." He balled his fists in his pockets. "A lot of boring stuff about contamination and food waste."

I chucked his shoulder. "Makes for a good restaurant owner."

"I want to cook." He sighed. "We have to wear masks too."

"At least it's only an eighteen-month school." I grabbed Nora's wine glass off the table and handed it to her.

Thomas and Seth emerged from the house. Spotting Jordan, they hurried over. "Hey Jordan. Want to play *League of Legends*?"

Jordan's eyes lit. "Yeah."

"Got room for two more?" Olivia asked.

"Sure," Seth said.

The five of them dashed into the house.

Charles strolled over. "You two look good together."

"Thanks." I glanced down at Nora. Her eyes were shining with happiness.

"Chief Dell said they arrested Luke Doric for cutting your brake line," Charles said. "I guess he admitted it right away."

My chest went cold. "He was a good customer at Simon's Place."

Charles pinned me with a stare. "Luke told Chief Dell Melissa left him because of you."

"Me?" I scowled. "She was your wife."

Charles shrugged. "She always told me she married the wrong brother."

"Charles, you have no idea…"

He clamped his hand on my shoulder. "I know. You don't have to tell me she was nuts."

"The woman is pure evil." I clenched my fists. "She probably sat back and watched. She loved drama and attention. Even negative."

"I can't picture Luke Doric killing a cat, and rubbing the carcass on the pickup engine," Nora shivered.

341

"Are you cold?" I drew my arm around her shoulders.

"It's probably the wine." She tucked herself against me, keeping a tight grip on her glass.

"Doric said he didn't kill the cat." Charles took a sip of whisky. "He confessed to cutting the brake line, but said he would never stoop low enough to killing an innocent animal."

I gave a laugh. "Of course not. You don't suppose Melissa might have done it?"

Charles scrubbed his jaw. "It's possible. I wouldn't put it past her."

Nora laid her head on my shoulder. "How many crazy people can one person attract, Simon?"

"A wise woman once said, if you're awake sixteen hours of the day, you're fighting a war sixteen hours of the day." I smiled at her.

She smiled back, the white lights from the windows shimmering in her golden eyes.

Kevin made his way over, and held his glass up. "I propose a toast to the bride and groom."

I reached for mine from the table next to us.

"Here's to my brother Simon, and his long awaited wife Nora. May you both live to a ripe old age with many happy years in between." Charles clinked his glass with mine.

Nora held up hers. "I'll drink to that."

97

It was nearly midnight before the guests left and the food was put away. Laughing, we made a mad dash to my bedroom. I pulled Nora inside and shut the door.

The laughter ceased.

Nora stood close, her eyes shimmered with longing.

My hands shook. I reached for her hips, gazing down at her upturned face. I kissed her as a man in love.

She kissed me back, sliding her hands up my neck, threading her fingers through my hair. It was everything a kiss ought to be. Soft, yet demanding.

She pulled away and reached for my hand, leading me towards the bed. I followed her down, brushing the hair away from her face.

"Do you remember the day I showed you the house?" I swallowed hard. "This is what I imagined. Seeing you like this, your hair spilling around you and onto my bed."

She gazed up at me, eyes glowing with desire. "What happens next?"

"I'll show you," I said in the time it took for my mouth to reach hers.

***

In the bathroom, food magazines were stacked in the rack next to the toilet. Tan and brown walls gave a masculine feel to the room. The lacy bra draped over the rung of the shower stall, a reminder I gained much more than I'd lost.

My cup overflowed.

I returned to the bedroom. The moonlight spilled through the window onto the quilted coverlet.

Tucked beneath the coverlet, the sound of breathing cut the silence. I crawled next to Nora, pulling her into my arms. I was amazed at her softness. *Flesh of my flesh.*

"Simon," she said sleepily.

"Yeah."

"Mm." She snuggled closer.

"You're so beautiful," I whispered, nuzzling her neck. She found my lips with hers, and kissed me thoroughly, completely. Totally. I kissed her back.

The next kiss was warm and delicious like coming home.

He who finds a wife finds a good thing

The sun peeking on the mid-December horizon, we shared breakfast on the veranda.

Stacking the dishes afterward, I considered mornings past. Breakfast with Harry and Hans, usually consisting of cold cereal, now a treasured memory.

In a red winter coat, Nora strolled out of the house with a tray of tea.

I took it from her grasp.

"This arrived." She held up *Eating Well* magazine. "It's a nice article. They did a good job."

"How many copies arrived?" I set the tray down on the table and poured two cups.

"Sadly ten. Not nearly enough for all your family members." Nora sat down.

"I'll buy one for everyone." I sat down next to her, scanning the index with a careful finger. "Here it is," I flipped to the story layout.

There was an aerial picture of Kevin's farm on one side. On the other side, eight smaller pictures amidst the article. One of Kevin and Gretchen, along with a few nice grain and vegetable pictures.

I began to read, *"With their family farm creating a place for fine dining, the Andersons are reimagining what a sustainable farm business can be."*

"They mention Simon's Place on the next page," Nora said.

I turned the page. "They used my ratatouille recipe."

"I'm glad." Nora held a hand against her temple.

"Me too. How's your head?" I asked, scanning the article.

"Better." She sipped her tea. "The shower and ibuprofen helped."

"Good." I reached for my tea. "Freaks me out some sicko rubbed a dead cat on the engine."

"The cops think it was Luke Doric, and that he lied to save his skin."

"Doesn't make sense he would admit to cutting the brake line, but lie about killing a cat." I thought of Luke Doric sitting in my restaurant, eating my food while plotting to kill me. Was the cat-killer also a customer?

"Doesn't make sense period." She sipped her tea. "Do you ever regret not going back to the dairy?"

"Nope."

"Preaching?"

I chuckled. "Sadly, not a bit."

"Do you remember the year I moved?"

I looked up from the magazine.

"I milked cows with you every day that summer," she said wistfully. "I saw a glimpse of what it would be like working with you when we grew up."

My gaze widened. "You mean, milking cows? Or being with me in general?"

She laughed. "What do you think?"

My chest squeezed. "I don't know. I mean, I knew you were the one for me, but I had no idea how you felt back then." I closed the magazine.

She uttered a soft sigh of contentment. "Having breakfast outside on the veranda with you is better than in my dreams."

We stared at each other for a long moment. Neither of us spoke.

"Anderson Bros. will be a huge hit with Mom at Thanksgiving," I said at last, rubbing my hands together.

"Simon's Place too. By the way, Kevin called when I was in the house. Thanksgiving is going to be at his house. Potluck style."

"Does Jordan need a ride?"

"Dane's got it covered."

"Sounds good. On Black Friday, the guys usually shoot clay targets while the women go shopping."

"Sounds like fun. I could shop for Christmas."

I stood. "I should be easy to shop for. I can't think of a thing I want I don't already have." I reached for my cap and tugged it on.

"Maybe a girl, Old Man." Then I saw she had something in her hand. A pregnancy stick with two lines.

"But you're...we're..." I stammered.

"You do know how babies are made?" She was looking at me with love, caring, and a hint of laughter.

I threw my hat up in the air and whooped.

Her eyes were full of morning sunshine. "I like to see you this way."

I reached for her hand, pulling her to her feet and into my arms, catching the scent of wildflowers.

"I've always loved you, Simon." She sighed.

My breath hitched. "I love you back."

Photo by Leah Meisch Photography

Hazel Mattice is the author of 3 novels, including *Where there is no Whisper* and *The Green Door*. When she isn't writing books, she can be seen on her porch in the summer enjoying the outdoors or riding her motorcycle. She is a sucker for cookies, cleverly written romance, and anime. *Thirsty Ground* is the third book in her series *The Chosen Five*.